Lisa Kleypas is the author of a number of his⸱
that have been published in fourteen languag⸱ ⸱ ⸱ ⸱ ⸱ ⸱ ⸱ was
named Miss Massachusetts and competed in the Miss America
pageant in Atlantic City. After graduating from Wellesley College
with a political science degree, she published her first novel at age
twenty-one. Her books have appeared on the *New York Times*
bestseller lists. Lisa is married and has two children.

Visit Lisa Kleypas online:

www.lisakleypas.com
www.facebook.com/LisaKleypas
www.twitter.com/LisaKleypas

Crystal Cove

LISA KLEYPAS

piatkus

PIATKUS

First published in the United States in 2013
by St. Martin's Press, New York, USA
First published in Great Britain in 2013 by Piatkus
Reprinted 2013

A CIP catalogue record for this book
is available from the British Library.

ISBN 978-0-749-95393-5

Printed and bound in Great Britain by
Clays Ltd, St Ives plc

Papers used by Piatkus are from well-managed forests
and other responsible sources.

MIX
Paper from
responsible sources
FSC® C104740

Piatkus
An imprint of
Little, Brown Book Group
100 Victoria Embankment
London EC4Y 0DY

An Hachette UK Company
www.hachette.co.uk

www.piatkus.co.uk

To Sue and Scott Carlson for being such wonderful and caring friends, and for creating a beautiful place where I can write and set my imagination free.

Love always,
L.K.

Acknowledgments

....

Special thanks to my friend Connie Brockway, for graciously allowing me to use a quote from her spectacular historical romance *The Other Guy's Bride* in the first chapter. You are a jewel, Connie—no wonder your words sparkle.

Crystal Cove

One

· ·

It was a safe bet, Justine Hoffman thought glumly, that after ninety-nine failed love spells, the hundredth wasn't going to work any better than the rest.

Fine. I give up.

She was never going to fall in love. She would never understand or experience the mysterious thing that fused one soul to another. It was something she'd always suspected deep down, but she had stayed too busy to dwell on it. The problem with staying busy, however, was that sooner or later you ran out of things to do, and then the thing you'd been trying so hard not to think about became the only thing you could think about.

Justine had wished on stars and birthday candles, thrown coins into fountains, blown the florets of dandelions to whisk the seeds upward on tiny feathered parachutes. With every wish, she had whispered a summoning spell . . . *These words bespeak*

*your fate . . . have no repose while I await . . . fate has found
you . . . love has bound you . . . Come to me.*

But her soul mate had never appeared.

She had pored over every page of the grimoire her mother had
given her when she was sixteen. But there were no rites or spells
for a witch with an empty heart. Nothing for a young woman
who yearned for something as extraordinary, and yet entirely
normal, as love.

Justine had tried to pretend to everyone, even herself, that she
didn't care. She had said she didn't want to be tied down, didn't
need anyone. In her private hours, however, she stared at the
little tornado of water at the drain of her bathtub, or the shadows thickening in the corners of her bedroom, and she thought,
I want to feel.

She wanted the kind of love that would take her on the ride
of her life. She dreamed of a man who would strip away her de-
fenses like silk garments, until at last she could surrender all of
herself. Maybe then the world wouldn't seem so small, or the
nights so long. Maybe then her only wish would be that the
night would never end.

The mournful parade of thoughts was interrupted as her
cousin Zoë entered the kitchen.

"Good morning," Zoë said cheerfully. "I brought the book you
asked for."

"I don't need it anymore," Justine said, barely looking up from
her coffee. She sat at the wooden worktable, leaning her chin on
her hand. "But thanks anyway."

A September morning breeze had swept inside the inn, the air
bitten with ocean salt and a hint of marine diesel from the nearby
docks of Friday Harbor. The scent was agreeable and familiar,

but it did nothing to improve Justine's mood. She hadn't slept well for the past few nights, and caffeine wasn't making a dent.

"No time to read?" Zoë asked sympathetically. "Just keep it for a while. I've read it so many times, I practically have it memorized." Her blond curls swirled on her shoulders as she set the paperback romance novel in front of Justine. The pages were tattered and yellow with age, some of them barely attached to the spine. A woman wearing a gold satin gown swooned languidly across the cover.

"Why read something over and over when you already know the ending?" Justine asked.

"Because a good happily-ever-after is worth reading more than once." Zoë tied on an apron and deftly pulled up her hair with a plastic clip.

Justine smiled reluctantly and rubbed her eyes, thinking that no one deserved happily-ever-after more than Zoë. Although they were distant cousins and had only seen each other at infrequent intervals during childhood, they had become as close as sisters.

It had been more than two years since Justine had asked Zoë, a talented chef, to come work at her Friday Harbor bed-and-breakfast, Artist's Point. Justine handled the business side of things, including the office work, cleaning, and building maintenance, while Zoë took care of inventory, food buying, and cooking. Zoë and her culinary skills had been so essential to the inn's success that Justine had offered her a share in the ownership.

Their partnership was a perfect balance—Justine's impulsive, outspoken nature was tempered by Zoë's diplomacy and patience. They shared a strong bond of loyalty, seeing each other at their worst, confiding their dreams and fears and insecurities. But the best part of the relationship wasn't all the things they agreed on—it was when they disagreed, when they helped each other look at things in a new way.

Together they had made a success of Artist's Point, which had become popular with both tourists and locals. They hosted weddings and private parties, and held monthly events such as cooking classes and wine tastings. During the island's tourist season, the inn was at or near full occupancy, and even in the off-seasons they averaged about thirty-five percent.

There was no obvious physical resemblance between the cousins—Justine was tall and slender, with brown hair and brown eyes, whereas Zoë was a blond bombshell who caused men to react like the old cartoon characters . . . the ones whose eyes launched out and tongues dangled and who had steam puffs that came out of their ears. Zoë's voluptuous appeal had always attracted men who had inflicted terrible pickup lines on her, and treated her as if she had the IQ of a houseplant.

Nudging the romance novel closer to Justine, Zoë said encouragingly, "Just try a few pages. You'll get so caught up in the story, you'll feel like you're in another time and place. And the hero is wonderful." She paused with a dreamy sigh. "He takes her on an adventure across the desert, looking for an ancient lost city, and he's so protective and sexy and brooding . . ."

"I'm afraid that reading about fantasy men might raise my expectations at a time when I need to lower them."

"Don't take this the wrong way, but I've never thought your expectations of men were all that high to begin with."

"Oh, yes they were. In the past, I would only go out with a

guy if he had a good personality, a decent body, and a job. Now I'd settle for a man who isn't currently married or incarcerated."

"Reading about fantasy men won't raise your expectations. It's just a nice escape."

"And of course you need an escape," Justine said dryly, "from your hideous troll of a fiancé."

Zoë laughed. Alex Nolan, a local builder, could be legitimately called many things, but "hideous troll" was not among them. He was a singularly attractive man, dark-haired and lean, with austerely perfect features and glacier-blue eyes.

No one would have paired the cynical and hard-drinking Alex with someone as gentle-natured as Zoë. But during the process of remodeling a cottage on Dream Lake for Zoë over the summer, Alex had surprised everyone, including himself, by falling deeply in love with her. He had stopped drinking and had straightened out his life. It was obvious to everyone that Zoë had him wrapped around her finger. She could manage him so sweetly that he didn't seem to notice—or care—that he was being managed.

Although Justine had never experienced real love, she knew it when she saw it. When Zoë and Alex were together, they tried to be casual, but the emotion was still too new and raw for either of them to be easy with it. Their intense awareness of each other was emblazoned in the air no matter how discreet they were. Sometimes it was even in their voices, as if love had filled them until they had to remind themselves to breathe.

You could feel terribly lonely, being around that kind of love.

Snap out of it, Justine told herself sternly. *You have a great life. You have everything you need.*

Most of the things she had longed for had finally come to her.

Caring friends . . . a home . . . a garden . . . a front porch with potted impatiens and trailing verbena. For about a year she'd even had a boyfriend, Duane, a biker with tattoos and big sideburns and an easy laugh.

But Duane had broken up with her just a few weeks ago, and now whenever they happened to cross paths, he was distantly friendly, his gaze never meeting hers. They had broken up when she had inadvertently scared the hell out of him.

Her gaze lowered to the romance novel. She pushed the book away like a sated diner refusing an extra piece of cake.

"Thanks for bringing the book," she said, while Zoë turned on the ovens and went to pour herself some coffee. "But I wasn't actually planning to read it in the first place."

Zoë cast a quizzical glance over her shoulder. "What were you going to do with it?"

Self-mocking amusement twitched the corners of Justine's mouth as she admitted, "Burn it and buy you a new copy."

Zoë fumbled with a spoon as she stirred cream into her coffee. Turning to Justine, she asked blankly, "Why were you going to burn my romance novel?"

"Well, I wasn't going to burn the whole thing. Just a page." Seeing her cousin's confusion, Justine explained sheepishly, "I was planning to sort of . . . well, cast a spell. And it called for setting fire to 'words of love scripted on parchment.' So I thought a page from a romance novel would do the trick."

"Who were you going to put a spell on?"

"Me."

Judging from Zoë's expression, an inquisition was about to start. "You've got some cooking to do," Justine said hastily, "and I need to roll out the coffee cart to the lobby—"

"The coffee cart can wait" came the gentle but inflexible reply.

Justine sighed and settled back in her chair. Silently she reflected that although she was known as the bossy and opinionated cousin, Zoë was the one who got her way more often. She just happened to be quieter about it.

"You've mentioned this stuff about spells before," Zoë said. "And I remember when I was having problems with Alex, and you offered to put a curse on him. I thought you were joking, trying to make me feel better. But now I'm getting the impression that you weren't kidding."

No. Justine had not been kidding.

She had never made a secret of the fact that she had been raised in the pagan tradition. What she hadn't admitted outright was that she, like her mother, Marigold, was a hereditary witch.

So many varieties of witchcraft existed that the word itself was practically meaningless without a qualifier. There was classic witchcraft, eclectic witchcraft, monotheistic witchcraft, Gardnerian, goth, Wiccan, and so forth. But Family Tradition witchcraft was a rare, centuries-old category of natural-born witches . . . those with magic in their DNA.

Throughout Justine's childhood, her mother had instructed her in the ways of the Tradition. She had taken Justine to festivals, camps, classes, often moving the two of them at a whim with no regard for school schedules. One year they had lived in Oregon, and the next they'd stayed in a pagan community in Sacramento . . . then a few months in New Mexico . . . Alaska . . . Colorado . . . Justine couldn't remember all the places they had stayed. But they had returned most frequently to Friday Harbor, which was the closest thing to a home that Justine had ever known.

If the soot pattern on the inside of a glass candleholder resembled a heart pierced by swords, Marigold would say it was time to leave again. She saw signs in footprints, the shape of a cloud, the path of a spider, the color of the moon.

Justine couldn't remember exactly when she had started to resent the nomadic pattern of their lives. She only knew that at some point, it had bothered her that they could pack up everything they owned in a quarter hour. "It's so much fun to go to new places," Marigold had told her. "We're free as birds, Justine. All we lack is wings." But even robins and starlings had stayed in their nests longer than Justine and her mother.

Things might have been different if Justine's father, Liam, had still been alive, but he had died when she was a baby. From what little Marigold had told her, Justine knew that Liam had been a farmer—an orchardist—who had grown apples, pears, and cherries. Marigold had met him when she was buying apples to celebrate the autumn equinox. A red bandana had been tied across his forehead to keep his long dark hair out of his eyes. He had peeled an entire apple in one long strand, and when the peel had fallen to the ground, it had made the shape of Marigold's initials, which she'd taken as a sign.

They had married right away. Liam had died before the next year was out. Their entire relationship had been as brief and intense as a lightning storm. Marigold had kept no photographs of him. She hadn't even wanted his wedding band or pocketknife, or the guitar he had played. His orchard had been sold, and his possessions had been disposed of. Justine was the only evidence that Liam Hoffman had ever existed. She had his heavy dark hair and brown eyes, and according to her mother, she had his smile.

Whenever Justine asked for stories about him, Marigold

shook her head and explained that when someone you loved was gone, all the memories went into a secret place in your heart. You could take them out and look at them only when you were ready. Eventually Justine had realized that Marigold would never be ready. All Marigold wanted to remember about her late husband was that love was the worst thing that could ever happen to you. It made you hate springtime breezes and guitar music and the taste of apples.

Reflecting on those years of constant upheaval, Justine thought she understood why her mother could never stay in one place. If you held still long enough, love might find you, and catch you so tightly that you couldn't slip free.

And that was what Justine wanted, with all the force of her will.

"Can we forget this whole thing?" Justine asked Zoë, rubbing her tired eyes. "Because you don't believe in this stuff, and if I try to explain, I'm only going to end up sounding crazy."

"It doesn't matter what I believe. What matters is that you believe in it." Her cousin's tone turned coaxing. "Tell me what kind of spell you wanted to cast on yourself."

Justine scowled and swung one of her feet, and muttered something under her breath.

"What?" Zoë asked.

Justine repeated it, more clearly this time. "A love spell." She darted a glance at her cousin, expecting derision or amusement. But this was Zoë. She only looked concerned.

"Is this because of the breakup with Duane?" Zoë asked gently.

"Not really. It's more . . . oh, I don't know. It's just that now Lucy's together with Sam, and you're engaged to Alex, and . . . I've never been in love."

"It takes longer for some people," Zoë said. "You're still a year younger than me, you know. Maybe by next summer—"

"Zoë, the problem isn't that I haven't fallen in love. The problem is that I *can't*."

"Why are you so certain?"

"I just know."

"But you're a very loving person."

"In terms of friendship, yes. But when it comes to romance . . . I've never felt that kind of love. It's like trying to understand what the ocean is like by holding a conch shell against my ear." She glanced morosely at the romance novel in Zoë's hands. "What's your favorite part of that book? The page you'd tell me to use in a spell."

Zoë shook her head, beginning to flip through the book. "You're going to make fun of me."

"I'm not going to make fun of you."

The page was located with an ease that implied many repeated readings. Zoë handed the open book to her, her cheeks turning pink. "Don't read it out loud."

"I won't even move my lips," Justine said. Her gaze swept down the page while Zoë busied herself at one of the counters, measuring ingredients into a mixing bowl.

"You," he whispered, "are my Solomon's mine, my uncharted empire. You are the only home I need to know, the only journey I want to take, the only treasure I would die to claim. You are exotic and familiar, opiate and tonic, hard conscience and sweet temptation."

The scene continued with escalating passion for pages afterward, compelling in its unabashed lyricism. Justine wanted to read more. "Are emotions like that even possible?" she asked. "I mean, even though you and Alex are in love . . ."—she gestured with the book—"real life can't be like *this*, right?"

Zoë's face turned pink as she replied. "Sometimes real life is even better. Because love is there not just in the big romantic moments, but in all the little things. The way he touches your face, or covers you with a blanket when you're taking a nap, or puts a Post-it note on the fridge to remind you about your dentist appointment. I think those things glue a relationship together even more than all the great sex."

Justine gave her a morose glance. "You're insufferable, Zoë," she muttered.

A grin curled her cousin's lips. "It'll be that way for you someday," she said. "You just haven't met the right man yet."

"I may have already," Justine said. "I may have already met and lost him without ever knowing."

Zoë's smile faded. "I've never seen you like this. I never realized it mattered so much. You've never seemed to care whether you fell in love or not."

"I've tried to make myself believe it wasn't important. Sometimes I almost managed to convince myself." Justine dropped her forehead to her folded arms. "Zo," she asked in a muffled voice, "if you could add ten years to your life, but the catch was that you could never love someone the way you do Alex, would you do it?"

Zoë's reply was unhesitating. "No."

"Why not?"

"It's like trying to describe a color you've never seen before. Words can't make you understand what real love is like. But until you've felt it . . . you haven't really lived."

Justine was silent for a long moment. She swallowed against the tightness in her throat.

"I'm sure you'll find true love someday," she heard Zoë say.

I'm just as sure that I won't, Justine thought. *Unless I do something.*

An idea came to her . . . a stupid, dangerous idea. She tried to unthink it.

But even so, she could feel the spellbook, stowed safely under her bed, calling to her.

I'll help you, it was saying. *I'll show you how.*

Two

. . . .

As she cleared breakfast plates and flatware from the tables, Justine paused to chat with some of the guests. There was an older couple from Victoria, a honeymooning pair from Wyoming, and a family of four from Arizona.

The family included two boys who were busy wolfing down Zoë's pumpkin pancakes. The boys were a couple of years apart in age, both small cyclones waiting to be set loose.

"How's breakfast?" Justine asked the children.

"Good," the older boy said.

The younger boy answered around a mouthful of pancake. "The syrup tastes weird."

He had filled his plate with syrup until the pancakes were practically floating. A gluey tuft of hair stuck up in front, and another at the side of his head.

Justine smiled. "That's probably because it's real. Most pancake syrup you buy at the stores doesn't have maple in it at all. It's all corn syrup and flavoring."

"I like that better," the boy said with his mouth full.

"Hudson," the mother scolded, "mind your manners." She glanced up at Justine apologetically. "He's made a mess."

"No problem at all," Justine said, and gestured to her empty plate. "May I take that for you?"

"Yes, thanks." The woman returned her attention to the boys while Justine removed her plate and glass. The boy's father, who was talking on his cell phone, paused his conversation long enough to say to Justine, "Take mine, too. And bring me some tea. Earl Grey, with nonfat milk. Do it fast—we have to leave soon."

"Of course," Justine said pleasantly. "Should I bring it in a to-go cup?"

He responded with a brief nod and a grunt, and resumed his phone conversation.

As Justine headed to the kitchen with the dishes, someone appeared at the doorway of the dining room.

"'Scuse me." The speaker was a young woman in a slim black skirt suit and sensible medium-height pumps, her penny-colored hair cut in a perfect shoulder-length bob. Her features were fine, her eyes luminous blue. She wore no jewelry except for a fine gold chain around her neck. Her appearance would have led Justine to expect a cut-glass British accent. Instead, she spoke in a West Virginia drawl as thick as diesel-spec engine oil. "I'm here for check-in, but there's no one in the office."

"Sorry," Justine said, "we're a little shorthanded at the moment. My breakfast help couldn't make it this morning. Are you with the group that's coming in today?"

A careful nod. "Inari Enterprises. I'm Priscilla Fiveash."

Justine recognized the name. She was the executive assistant who would handle the advance check-in for Jason Black and his entourage. "I'll be free in about ten minutes. Would you like a cup of coffee while you wait?"

"No, thank you." The young woman didn't seem unfriendly so much as guarded, her emotions tightly laced and double-knotted. "Is there a place where I could make some calls in private?"

"Sure, you can use the office. It's unlocked."

"Thank you."

The father of the two boys asked irritably from the table, "My tea?"

"Right away," Justine assured him. But before leaving the room, she paused to say to the woman, "Fiveash . . . that's an unusual name. English, Irish?"

"I'm told it came from England. A village they can't find anymore, with five ash trees in the center."

It sounded like a Tradition name. Ash trees were nearly as powerful as oak trees. And the number five was especially significant to those in the craft, whose symbol was the five-pointed star enclosed in a circle. Although Justine was tempted to ask more, she only smiled and headed toward the kitchen.

A few moments later, she heard alarming sounds from the dining room. A mother's cry, a clatter of plates and flatware, a chair overturned. Turning swiftly, Justine hurried back and dumped the armload of dishes onto a table.

The younger of the two boys appeared to be choking. His eyes were wide and white with panic, his hands pawing at his throat. The mother patted his back helplessly.

Priscilla had already reached the boy. Locking her arms around him from behind, she jerked her fist upward and inward in a sharp movement. The procedure was repeated three more times, but the obstruction was not dislodged. The boy's face was gray, his lips moving in spasms.

"You're hurting him," the mother cried. "Stop—she's hurting him—"

"He's choking," the father snapped. His fists clenched as he watched Priscilla. "Do you know what the hell you're doing?"

Priscilla didn't answer. Her mouth was grim, her face white except for two patches of red color high on her cheeks. Her gaze met Justine's. "Won't come loose," she said. "Might be stuck all the way along his gullet."

"Call 911."

While Priscilla snatched up her nearby bag and rummaged for a phone, Justine took her place behind the boy's heaving body. She tried a couple of steep-angled jerks up into the surface of his upper abdomen, and muttered a few words under her breath. *"Sylphs of air I conjure thee, help him breathe, so mote it be."*

The plug of food was abruptly expelled. The boy stopped writhing and began to draw in huge breaths. Both parents rushed forward and pulled him close, the mother sobbing in gratitude.

Justine pushed back a lock of hair that had come loose from her ponytail. She let out an unsteady sigh, trying to quiet the clackety rhythm of her heart.

Priscilla's black leather pumps came into the periphery of her vision. Justine glanced upward with a weak smile. Relief had drained all the strength out of her until she was as limp as a pillowcase on a clothesline.

The moonstone-blue eyes looked down at her intently. "You sure got a funny way of doing the Heimlich," Priscilla said.

After the commotion was settled and breakfast had been cleared, Justine sat with Priscilla in the small office. The entire inn had been rented out for the next five days to a half-dozen employees and colleagues of Inari Gaming Enterprises, an in-house development team of a major software company. The rest of the inn would go unoccupied even though it had been paid for.

"Jason likes his privacy," Priscilla had explained, which had hardly been a surprise. Jason Black, who had produced the most successful fantasy video-game series ever released, was notoriously elusive. He never attended promotional events. He turned down all interview requests from broadcast media, and only agreed to the occasional print interview with the provisions that his private life would not be discussed and he wouldn't allow his picture to be taken.

In fact, Justine, Zoë, and the two women who helped to clean the inn had all been required to sign nondisclosure agreements in advance. As a result, they were legally prohibited from revealing details about Jason Black. If they so much as revealed the color of his socks, they would be sued into the next century.

After typing his name into a few Internet search engines, Justine had found reams of information about the gaming company and its achievements, but only a sparse handful of facts about the man himself. He'd been brought up in California and had gone to USC on a football scholarship. Halfway through sophomore year, he'd taken a leave from college and had gone, of all places, to live at a Zen monastery near the Los Padres National

Forest. He had dropped off the radar for a couple of years and had never returned to school. Eventually he had applied for a job in the game-development division of a software company. After several successes, he had taken another job with Inari Software to head its gaming division, and he had become the project leader and developer of the top-selling video-game series of all time.

As far as Jason Black's personal life went, there had been a few discreet relationships, but he'd never been engaged or married. There were a few candid photos of him available on the Net, getting in and out of a car, escorting someone to a social function, but his face was averted in most of them, his dislike of the camera obvious. The best shot of him had been a pixelated blur.

"Why's he so publicity shy?" Justine asked Priscilla.

"You can ask, but I can't say."

"Is he handsome?"

"Too much for his own good," Priscilla said darkly.

Justine's brows lifted. "Are you involved with him?"

Priscilla's brief huff of laughter held no amusement. "Never. My job is too important to me—I'd never risk it for anything. 'Sides, he and I wouldn't suit."

"Why not?"

Priscilla began to check off reasons on her fingers. "He's too used to having his way. And basically I wouldn't trust him with my left shoe." She pulled an electronic tablet from her briefcase and brought up a file. "Here's the updated list for Jason's room. Let's go over it."

"It's already taken care of. You e-mailed the updated list to me a few days ago."

"This is the updated updated list."

Jason Black required a west-facing second-floor room maintained at a temperature of sixty-eight degrees. A king-size bed with high-thread-count sheets and goose-down pillows with no feathers. Two bottles of chilled spring water were to be brought to his room every morning, along with a health shake. He also required two white bath towels per day. Unscented soap and shampoo. An LED desk lamp on the table in his room, wireless access, a white flower arrangement, and a package of foam earplugs on the nightstand. A selection of organic unwaxed fruit. No newspapers or magazines—he preferred digital formats. And every night at nine, two shots of chilled Stolichnaya vodka were to be delivered to his room.

"Why two?" Justine asked.

Priscilla shrugged. "I don't usually ask Jason why he wants something. It makes him ornery, and he never explains anyway."

"Good to know." Justine returned her attention to the list. "I think I've got everything. Except for the flower arrangement. What kind of white flowers? Daisies? Lilies?"

"That's up to you. Nothing too strong-smelling, though."

"I have one more question. You know how each room at the inn pays homage to a different artist? Well, there are two second-floor west-facing rooms. One is the Roy Lichtenstein, and the other is the Gustav Klimt. Which one do you think Mr. Black would prefer?"

Tucking a coppery sweep of hair neatly behind her ear, Priscilla considered the question. "To me they both sound like something you'd take antibiotics for," she said. "Could you tell me about 'em? I don't know art from apple butter."

Justine liked her frankness. "Roy Lichtenstein was an American

19

pop artist. His most famous paintings looked like comic strips, with lettering and thought balloons. His work is more about irony and technique than emotion. Klimt, on the other hand, is all about sensuality. He was an Austrian painter in the 1800s, and his style was what they call Art Nouveau, with lines and curves inspired by Japanese woodblock prints. His best-known painting is *The Kiss*—there's a print of it in the room. So . . . which one would suit Mr. Black? Lichtenstein or Klimt?"

Priscilla frowned.

Justine waited patiently.

"Klimt," the woman finally said, her eyes narrowing. "But don't read nothin' into it."

"I signed the nondisclosure contract," Justine reminded her. "But even if I hadn't, you wouldn't need to worry. I'm good at keeping secrets."

"I imagine so." After a deliberate pause, Priscilla shot her a direct glance and asked, "What's a sylph, anyways?"

So she *had* heard the incantation. Justine answered casually, "An elemental spirit that represents air. There's another one for earth, one for water, and so on."

"Are you one of those tree-hugger types?"

Justine smiled. "I've never technically hugged a tree, but I've discovered they make great listeners. What faith are you?"

"I was brought up in the Angels on Fire Ministry."

"I'm not familiar with that one."

"They preach sexual abstinence and the apocalypse. And our pastor was convinced that Satan put dinosaur fossils in the ground to fool people." Not without pride, Priscilla added, "I was exorcised twice before I was fifteen."

"Really? What for?"

"I was caught listening to rock music."

"Both times?"

"First one didn't take." Priscilla paused as a ringtone sounded from the depths of her bag. " 'Scuse me." She pulled out her phone and glanced down at the tiny screen. "I've got some e-mails and texts to take care of."

"Stay in the office for now, if you'd like. I'll get one of the rooms ready for you."

"Thank you. If you wouldn't mind, I'd like to collect all the room keys once they're ready."

"Okay. Usually I show the guests to their rooms when they arrive."

"Jason prefers me to take care of that. He's not much on chin-wagging."

"No problem. I'll stay out of the way when they get here."

"Thank you." Priscilla's head bent over the phone as she began texting. "What room will you put me in?" she asked without looking up.

"Degas," Justine said. "A French Impressionist who painted ballet dancers. It's not the biggest room we have, but it's the prettiest. Lots of white lace and pink roses, and a crystal chandelier."

Priscilla didn't pause in her texting. "What makes you think I'd like a girly type room?"

"Because I saw the background picture on your tablet." Justine lifted her brows in teasing arcs. "A row of kittens sitting on a piano? Really?"

As the young woman's discomfited gaze met hers, Justine laughed quietly. "Don't worry. I won't tell."

Three

· ·

Later in the afternoon, Justine sat in the kitchen and drank mint tea, while Zoë took inventory of the refrigerator and pantry.

"Do you have everything you need for tomorrow morning?" Justine asked. "I finished cleaning the rooms, so I'm free to run errands."

"We're all stocked up." Zoë brought a cardboard carton to her. "Take a look at these—the farm down the road added a couple of Araucana hens to the flock."

Three pale turquoise eggs were nestled among the cream and brown ones.

"Those are fantastic," Justine exclaimed. "Zoë, we have to start keeping chickens."

"No we don't."

"Think of the free eggs."

"Think of the smell and the noise. We'd have to build a coop.

The expense of keeping chickens would cancel out any money we'd save on eggs."

"One chicken. It would be like a pet."

"It would be lonely."

"Okay, two chickens. I could call them Thelma and Louise—"

"We are not getting chickens," Zoë said, her tone soft but inflexible. "You have more than enough to do around here. You can barely keep up with the garden as it is. And I don't think you need a pet. As you used to tell me before I got together with Alex . . . you need a boyfriend."

Justine lowered her head to the table. "There's no point," she said dolefully. Her mint-infused breath collected in the space between the scrubbed wood and her chin. "It would end up the same way it did with Duane. From now on I'm swearing off men. Maybe I should become a nun."

"You're not Catholic."

"I'd have to convert," Justine said against the table. She sighed as another thought occurred to her. "But I'd probably have to wear a habit. And the floppy hat."

"Wimple," Zoë said. "And don't forget, you'd have to live in a convent. All women and lots of gardening."

I might as well join the coven, Justine thought glumly.

At this point in her life, Justine had been expected to become initiated into the Circle of Crystal Cove. Her mother, Marigold, belonged to it, and the rest of the coven were honorary relatives—most of them had known Justine all her life. As much as Justine loved the coveners, however, she had never wanted to become one of them. She liked to cast an occasional spell or brew a potion now and then, but the idea of centering her entire life around the study and practice of magic was not at all appealing.

Unfortunately Justine's reluctance had caused a rift with Marigold that had lasted at least four years and showed no signs of healing. In the meantime, Justine had received support from Rosemary and Sage, a pair of elderly crafters who were the closest thing to family that Justine had besides Zoë. The two women lived together in a lighthouse on Cauldron Island, where Sage's late husband had served as a lightkeeper.

She sat up as she heard the sound of people entering the inn . . . voices, the rattle of luggage wheels.

"The guests are here," Zoë said. "I'll go with you to meet them."

"No, we're supposed to keep our distance. Priscilla is showing them to their rooms. She has the keys."

Zoë looked bewildered. "We're not supposed to welcome them?"

Justine shook her head. "Mr. Black is all business. He doesn't want to be bothered with trivial social customs like saying hello and shaking hands and making small talk. The group will be down for breakfast in the morning, but he wants a health shake brought up to him at six. Priscilla said she would e-mail you the instructions."

Zoë went to pick up her phone from the counter to check her e-mails. "Yes, it's here." She did a double take as she read the e-mail. "There must be a mistake."

"Why?"

"Spinach . . . protein powder . . . peanut butter . . . soy milk . . . I won't tell you the rest, because your stomach is already upset."

24

Justine grinned at Zoë's appalled expression. "That sounds like a variation on the Green Monster smoothie. Duane drank them all the time."

"This will look like blended-up swamp."

"I think the point is to make it as nutritious and disgusting as possible."

"That won't be a problem." Zoë wrinkled her nose as she looked over the recipe. "I thought I would probably meet Mr. Black, since he's negotiating with Alex. Now I'm not even sure I want to meet him."

"Zoë, if this deal goes through, you and Alex are going to make so much money, you'll want to name your firstborn child after him."

The purpose of Jason Black's visit to the island was to view a twenty-acre parcel of land bordering Dream Lake, which Alex had once bought with the intention of developing it as a residential area. Although the crash of the housing market had cleaned him out financially, Alex had managed to hold on to the Dream Lake acreage.

This past summer, a Realtor had approached Alex with an offer for the Dream Lake parcel. It seemed that Jason Black planned to establish a community retreat for education, innovation, and inspiration. The proposed development would include several buildings and facilities, all of them environmentally low-impact. Alex was LEED certified, which meant he could build according to the strictest environmental and energy regulations. As a result, the negotiations involved a stipulation that, along with the sale of the property, Alex would be hired as the retreat's managing contractor.

Justine hoped the deal would go through, for Alex's sake but especially Zoë's. After the tough times Zoë had been through, including the recent death of her grandmother, she was due for some luck.

And Justine had a personal interest in the deal: In the summer she had bought and renovated a small lakeside cottage on Dream Lake Road. The cottage had been boarded up and decaying from decades of neglect. Zoë had wanted to live there with her grandmother, who had been diagnosed with vascular dementia. To help out, Justine had bought the cottage and paid for the renovations, and had let Zoë and her grandmother stay there rent-free.

If the Dream Lake land were eventually turned into an upscale community retreat and learning center, the value of Justine's cottage, which bordered the property, would increase substantially. A win-win for everyone.

"I told Alex that Mr. Black must be a very nice person," Zoë told Justine, "because the idea of creating an educational institute is a very noble goal."

Justine sent her a fond smile. "And what did Alex say?"

"He said there's nothing noble about it—Mr. Black is doing it for the tax-exempt status. But I'm still trying to give him the benefit of the doubt."

Justine laughed. "I guess it's possible that Jason Black has some redeeming qualities. Though I wouldn't hold my breath." She gulped the rest of her tea, stood, and went to put the cup into the dishwasher. "I'll put out some wine and snacks in the lounge area."

"No, I'll do it. You've been busy enough today, cleaning all those rooms with only Annette to help. Did you find out what was wrong with Nita earlier? Was it the twenty-four-hour flu?"

"It's not quite that temporary," Justine said with a smile. "She texted me a little while ago. It was morning sickness."

"She's pregnant? Oh, that's wonderful! We'll give her a baby shower. Do you think we'll need to hire someone to fill in for her when she gets past the first trimester?"

"No, we're heading into the winter season, so business will slow down. And I can easily pick up the slack." Justine heaved a sigh. "It's not like I have a personal life to get in the way of work."

"Go to the cottage and relax. And take these with you." Zoë went to the pantry and unearthed a plastic container filled with treats left over from yesterday's afternoon tea: icebox cookie squares studded with cranberries, buttery nuggets of short-bread, dark and chewy molasses rounds, and French-style mac-arons sandwiched with layers of homemade marionberry jam. It was a wonder that any were left—Zoë's cookies were so delec-table that guests at the inn's afternoon teas usually showed no compunction about slipping cookies into handbags and pock-ets. Once Justine had seen a man fill his baseball cap with a half-dozen peanut butter blossoms.

She held the box as if it contained a lifesaving organ dona-tion. "What kind of wine goes with cookies?"

Zoë went to the refrigerator and pulled out a bottle of Gewürz-traminer. "Don't have too much. Remember, you might have to bring Mr. Black his vodka tonight."

"He'll probably want Priscilla to do it. But I'll take it easy just in case."

Zoë glanced at her with an affectionate frown. "I can tell you've already made up your mind about what you can't do, and what you'll never have . . . but you can't give up. When there's no reason to hope, that's when you need to do it the most."

"Okay, Mary Poppins." She gave Zoë a quick hug before heading out through the back door.

She walked across the yard, past the herb garden that separated the backyard cottage from the main building. It had originally served as a writer's retreat, back in the days when the inn had been a private residence. Now Justine lived in the tiny two-bedroom dwelling.

"There's plenty of room here for a chicken coop," Justine said, even though Zoë couldn't hear her.

The afternoon was deep and full-slip ripe. Dandelion light slanted through the scalded red branches of a single madrone, and gilded the brown tassels of alder catkins. The pungent green scents of a raised-bed herb garden steamed through screens of pestproof fencing.

Justine had fallen in love with the former hilltop mansion as soon as she'd seen it, and had bought it for a steal. As she had painted the rooms and decorated each one according to a different artist such as van Gogh or da Vinci, she'd felt as if she were creating a world of her own. A quiet, welcoming place where people could relax, sleep well, eat well.

After a childhood of constant wandering, the weight and feeling of home was deeply satisfying. Justine knew practically everyone on the island. Her life was filled with all kinds of love . . . she loved her friends, the inn, the islands, walking through forests thick with pine and sword fern and Oregon grape. She loved the way Friday Harbor sunsets seemed to melt into the ocean. With all that, she had no right to ask for anything more.

She paused before the doorstep of the cottage, her lips quirking at the sight of a disappointed brown rabbit staring through the steel mesh at the plants it couldn't reach. "Sorry, buddy. But after what you did to my parsley last June, you can't blame me."

She reached for the doorknob, but hesitated as she felt something catch at her senses. Someone was watching her.

A quick glance over her shoulder revealed that no one was there.

Her attention was drawn to one of the second-floor windows of the inn, to the dark, slim silhouette of a man. Instantly she knew who he was.

There was something predatory in his stillness, something ominously patient. The chilled wet neck of the wine bottle dripped condensation over the tightening circle of her fingers. With an effort, she shook off the feeling and turned away. The rabbit broke for cover, streaking to its burrow.

Justine walked into the cottage and closed the front door, which had been painted sky blue on both sides. The furniture was comfortably worn with layers of paint gleaming through the scuffed places. The upholstery was covered in linen printed with vintage flower patterns. A pink and beige rag rug covered the wood floor.

Setting the wine and cookies on a bistro table, Justine went into her bedroom. She sat on the floor by her bed, pulled out the spellbook, and held it in her lap. A slow, unsettled breath escaped her.

What's wrong with me?

She had felt this ache before, but never so intensely.

As Justine unwrapped the linen, a wonderful perfume rippled upward, honey-sweet, greeny-herbal, lavender-musty, candle-waxy. The cloth, with its frayed selvage and ancient fingerprint smudges, fell away to reveal a leather-bound book with ragged deckle-edged pages. The leather binding gleamed like the skin of black plums and cherries. A design of a clock face had been tooled on the front cover, with a small copper keyhole in the center.

She traced the single word emblazoned on the book's spine: *Triodecad*. It was the word for a group of thirteen, a number that bonded multiplicity into oneness. The ancient book, more than two centuries old, was filled with spells, rituals, and secrets.

Usually a grimoire was burned upon its owner's death, but a few, like the Triodecad, were too powerful to destroy. Such rare and revered volumes had been passed down through generations. Since a grimoire preferred to remain with its keeper, it was almost impossible to steal one. But even if someone did manage such a feat, he or she would never be able to open the book without a key.

"Never read page thirteen," her mother had warned on the day she had given the spellbook to Justine. .

"What's on page thirteen?"

"It's different for everyone. It will show you how to achieve your heart's desire."

"What's so bad about that?"

"It never turns out the way you expect," Marigold had said. "Page thirteen teaches one lesson only: Be careful what you wish for."

Justine had looked down at the grimoire with a chiding grin and jostled it playfully. "You wouldn't get me into trouble, would you?"

And she had felt the Triodecad's cover flex as if it were smiling back at her.

Now, as she stared guiltily at the spellbook, she knew that what she was considering was wrong. But she wasn't trying to hurt anyone. She wasn't asking for anything extraordinary. Was it so terrible to want to change her own heart?

I should leave well enough alone, she thought uneasily.

Except that leaving well enough alone was only an option as long as things really were well enough. In Justine's case, they weren't. And if she didn't do something, they never would be.

She reached beneath the neck of her T-shirt and pulled out the copper key on a chain. Leaning forward, she unlocked the Triodecad. Instantly, the book rustled and flipped of its own accord, fanning her with the resinous perfume of vellum and ink. The rag paper pages revealed a rainbow blur of illustrations . . . sunflower yellow, peacock blue, medieval red, soot black, deepest emerald.

The spine of the volume slumped abruptly as it reached 13. Unlike the rest of the book, this page was blank. But beneath Justine's curious gaze, symbols appeared in random places like bubbles rising to the surface of champagne. A spell was forming. Justine stared at the page, her pulse thumping hard at the base of her throat.

The first line, written in elaborate and archaic letters, puzzled her:

TO BREAK A GEAS

Justine knew little about a geas, except that it was pronounced like "guest" with a *sh* sound instead of a *t*. A geas was a lifetime enchantment, most often a curse. The effort to break one was so difficult and dangerous that the results were potentially even worse than the original curse. The unlucky victim of a geas was usually better off learning to live with it.

"This can't be right," Justine said in bewilderment. "This won't fix my problem. What does a geas have to do with anything?"

The page rippled emphatically, as if to say, *Look at me*. Slowly it dawned on her: This was the answer.

The words played through her mind with strange variations on emphasis . . . *this* was the answer . . . this *was* the answer . . .

"I've been *cursed*?" she asked after a long time, in the insulated silence. "That's not possible."

But it was.

Someone had condemned her to a lifetime of solitude. Who would have done such a thing to her? And why? She had never hurt anyone. She didn't deserve this. No one did.

Too many feelings were coming to her at once. The cage of her chest was too small to contain them, pressure building behind her ribs. She trembled, breathed, waited, until the shock and pain burned down to a white-hot core of fury.

It took considerable skill and power to cast a spell of lifelong duration. The crafter would most likely have had to permanently sacrifice a portion of her power, which was sufficient deterrent to make a geas a rare spell, indeed.

All of which meant that this had been done to Justine by someone who had *hated* her.

But a geas wasn't unbreakable. Nothing was. And no matter what it took, Justine would break this one.

32

Four

· ·

Justine didn't give a damn about what it would cost her to get rid of the geas. She would do whatever it took. *So mote it be.* A blaze of injustice filled her. She had spent the past few years waiting and wishing for something that was never going to happen. Because that choice had already been made for her, regardless of what she might have wanted or dreamed of.

She would find out who was responsible. She would turn the geas right around back on them. She would . . .

Her plans for vengeance faded as she blinked hard against a salty blur. She pressed her palms hard against her eyes. A headache throbbed behind the front and sides of her skull, the kind of pain that no medicine could ease. She thought briefly of calling her mother, even though she and Marigold had been estranged for four years. Even knowing it would do no good. Marigold wouldn't be sympathetic, and even if she knew something about the geas, she wouldn't admit it.

Some women gave their children unconditional love. Marigold, however, had meted out affection to Justine like expensive arcade tokens, withholding it whenever Justine had disagreed with her. Since traditional education didn't interest Marigold, she had done everything possible to discourage Justine from going to community college. She had mocked and criticized Justine's job as a hotel desk clerk. The last straw, however, had been Justine's decision to buy the inn.

"Why have you always been so impossible?" Marigold had demanded. "You've never wanted to do the one thing you're good at. Are you really telling me that the biggest dream you can come up with for yourself is *housework*? Cleaning toilets and changing dirty sheets?"

"I'm sorry," Justine had said. "I know how much easier it would be for both of us if I'd turned out the way I was supposed to. I don't belong anywhere . . . not in a magical world and not in an ordinary one. But between the two, this makes me happier. I like taking care of people. I don't mind cleaning up after them. And I want a place that's all my own, so I'll never have to move again."

"There's more to consider than what *you* want," Marigold had shot back. "Our circle is the oldest lineaged coven on the West Coast. Once you're initiated, we'll have a total of thirteen. You know what that means."

Yes, Justine had known. Thirteen witches in a coven would result in a power greater than the sum of its parts. And she had felt horribly selfish for not wanting to join, for putting her own needs above the others'. But she had known that no matter how hard she tried, she would never be like them. A lifetime was an awfully long time to be miserable.

"The problem is," Justine had said, "I'm not interested in learning any more about the craft than I already know."

That had earned her a scornful glance. "You're satisfied with knowing a handful of bottle spells and crystal runes? With having barely enough magical ability to entertain children at a birthday party?"

"Don't forget, I also do balloon animals," Justine had said, hoping to coax a smile from her.

But Marigold's face had remained stony. "I never would have had you if I'd thought there was a chance you wouldn't be part of the coven. I've never even heard of a natural-born witch who turned away from the craft."

The impasse had been hopeless. Marigold was convinced that her plans for Justine's life were infinitely better than anything Justine could have come up with. Justine had tried to make her understand that it was every person's right to make those decisions for herself, but eventually she had realized that if Marigold had been capable of understanding the point, she never would have been controlling in the first place.

And if Marigold couldn't have the kind of daughter she wanted, she didn't want a daughter at all.

As a consequence, Justine had developed an ambivalent relationship with magic, which was inherently an all-or-nothing proposition. Trying to remain a magical dilettante was like trying to stay a little bit pregnant.

She read the spell again. If she were reading correctly, the rite had to be performed beneath a waning moon at midnight. That made sense: The last phase before the new moon was the ideal time for banishing, releasing, reversing. To succeed in lifting a curse as powerful as a geas, it was best not to cut corners.

Standing, Justine went to the antique writing desk by the window to consult a lunar phase Web site on her laptop.

As luck would have it, tonight was the last night of the waning crescent. If she didn't try to break the geas now, she would have to wait a full month before she could have another shot. Justine was certain that she couldn't make it that long. Every cell in her body screamed for action. She felt off course, like a comet that was about to break free of its solar orbit and hurtle out into space.

She should call Rosemary and Sage for advice, except they might try to talk her out of it, or at least tell her to wait, and Justine didn't want her mind to be changed for any reason. Even a good one. The geas had to be broken *now*.

For the rest of the evening, Justine studied the spell and pored feverishly through the Triodecad. If she was going to do this, it had to be done right. Many factors played into the art of magic. If any of the steps of a spell were conducted in a haphazard manner, if words were mispronounced or left out, if the crafter's focus wavered, if her magic supplies were of poor quality, the spell might not work. Or it might work in reverse, or on the wrong person. A mistake as apparently minor as using a candle made with paraffin instead of beeswax could lead to disastrous consequences.

Justine concentrated so deeply on the Triodecad that the sound of her cell phone caused her to start. She reached for it with her heart racing unpleasantly, and read the caller ID.

"Hi, Priscilla," she said. "How's it going?"

"Everything's fine. Got everyone settled into their rooms, and then they walked to Downrigger's for dinner. Most of them are back. I'm calling to remind you to bring the vodka to Jason's room in fifteen minutes."

36

"Oh." Justine looked down at her T-shirt and jeans, which she hadn't changed since cleaning the rooms earlier in the day. She smelled like ammonia and floor wax. The knees of her jeans were filthy, and her ponytail had come loose. "I thought he'd probably want you to do it," she said hopefully.

"Nope. He wants you."

Justine sighed inaudibly. "I'll be there."

"Nine o'clock on the dot," Priscilla reminded her. "He doesn't take well to people being late."

"I'll be there. Bye."

Ending the call, Justine scrambled to the bathroom, tore her clothes off, and jumped into the shower. After a brief but thorough scrubbing, she got out and towel-dried her hair.

She rummaged through her closet until she found a sleeveless knit dress with a drawstring waist, and a pair of flat white sandals. Pulling her hair back into a low ponytail, she swiped on some ChapStick and applied a couple of flicks of mascara to her upper lashes.

As Justine strode across the small yard, she risked a glance at the second-floor window, but it was empty. She had to admit it: She was curious about Jason Black, who kept his private life under such tight control.

Entering the back door of the inn's kitchen, she pulled the bottle of Stoli from the freezer. She measured two shots of biting-cold vodka into shot glasses, and settled them into a small high-sided silver tray filled with crushed ice. Carefully she carried the tray upstairs.

The quietness of the inn was disrupted only by discreet sounds: the opening and closing of a drawer, the muffled ring of a phone. As Justine approached the Klimt room, she heard a man's voice

37

inside. It sounded like he was in the middle of a phone conversation. Should she knock? She didn't want to interrupt, but it was nine o'clock. Schooling her features into a polite mask, Justine rapped her knuckles lightly on the door.

Footsteps approached the threshold.

The door opened. Justine had a brief, dizzying impression of midnight eyes and hard features, and a sexy disorder of short black hair. He gestured for her to enter the room, pausing just long enough to tell Justine, "Don't leave yet." He looked at her directly.

The glance lasted only a half second, but it was nearly enough to knock Justine backward. His fathomless eyes—shrewd and opaque as blackstrap molasses—could have belonged to Lucifer himself.

Justine responded with a dazed nod and managed to set the tray on the table without spilling it. She was so unsettled that it took her a minute to realize he was speaking in Japanese. His voice was mesmerizing, a quiet baritone wrapped in shadow.

At a loss for what to do, she went to one of the windows and looked outside. The vestigial light was melon colored at the horizon, darkening to a black-plum meridian overhead. The fissure of a crescent moon gleamed white and clear like a claw mark in the sky.

A night made for magic.

Her attention returned to Jason Black, who paced slowly as he talked. He was a big man, elegantly lean, the easy athleticism of his movements hinting at deep tracts of muscle beneath the crisp white button-down shirt and khakis. Leaning over the table, he scrawled a few words on a notepad. A stainless-steel Swiss Army watch gleamed on his wrist.

His face could have been honed from amber, the cheekbones steeply angled. Weathering at the outward corners of his eyes betrayed a pattern of sleepless nights and restless days. Although his mouth was set in ruthless lines, his lips looked soft, as if erotic tenderness had been kneaded into the surface.

"Forgive me," he said, shutting off the phone as he approached Justine. "Tokyo is sixteen hours ahead of us. I had to get in one last call."

His manner was relaxed, but Justine had to fight the instinct to step back from him. Even though she knew he posed no threat to her, she had the sense of him as a dangerous creature, a tiger behind a thin glass wall.

"Of course," she said. "Your Stoli is right over there."

"Thank you." His gaze didn't move from hers. He extended a hand. "Jason."

"Justine." Her fingers were swallowed in a deep grip that sent a jolt of warmth to her elbow. "I hope your room is satisfactory."

"Yes. However . . ." Releasing her hand, he said, "I'm curious about something." He nodded toward the glazed earthenware flowerpot on the table. It contained a double-stemmed moth orchid, each stem bearing an inflorescence of snowy-white blooms. "I asked for an arrangement of white flowers. But this—"

"You don't like it? I'm sorry. First thing in the morning I'll get you another—"

"No. I—"

"It would be no trouble—"

"Justine." He lifted a hand in the peremptory gesture of a man who wasn't used to being interrupted. She fell instantly silent. "I like the orchid," he said. "I just want to know why you chose it."

"Oh. Well, it's nicer to have a living, breathing plant in the room instead of a cut bouquet. And I thought an orchid would go with the Klimt artwork."

"It does. Clean, elegant . . ."—a barely perceptible pause—"suggestive."

Justine smiled wryly. The orchid bloom, with plush petals resembling lips and furled folds and delicate apertures, was nothing short of flower porn. "If there's nothing else," she said, "I'll be going now."

"Do you have to be somewhere?"

She glanced at him in bemusement. "Not really."

"Then stay."

Justine blinked and knitted her fingers together. "I was told you're not much on small talk."

"It's not small talk if it's someone I want to talk to."

She gave him a carefully neutral smile. "But you must be tired."

"I'm always tired." Jason gripped the back of the chair, lifted it easily with one hand, and placed it near the bed. He sat on the edge of the mattress, and gestured to the chair. "Have a seat."

Another command. Justine was half amused, half annoyed, thinking that he was entirely too used to telling people what to do. Why did he want to talk to her? Was he hoping to find out something about Zoë or Alex, something he could use during the negotiations for the Dream Lake development?

"Only for a few minutes," she said, lowering to the chair. "It's been a long day." Pressing her knees together and folding her hands in her lap, she looked at him expectantly.

Jason Black was so darkly beautiful, so striking in his cool self-assurance, that he seemed more like a fantasy figure than an actual human being. He appeared to be on the early side of his thirties, wearing an air of disenchantment like a bulletproof vest. "Too handsome for his own good" was how Priscilla had put it . . . but it would have been more accurate to say he was too handsome for anyone's good.

"Why are you staying here?" she asked bluntly. "You could have chartered a luxury yacht and moored it in the harbor. Or gotten a hotel penthouse in Seattle and flown in for the day."

"I'm not the luxury-yacht type. And the inn looked like the right place for a vacation while we negotiate terms for the Dream Lake project."

Justine smiled at that. "You're not on vacation."

One dark brow lifted slightly. "I'm not?"

"No, a vacation is when you spend entire days doing nothing productive. You take pictures of scenery, buy stuff you don't need, eat and drink too much, sleep late."

"That sounds . . ."—he paused in search of the right word—"grotesque."

"You don't like to relax," she said rather than asked.

"I don't see the point."

"Maybe the point is that every now and then you should take a break to look back and enjoy what you've accomplished."

"I haven't accomplished enough to be able to enjoy it."

"You're the head of a big company and you're a gazillionaire. Most people wouldn't complain about that."

"What I meant," he said evenly, "is that I can't take credit for the company's success. I have a good team. And we've had some luck." He took one of the vodka shots and nudged the silver tray toward her. "Here."

Justine blinked. "You're asking me to have a drink with you?"

41

"Yes."

She gave a disconcerted laugh.

His eyes narrowed. "Why is that funny?"

"Usually when you invite a person to do something, you don't give orders. 'Sit there, do this, have that . . .'"

"How do you want me to say it?"

"You could try something like 'Would you like to have the other shot of vodka?'"

"But if I asked you that way, you might turn me down."

"Do you ever get turned down?" she asked skeptically.

"It's been known to happen."

"I find that hard to believe. Anyway, I'm not good at following orders. I need to be asked."

Jason's gaze was steady and intent on hers. After a moment he asked, "Would you stay and have a drink with me?"

Heat climbed up her cheeks until the skin felt tight and burnished. "Yes, thank you." She reached out to take the vodka. "Do you usually drink both shots?"

"Sometimes I only need one. It helps me wind down at the end of the day. If I still can't get to sleep after that, I have the second shot."

"Have you ever tried herb tea? A hot bath?"

"I've tried everything. Pills, progressive relaxation, sleep music, books about golf. I've counted sheep until even the sheep can't stay awake."

"How long have you had insomnia?"

"Since birth." Finespun amusement played at the corners of his mouth. "But there are benefits. I'm a champ at online Scrabble. And I've seen some great sunrises."

42

"Maybe you'll have luck getting some sleep while you're here. The island's quiet, especially at night."

"I hope so." But he sounded unconvinced. It wasn't external stimuli that kept him awake.

Lifting the small glass to her nose, Justine sniffed cautiously and detected a slightly sweet odor like cut hay. "I've never had straight vodka before." A cautious sip of the glacier-cold liquid set her upper lip on fire. "Wow. That burns."

"Don't sip it. Take it in one swallow."

"I can't," she protested.

"Yes you can. Breathe out, knock it back, and wait ten or fifteen seconds before breathing in. That keeps it from burning." To demonstrate, he downed his shot efficiently. She could see the movement of his swallow at the front of his throat, where his skin was smooth and sun glazed.

Tearing her gaze away, Justine concentrated on the tiny glass in her hand. "Here goes nothing," she said, and expelled her breath. Swallowing the vodka, she tried to hold her breath, but her lungs spasmed as if they were about to explode. Giving up, she took a deep gasp of air, and was instantly sorry as her throat was scorched with wintry fire. She choked, her eyes watering.

"You breathed too soon," Jason said.

A laughing cough escaped her before she could reply. "I have this habit of needing to take in oxygen at regular intervals." She shook her head, wiping a trace of moisture from beneath her eyes. "Why vodka? Wine is so much nicer."

"Vodka is efficient. Wine takes too long."

"You're right," Justine said. "Vile, inefficient cabernet—I can't believe all the time I've wasted on it."

He continued as if he hadn't heard her. "Vodka also makes food taste better."

"Seriously? How?"

"Ethyl alcohol is a solvent for flavor chemicals. If you eat something right after a sip of vodka, the flavor is stronger and lasts a longer time on your taste buds."

Justine was intrigued. "I'd like to try that."

"It works best with spicy or salty food. Something like caviar or smoked salmon."

"We don't have caviar. But we can almost always put together a cold plate." Justine studied his inscrutable face. "You probably didn't go out to dinner with the others, did you? I'll bet you stayed in your room and made phone calls."

"I stayed here," he admitted.

"Are you hungry?"

The question seemed to merit careful consideration. "I could eat," he finally said.

Without a doubt, he was the most guarded person she had ever met. Did he ever relax and let go? It was hard to imagine. She wondered what he sounded like when he laughed.

"Hey," she said gently, following an impulse. "When was the last time you raided a pantry?"

"I can't remember."

"Why don't you come downstairs with me? I'm hungry, too. We'll find something to eat. Besides, I owe you a second shot of vodka."

To her surprise—and undoubtedly his—he agreed.

Five

···

Jason sat at the scarred wooden table and glanced around the kitchen. It was a spacious and cheerful room with painted cabinets, retro cherry-printed wallpaper, and soapstone counters. The massive pantry was filled with baking ingredients stored in penny-candy jars, and canned goods stacked three and four rows deep.

He watched as Justine unearthed glass Mason jars filled with pickled vegetables and brought them to the table.

Pulling a bottle of Stolichnaya from the freezer, she set it in front of Jason along with two glasses. "You pour," she said, and went to slice a baguette into delicate ovals. He could barely tear his gaze from her long enough to comply.

So far in their brief acquaintance, Justine Hoffman had teased and mocked him in a way that no one else dared. She had no idea how much latitude he was giving her, how easily he could have crushed her. But the truth was, she interested him more than anyone had in a very long time.

She was a beautiful woman, with a slender build, long, dark hair and fine skin, and a delicately angular face. She gestured as she talked. Had there been a blackboard in front of her, it would have been erased several times over by now. He should have found that annoying, except that he couldn't stop imagining ways to slow her down with his mouth, hands, body.

A background check had revealed a woman who wasn't given to excesses of any kind. She had grown up without a father, which would have made her more likely to have had behavioral problems, drop out of school, abuse alcohol or drugs. But there had been no signs of trouble. No credit issues. No prolific sexual history, only a couple of quiet relationships, neither of which had lasted more than a year. No arrest records, medical issues, or addictions. Only a parking ticket issued by her college's campus security. So the usual things that made people tick—lust, greed, fear—none of that seemed to apply to Justine Hoffman.

But everyone had something to hide. And everyone wanted something they didn't have.

In Justine's case, he knew what the first thing was. The second thing, however . . . that was the question mark.

Standing at the table, Justine arranged food on a large sectioned plate. "You're a vegetarian, right?"

"When it's possible."

"Did you start eating that way when you went to stay in the Zen monastery?"

"How do you know about the monastery?"

"It's on your Wikipedia page."

He frowned. "I've tried to get rid of that page. The administrators keep overturning the deletion. Apparently a person's right to privacy doesn't bother them."

"It's hard enough for regular people to have privacy these days. It must be impossible for someone like you." Justine unwrapped a wedge of cheese and set it on a cutting board. She began to cut it into thin translucent slices. "So did you become a vegetarian for karmic reasons? You got worried you might come back as a chicken or something?"

"No, it was what they served at the monastery. And I liked it."

Holding up a hard-boiled egg, Justine asked, "Are eggs and dairy okay?"

"They're fine."

Justine loaded the plate with pickled yellow wax beans and cauliflower, salted Marcona almonds, buttery green Spanish olives, coral slivers of home-cured salmon, hard-boiled farm eggs, translucent triangles of Manchego cheese, a fat gleaming wedge of triple-crème Brie, a handful of plump dried figs. The plate was accompanied by a basket of baguette slices and salted rosemary crackers.

"Bon appétit," she said cheerfully, and sat beside him.

As they ate and talked, Jason found himself enjoying Justine's company. She was engaging, quick to laugh, the kind of woman who would call you on your bullshit. Her face was as cleanly structured as a haiku, the eyes velvety brown, the mouth as plush and pink as a cherry blossom. But there was something intriguingly unsensual about her, a delicate frost of remoteness. It made him want to burn through that vestal coolness.

"Why did you decide to run a bed-and-breakfast?" he asked, centering a slice of radish on a buttered cracker. "It doesn't seem like something a single woman your age would want to do."

"Why not?"

"It's a quiet life," he said. "Isolated. You live on an island with no more than eight thousand year-round residents. You must get bored."

"Never. My entire childhood was spent moving from place to place. I had a single mom who couldn't stay put. I love the comfort of familiar things . . . the friends I see every day, the pillow that feels just right under my head, my herb garden, my mountain bike. I've run on the same trails and walked on the same beaches until I can tell whenever there's the slightest change. I love being connected to a place like this."

"I understand."

"Do you?"

"Yes. The Japanese believe that you don't choose the place, the place chooses you."

"What place has chosen you?"

"Hasn't happened yet." By now it wasn't likely. He owned a condo on San Francisco Bay, an apartment in New York, and a lodge on Lake Tahoe. Each of them was beautiful, but none had ever given him a feeling of belonging when he walked through the front door.

Justine stared at him speculatively. "Why did you go to the Zen monastery?"

"I needed the answer to a question."

"And did you get it?"

That brought a faint smile to his lips. "I found the answer. But also several more questions."

"Where did you go after that?"

Jason lifted his brows into mocking arches. "It's not on my Wikipedia page?"

"No. Your life is a big blank for a couple of years. So what were you doing?"

Jason hesitated. The habit of protecting his privacy wasn't easy to set aside even when he was willing.

"I signed a *massive* confidentiality agreement," Justine told him. "You can spill your guts and I won't say a word."

"What happens if you break the agreement?" he asked. "Jail time? Monetary damages?"

"You don't know? It's your contract."

"We have three versions with different fine print. I want to know which one Priscilla gave you."

Justine shrugged and grinned. "I never read the fine print. It's always bad news."

Her unguarded smile went through him like slow-motion lightning.

He hadn't expected her effect on him. He'd never felt anything like it before. Something about her had set his nerves on tripwires, unknown feelings ready to be sprung. Carefully he closed his fingers around his second shot of vodka and drank it in a practiced gulp.

Justine tilted her head, studying him. "Why did you go into the video-game business?"

"I started as a game tester when I was an undergrad and wrote a couple of simple 2-D games. Later a friend of a friend was setting up a studio and needed someone to help with designing and programming. Eventually I was hired to launch the gaming division at Inari."

"That explains how you got into the business," Justine said, "but I'm curious about *why*. What is it about video games?"

"I'm competitive," he admitted. "I like the aesthetics of a well-designed game. I like world-building, setting up challenges, pitfalls . . ." He paused. "Do you like gaming?"

She shook her head. "Not my thing. The couple of games I've tried are complicated and violent, and I really don't like the sexism."

"Not in the games I produce. I don't allow story lines that include prostitution, rape, or demeaning language toward women."

Justine seemed unimpressed. "I've seen some of the ads for Skyrebels—that's one of yours, right?—and most of the female characters are dressed like space hookers. Why do they need to wear leather minis and boots with five-inch heels to fight off an attack of armored soldiers?"

She had a point. "The teenage male demographic likes it," Jason admitted.

"Thought so," she said.

"But no matter how they're dressed, the female characters are just as tough as the males."

"Sexism is about presentation and tone as well as actions."

"Are you a feminist?"

"If you define a feminist as someone who wants to be treated with equality and respect, yes. But some people tend to think of feminists as being angry, which I'm not."

"I'd be angry if someone sent me to war in five-inch boots and a leather mini."

Justine burst out laughing and poured more vodka. She took a sip and nibbled at a big green olive. As Jason watched the movements of her mouth, her lips pursing around the plump swaddle of the fruit, he felt a deep, disconcerting tug of response.

"Have you ever played truth or dare?" Justine asked, setting aside the pit.

"Not since high school," he said. "I can't say I've missed it."

"Me, neither. Still . . . want to play a couple of rounds?"

Settling back in his chair, Jason gave her an assessing glance. No doubt she thought it would disarm him, coerce a couple of answers he wouldn't have given otherwise. But it would work both ways. "I never take dares," he said.

"Okay, then for you, it's all truth. Now, about limits, I think we should—"

"No limits. It's not worth playing otherwise."

"No limits," Justine agreed, a new and faintly wary edge to her tone. "What about penalties?"

"Whoever loses a round has to remove an item of clothing." He had the satisfaction of seeing Justine's eyes widen.

"Okay," she said. "I'll start: Tell me your idea of true happiness."

He reached for a small white paper napkin and folded it diagonally, using the flat of his thumbnail to sharpen the crease. "I don't believe in happiness." Turning the napkin over, he folded it into a small square. "People think they're happy when something like a box of doughnuts, a Lakers win over the Spurs, or a sex position with a Latin name causes certain chemicals to attach to receptors in the brain to stimulate electrical impulses in neurons. It doesn't last, though. It's not long-term. It's not real."

"What a downer," Justine said, laughing.

"You asked." He folded the sides of the napkin inward to form a compressed triangular base. "Next round: truth or dare?"

"Truth," she said promptly, watching the careful, deliberate movements of his hands.

"Why did you break up with your last boyfriend?" He began to fold and crease the flaps of the triangle.

A swift tide of pink swept up to her hairline. "It just . . . didn't work out."

"That's not an answer. Tell me the reason."

"Sometimes there is no reason for why people break up."

He paused in the middle of folding the points of the paper shape and gave her a mocking glance. "There's always a reason."

"Then I don't know what it is."

"You know what it is. You just don't want to admit it. Which means you lose the round." He looked at her expectantly.

Frowning, Justine wriggled her foot out of a delicate white sandal and pushed it toward his chair.

The sight of her bare foot, beautiful and long-toed, the nails painted with glittery pale blue polish, seized Jason's attention.

"Your turn," he heard her say, and reluctantly he dragged his gaze back to her face. "Where were you during those two years after you left the monastery?"

He peeled the edges of paper away from the folded model until they resembled flower petals. "I went to stay with relatives in Okinawa. My mother was half Japanese. I'd never met any of her family, but I'd always wanted to. I thought it would help me feel closer to her." Before Justine could respond, he gave her the finished origami.

She took it hesitantly, her eyes round and wondering. "A lily."

"*Yuri*," he murmured. "The name comes from a Japanese word that describes how the flowers move in the wind. Truth or dare?"

She blinked, caught off guard. "Truth."

"What caused the breakup with your last boyfriend?"

Justine's mouth dropped open. "You already asked me that."

"Still not going to answer?"

"*No.*"

"Then hand over another piece of clothing."

Indignantly Justine removed her other sandal and flipped it to him. "You're going to keep asking the same thing over and over, aren't you?"

He nodded. "Until you've answered, or you're naked."

"You can't think of *anything* else you'd like to know about me?"

"Afraid not." He tried to look contrite. "I tend to hyperfocus. One-track mind."

Justine gave him a fulminating glance. "Next round. You said you went to the Zen monastery to learn the answer to something. What did you find out?"

"I found out," he said slowly, "that I have no soul."

Six

· ·

Justine stared at him in astonishment. "You mean like . . . you're no good at dancing?"

"No, then I would have said I have no rhythm. Which is also true. But I meant it literally—I have no soul."

"If you didn't, you couldn't be sitting here and talking to me. You wouldn't be alive."

"What do you think a soul is?"

"The thing that makes your heart beat and your brain work and your body move around."

"Actually, the human body runs on thermoelectric energy. About a hundred watts—the equivalent of a standard lightbulb."

"Yes, I know that," she said. "But I've always thought of the soul as the power source."

"No. The soul is something separate."

She looked bewildered and troubled as she contemplated Jason, absently tapping a forefinger against the tip of her nose.

Abruptly she asked, "What do Buddhists believe about the soul?"

"That speculation is useless . . . that when you focus on the idea of self, and the pleasure of self in heaven, it blocks your view of truth and the eternal."

"Oh." Her forehead smoothed out. "So for all you know, you might have a soul."

He gave her a neutral look and didn't reply.

"You are an interesting guy," Justine said, in a way that didn't sound remotely like a compliment.

"Next round. You know the question."

She was starting to look nettled, uneasy. "You're going to ask me the same thing about my boyfriend again?"

"You could lie," he suggested.

"I'm a bad liar. Ask me something else."

He shook his head.

"Then give me a dare." She paused and added with difficulty, "Please."

Another negative shake. And he watched every visible inch of her skin turn pink.

"Why is it so tough to answer?" he asked.

Although he was pretty certain he already knew.

Justine stood and went to a nearby cabinet, pulling out a roll of plastic wrap. She tore off lengths of wrap with agitated movements, covering the cold plate. "Your question has to do with something I hate talking about, so naturally I'm reluctant."

"It appears to be more than simple reluctance," he said, reaching beneath the plastic wrap to steal one last olive. "It seems more like something you *can't* talk about."

Justine picked up the plate, took it to the refrigerator, and shoved it onto a shelf. "I'm going back to my cottage. I have to get up early, and I still have a couple of things to do tonight."

"Such as?"

"None of your business," she said curtly. "Leave the kitchen, please, so I can turn out the lights."

Jason stood, bringing the vodka bottle and the shot glasses to the counter. "You're going to bail before the game is finished? You owe me an answer . . . or you have to take the penalty."

"Well, I can't answer. And since I didn't dress in layers and you've already gotten my shoes, I can't take the penalty. It's a no-win situation."

They both knew she wanted him to let her off the hook. A gentleman would have.

"We agreed to the rules," he reminded her.

"Yes, but the point was to get to know something about each other, and . . . pass the time in a friendly way . . ."

"What should I have asked you? I'm interested in what makes you uncomfortable."

"At the moment, that would be you."

Jason approached her, his gaze flickering to the visible pulse at the base of her throat. Quietly he said, "If you won't give me an answer, ante up."

Justine faced him fully, pressing back against the countertop as if she needed it for balance. Her eyes were huge, depths of bittersweet brown swirled with dread and curiosity. As he stood close, he became aware of her trembling.

"Touch me and I'll sue you," she said gruffly.

"I'm not going to take your dress." Slowly Jason lifted a hand and ran his fingertips along the side of her neck. Her skin was silky and impossibly fine. He let his thumb dip gently into the hollow at the front of her throat, where panic throbbed.

Justine stiffened, her face filled with rioting color. "I'll do it," she muttered, evidently having come to some conclusion. Reaching beneath the shoulder of her sleeveless dress, she hooked her thumb around a slender white bra strap and pulled it out. With a hasty wriggle, she tugged her elbow through. After repeating the procedure on the other side, she delved beneath the neckline of her dress, unfastened the front closure, and fished out a white bra.

"Here," she said, a defiant flash in her eyes as she gave him the bra. "Game over."

Jason took it automatically, his hand closing over the unlined elastic fabric, straps dangling between his fingers. The garment was still permeated with the warmth of her body.

He couldn't keep from glancing at the front of her dress, where the tips of her breasts pressed distinctly against the thin cotton. The small act of uncovering something private, holding an article of clothing that had just been stretched intimately around her, stirred the most profane thoughts in him. He wanted to touch her, tease her. He wanted her under him, flushed and writhing. Arousal dilated his veins, his flesh thickening. It was going to become obvious in a few seconds, if he didn't put an end to this.

He went to the table, bent to scoop up her discarded sandals, and brought them back to her, along with the bra and the folded origami flower.

"I was only going to take down your hair," he said blandly, which was the truth, and she gave him a sullen glance, her cheeks bright.

"Good night." She pointed to the door leading back to the hallway. "You'll have to find your room by yourself."

He bit back a grin, enjoying her discomfort. "Are you going to bring up my health shake in the morning?"

"No, I'll give it to Priscilla." She paused at the back door, her free hand hovering near the light switches. "Go."

Obligingly he went to the opposite threshold. "Good night," he said, just as the lights switched off and the back door closed firmly.

Jason went back upstairs at a slow pace, his mind occupied with the revelation of Justine Hoffman.

He had already known more about her than she would have guessed, certainly more than she would have preferred. It had been easy to uncover the basic information: date of birth, past places of residence—of which there were many—level of education—a degree in hotel management from a community college—financial situation—modest and carefully managed.

But that skeleton of factual knowledge couldn't begin to convey the uniqueness of a woman like Justine. Vivid, glowing, with the raffish spirit of an adventuress. And yet there was something agreeably settled about her . . . she had found her place in the world, and was happy in it.

Happy, but not altogether content. He wanted, on the most instinctual level, to fill that space between what she had and what she needed.

It was an unwanted complication, this compelling attraction to her. It made him regret the necessity of having to use her, to take what she valued most.

But he needed magic in the most literal sense, and it could only come from a witch, a spellbook, and a key.

Justine felt shaken and hollow as she went into her cottage. She wasn't entirely certain what had just happened, only that she had started a casual game and Jason had turned it into something threatening. Something sexual.

Her gaze went to the clock on the wall. A quarter to midnight. Just enough time to prepare for the spell.

All thoughts of Jason Black fled from her mind as she glanced at the shadowy space beneath her bed, where the Triodecad waited.

Am I really going to do this?

She had to try. There was no choice, now that she knew about the geas. She couldn't rest until it was broken.

She went to her bedroom closet to pull out a besom broom with a cedar handle. Cinnamon fragrance flourished upward as she began to sweep the floor in a counterclockwise direction, widdershins as it was called in the craft. The ritual broom would whisk away negative energies.

After a few minutes of vigorous sweeping, Justine replaced the broom in the closet and stood on her toes to reach the top shelf. She took down a Mason jar filled with a mix of stone and crystal . . . quartz, calcite, pyrite, obsidian, agate, turquoise, and other varieties poured around a candle in the center. After lighting the candle, Justine set the jar on the floor. The last necessary element for spell-casting was to create a protected area. She retrieved a bundle of soft hemp rope cord from the closet and unwound enough to form a large circle on the floor.

She retrieved the Triodecad from under the bed. The book felt warm and vibrant in her hands. Unwrapping the book from its linen covering, she carried it to the center of the circle and sat with it in her lap.

She grasped the fine chain around her neck, withdrew the key from beneath her shirt, and unlocked the spellbook. It opened immediately to page 13. Justine stroked her fingers across the parchment as words appeared. She had always wondered why anyone would cast a spell that had been predestined to end in disaster, and now she understood: Sometimes you wanted something so much that you didn't care about the consequences.

She concentrated on the candle flame, the flick of blue at its heart, the radiant yellow outer layer, the dancing white summit. Her mouth was dry. She was nervous. Not because she was afraid the banishment would fail, but because she knew it was going to work. And nothing would be the same afterward.

She read the banishing rite once . . . twice . . . thrice.

But it wasn't enough. Her heart was still a tight knot. Nothing had changed.

Something more was needed.

A tear slipped down her cheek as she cradled the spellbook in her lap. She remembered watching Marigold in the middle of a particularly tricky act of spell-casting. *"These are the bones of magic,"* Marigold had once told her, sifting through handfuls of minerals and crystals in a bowl. *"Everything taken from the earth . . . stones, fibers, roots . . . all are the tools of our art. Let their energy guide you. When a spell isn't working, it means you're not focusing clearly on your goal. Use the crystals as the spirits direct."*

Following instinct, Justine blew out the candle flame, poured the jar of stones and crystals into a heap on the floor, and combed through them with her fingers. She closed her eyes and picked one that seemed especially vibrant, its energy singing to her.

A hematite, its surface silvery and liquid-smooth. An easily magnetized stone, good for improving the blood's circulation and for turning negative energy into love.

She pressed the hematite to the center of her chest, over her heart. She covered it tightly with her palm. "Help me, spirits," she said humbly, swallowing against a lump in her throat. "I need to love someone. Even if it doesn't last. Because one day of something wonderful is better than a forever of nothing special."

Slowly a white glow collected outside the window. Moonlight. It broke into separate rays, thin silver splines that reached through the glass and trailed down the wall and along the floor. The light moved toward her like outstretched fingers, sliding through the circle.

Justine felt dizzy, unable to catch up to her own heartbeat. Her thoughts darted out of reach, hummingbird-fast. She closed her eyes against a sensation of falling slowly, a tumble into clouds and midnight and soft-carded dreams.

It could have been minutes or hours as she lay there. Eventually the moonlight awakened her, teasing her closed lids and playing with her lashes until she stirred. She discovered that she was lying on her side, on the floor, her head cradled on the spellbook. The pages were smooth beneath her cheek, wafting out a crisp scent of cloves. She was cold, but it was a pleasant sensation, like drawing in fresh air after having been trapped beneath a smothering blanket. She felt vulnerable. She felt . . . free.

Uncurling her fingers, she stared at the silvery hematite in her open palm.

A curse contained in stone.

Seven

· ·

Justine started the day by walking down to the Spring Street dock. The morning mist had diffused the sunrise into layers of pink and peach. The tide was slack, the water pinned by the reflected bristle of boat masts. A boat loaded with crab pots headed out of the harbor, followed by a pair of seagulls that split the air with squeaky-hinge cries.

Justine went out to the farthest boat slips with the hematite in her hand. She drew back her arm and threw the stone as far as possible. As it disappeared beneath the surface of the water, taking the geas with it, she took a deep breath and let it out slowly.

No excuses now. Nothing to stand in the way of whatever life dared to throw at her.

She felt as if she could jump up into the sunrise and be caught by a cloud. She felt fragile and raw. Newborn.

A fractious breeze came out of nowhere, carrying the promise of rain. Narrowing her eyes against the cool rush, she saw that the sky had darkened near the horizon. Waves slapped against the dock pilings like a dog lapping from its bowl.

By the time Justine walked into the kitchen at Artist's Point, Zoë had arrived and started breakfast. The air was laced with the tang of coffee and the scents of browning butter and hot ovens.

"Good morning," Justine said exuberantly. "What are we having?"

"Brioche French toast with berry compote."

"Yum." Justine's attention was caught by the sight of the nearby blender, half filled with vivid green sludge.

"Mr. Black's health shake," Zoë said with a grimace.

Justine poured a small quantity into a glass and sampled it. The flavor was fresh and fruity, the texture light. "Did you remember to put in the hemp protein powder?"

"Yes, why?"

"Because a Green Monster smoothie is supposed to be a glutinous slop . . . and this is delicious."

"I may have adjusted the ingredients a little," Zoë said. She frowned as she saw Justine's reaction. "I know. But it was so disgusting."

Justine grinned. "It's supposed to be. Has Priscilla already taken a glass up to Jason?"

"Yes." Zoë began to slice homemade brioche loaves, golden and cakelike with shiny puffed tops. "I've never seen anyone multitask the way Priscilla does. She just drank a triple-shot espresso and had conversations on two cell phones *and* texted on a third. Simultaneously."

"According to Jason, they're all on a working vacation,"

Justine said dryly. "Makes you wonder what their normal day is like."

"Alex and his lawyer are going to spend most of today with him."

"That should be interesting," Justine said. "I'd love to hear Alex's take on him."

"Did you get to meet him last night? What did you think?"

"My first impression was that he's a smug, self-aware, manipulative narcissist with spectacular cheekbones."

They both jumped a little as a new voice entered the conversation. "I disagree," Priscilla said, walking into the kitchen, carrying a glass of the green health shake.

Justine gave her a contrite glance, but before she could apologize, Priscilla continued, "Once you get to know him, the cheekbones are only a little above average."

Zoë came forward to take the full glass from her. "He didn't like it?" she asked in concern.

Priscilla shook her head, her copper-colored hair swinging. "He says it tastes too good," she said. "I swear, he'd complain if someone hung him with new rope."

"I took liberties with the recipe," Zoë confessed sheepishly. "I'm sorry. I'll make another one."

"I'll do it," Priscilla began, but she was forced to pause as her cell phone rang. " 'Scuse me." She retreated to the corner of the kitchen, muttering fiercely into the phone. "Toby." A brief pause. "Don't even try. You really expect I would give that sorry excuse to Jason? The software patch we sent out to fix the framerate problem made everything worse and now people are raisin' hell 'cause they got weapons malfunctioning and dragons flying ass-backward. You'd better come up with some kinda brand-new patch to fix it, or . . . *hold on.*" Another cell phone went off, and she grabbed it out of a bag slung over her shoulder. "Yeah," she said into the second phone. "I got the asshole on the other line, trying to convince me everything is all MoonPies and salted peanuts."

Justine caught her eye, gestured to the blender, and said sotto voce, "I'll take care of it."

Priscilla nodded and kept talking with quiet ferocity.

Zoë brought a colander of freshly washed spinach leaves to the blender. "I can give it another try," she said, heaving a sigh.

"No, leave it to me," Justine said. "You need to make breakfast for everyone else. Where's the recipe?"

"I printed it out," Zoë said, nudging a piece of paper to her.

In less than five minutes, Justine had blended the ingredients into a smoothie that approximated the color of an oxidized avocado, and poured it into a glass. Seeing that Priscilla was still talking and making furious notes, she said, "I'll take it up to him."

The assistant sent her a grateful glance and snarled into the phone, "Oh, really? 'Cause about a million geeks have e-mailed about the PS3 version freezing up every ten or fifteen minutes. Here's an idea—why don't we get the dadgum game right *before* we start selling it?"

Justine left the kitchen quietly and carried the shake upstairs. On the way, she passed a couple of guys who were descending to the first floor. "Good morning," she said. "The coffee cart is in the lobby."

"Great," one of them said, his eyes friendly behind wire-rimmed glasses. "I could use some caffeine."

The other, who was stocky and middle-aged, gave Justine a blatant once-over and said, "I could use some room service."

Both men chuckled.

Justine was in such a good mood that she only smiled and said, "Trust me, you'd rather have breakfast downstairs."

Making her way to the Klimt room, she saw that the door was ajar. She knocked on the jamb.

"Priscilla," came a curt voice. "I need the report from the emerging-markets group. And I want to know who we're sending to the E3 Expo. Also, get me a hard copy of the exhibitor list and a plan of the show floor—"

"Save your breath," Justine said. "It's me. I have your breakfast shake."

A short silence ensued. "Are you coming in?"

"Are you decent?"

The door opened fully to reveal Jason dressed in jeans and a white T-shirt printed with the Inari logo, the *I* formed in the shape of a stylized dragon. "I'm clothed," he said. "Decency is open for debate."

His black hair was damp from a recent shower, his face clean-shaven. Forcing herself to look into those cool coffee-dark eyes, Justine felt her heart jam up against her ribs until every throb was a sharp little pain. Even though she kept her gaze on his, she was aware of every detail of him, the carnal mouth, the long, superbly conditioned body. The indefinable threat was still there, raising the fine hairs on her arms and neck . . . something physical, something shadowy.

Something erotic.

She extended the drink to him, careful not to let their fingers touch.

"Who made this one?" Jason asked.

"I did." She smiled at his dubious expression.

Taking a sip of the shake, he nodded in approval. "Just the way I like it."

"What a relief," she said. "Because if I'd had to bring up a third one, I might have added a splash of hemlock."

"You wouldn't poison me," he said, and took another swallow.

"You have that much faith in my integrity?"

"No. It would be too much trouble for you to drag me outside and bury me in the yard."

Justine grinned reluctantly.

Jason stared at her in the unsettling way he had, taking in every detail. "I made you uncomfortable last night," he said.

Her smile faded instantly. "No harm done."

"So . . . we're good now."

"No, I still don't like you."

A glint of humor entered his eyes. "Justine, you have to admit—" He broke off, appearing to think better of what he'd been about to say.

"What?"

Jason set the health shake on the table beside his laptop. "You were the one who suggested playing truth or dare."

"And you were the one who turned it into a cat-and-mouse game."

He didn't bother to contradict her. They both knew she was right. And he didn't look the least bit remorseful. "I should have warned you that I don't play well with others."

"Yeah, I'm clear on that now," Justine muttered, turning away. "Let Priscilla know if you want the rest of what's in the blender. God knows no one else will touch it."

"Wait," he said as she began to leave.

She turned back to him reluctantly. "Yes?"

Jason approached slowly, his gaze holding hers. A visceral pulse awakened in all the vulnerable places of her body. All she could do was stand there helplessly, wondering how his mouth might feel against hers, if his kisses would be hard or soft, if his hands would be impatient or gentle. Taking a deep breath, she fastened her gaze on the logo of his T-shirt. She couldn't help wondering what it would be like, with a man like this. She would be at his mercy as she had never been with Duane or any other man. He would demand total surrender—

"Would you go out to dinner with me tonight?"

Thrown off balance, Justine stared at him blankly. "Just the two of us?"

Jason gave a single nod, his expression unfathomable.

She shouldn't. There was a complexity in him that was beyond her ability to untangle. Secrets contained like some volatile substance. If she were stupid enough to have anything to do with him, she would deserve whatever she got.

"No, thank you," she said unsteadily. "But if you want company, I know some great women I could fix you up with."

"I don't want another woman. I want you."

"You can't always have your way."

"Actually, I do most of the time," he told her.

That drew a reluctant smile from her. "I can see that's done wonders for your personality. What about your girlfriends? Do they have to pander to you and let you have your way?"

"My favorite ones do."

Justine's smile turned rueful. "About the question you asked me last night . . . the most I can tell you is that we were together almost a year. He's a nice guy. I was lucky to be with him. But we broke up because . . . I don't do well with nice guys."

"Good," he said promptly. "You can go out with me, then."

She shook her head.

"Justine," he chided, a wicked glint in those dark eyes. "What will it take to soften you up?"

"I'm sorry. Really. Any woman would be thrilled by the idea of going out to dinner with you. But you and I are not just from different worlds, we're from different realities."

"In these matters, I've learned not to factor in reality," he said. "It's very limiting."

"The whole thing is pointless. I don't do vacation flings or spontaneous hookups, and I don't have any Cinderella fantasies about some rich guy sweeping me off my feet. So thanks for asking, but I think it's better for both of us if I turn you down."

"All I want is to spend a little time with you," he said gently. "No games. We can talk about anything you want. Or not talk at all. Just you and me in a quiet place with a bottle of wine and maybe some candlelight." Reading the uncertainty in her gaze, he added huskily, "Don't say no. Because this has never happened to me before."

"What hasn't happened?"

Jason smiled into her puzzled face, a sincere and unexpectedly charming smile. "I can't put it into words yet. But it may be as close as I'll ever get to having a soul."

Eight

Immediately after Justine had agreed to go out with Jason, she had known it was a mistake. Now that she'd committed to it, however, there was no backing out. *"It may be as close as I'll ever get to having a soul."* How was she supposed to refuse him after *that*?

After clearing the breakfast dishes and bringing them to the kitchen, she carried a bucket of cleaning supplies upstairs. Annette and Nita, local women who came to help clean the inn, were already busy stripping the beds.

"Nita, how are you feeling?" Justine asked, entering the Degas room and setting the bucket on the floor.

The petite young woman, whose Coast Salish heritage was evident in her gleaming black hair and smooth cinnamon skin, smiled and patted her still-flat stomach. "Pretty good. I'd be better if I didn't have to take horse-pill vitamins."

"Make sure not to overdo it today, Nita," Justine said. "Take a break whenever you need to."

"Annette and I already have it worked out. She's going to do the heavy lifting, and I'll handle all the dusting."

Annette grinned and told Justine, "Nita was determined to come to work today, no matter what. She wanted to get a look at Jason Black."

"Did you?" Justine asked.

Nita nodded, her expression turning dreamy. "Sweet, sweet man-candy."

"He's pretty good-looking," Justine admitted with a rueful grin.

"He's *hot*," Annette said fervently. "The Inari people were leaving the bed-and-breakfast just as we were heading in, and Mr. Black held the door open for us, and the second he looked at me, I felt my ovaries explode while that Seal song 'Kiss from a Rose' started playing in the back of my head."

"Jason Black is mine," Nita said, spraying ammonia solution onto the bedroom mirror. "We're like one of those movies where fate wants us to meet and we keep missing each other, and then when we find each other, I'm accidentally engaged to John Corbett. But John Corbett lets us off the hook because he never stands in the way of true love." She ran a squeegee over the glass in expert strokes.

"Nita," Annette said, "you're happily married and pregnant."

"For Jason Black, I would kill my husband with this squeegee." Nita paused reflectively. "I might even kill him for John Corbett."

Justine was laughing. "Death by squeegee . . . how does that work, Nita?"

"Well, basically you—"

"No, never mind. I don't need to know. I have to sweep and mop downstairs." And she fled while Annette and Nita argued over who was going to end up with Jason.

After working for the rest of the morning and the first part of the afternoon, Justine went into the office and closed the door for privacy. Picking up her cell phone, she autodialed the Cauldron Island lighthouse where Rosemary and Sage lived.

She called frequently to ask how they were and to find out if they needed anything. In good weather, she would paddle her sea kayak across the nautical mile between the north of San Juan Island and Cauldron Island to visit them weekly.

The elderly women, who had lived together for almost forty years, refused to consider moving to a less isolated place. Cauldron Island was approximately two square miles in size, with only a handful of full-time residents. The only way to reach the island was by private boat, or to land a small aircraft on a mown grass landing strip.

Coven meetings were held at the lighthouse about a half dozen times a year. Marigold attended the meetings, of course, and according to Rosemary and Sage, she was doing well. She had started an Internet store that sold magical supplies, including herbs, stones, candles, divination tools, and even some bath and cosmetic products.

"Does she ever mention me?" Justine had asked Rosemary recently.

"She asks how you are," Rosemary had said. "But she's as stubborn as ever. Until you agree to join the coven, she says there's nothing for you to discuss."

"What do you think I should do?"

"I believe you should decide what's best for yourself," Rosemary had said, "and don't allow anyone, even your mother, to pressure you into making a commitment you're not ready for. I've said as much to Marigold. If you don't feel called to it, you shouldn't join."

"What if I never feel ready?"

"Then the coven will go on as we always have. Maybe it's fate's way of telling us that we're not ready for the power of thirteen."

Sage had agreed. "No one can tell you what your path is," she had told Justine. "But someday you'll discover it." She had smiled pensively. "And it won't be at all what you expected."

In her twenties, Sage had met and married Neil Winterson, a lighthouse keeper, and had gone to live on Cauldron Island with him. The lighthouse had been built at the turn of the century to guide shipping in the active waters of Boundary Pass, between Washington State and British Columbia. Every night Neil had climbed the curving staircase to the glass cupola, and had lit the Fresnel kerosene lamp, made with forty pieces of French crystal. Once lit, it could be seen from fourteen miles away. In heavy fog, Neil and Sage had taken turns ringing the lighthouse's thousand-pound bell to warn approaching ships.

Sage and Neil's marriage had been a happy one despite their disappointment over not having children. Five years after the wedding, Neil had gone out in a small wooden dory in good weather, and had never returned. His boat was found capsized, and his body was later found still wearing a life jacket. Most likely a gust of wind had knocked the dory over, and Neil hadn't been able to right it.

The members of the coven had all helped Sage through her

mourning, some of them living with her at the lighthouse for short periods of time. Sage had assumed her husband's job as lightkeeper, and she also taught a half dozen children in the one-room schoolhouse on the island.

Approximately a year after Neil's death, Rosemary had come to stay at the lighthouse for a week. Sage had asked her to stay another week, and another, and somehow that visit had turned into a lifetime together. "Love will break your heart," Sage had once told Justine, "but love can also mend it. Not many things in life are both the cause and the cure."

The phone rang twice, and someone picked up. "Hello?" came Sage's familiar voice, sweetly frayed like antique lace and faded roses.

"Sage, it's me."

"I was expecting your call. What's the trouble?"

"Why do you assume there's trouble?"

"I was thinking about you last night. And I saw blood on the moon. Tell me what's happened."

Justine blinked and frowned. A red-hazed moon was a bad sign. She wanted to contradict Sage and tell her that nothing had happened, and the sign had nothing to do with her. But she was more than a little worried that it might.

"Sage," she asked carefully, "do you know anything about a curse that someone might have cast on me? A geas?"

The silence was as thick as molten tar.

"A geas," Sage finally repeated in a meditative tone. "What in the world would give you that idea, dear?"

"You're not fooling me, Sage. You're an even worse liar than I am. Tell me what you know."

"Some conversations," Sage observed, "aren't meant to fly

through the air between telephones. They're meant to happen in a civilized way with people talking face-to-face."

Justine had sometimes found Sage's evasiveness charming. However, this was not one of those occasions. "Some conversations have to happen on the phone because some people are busy working."

"We haven't seen you in so long," Sage said wistfully. "It's been months since you visited."

"It's been three weeks." Anxiety spread inside her like an ink stain. "Sage, you have to tell me about this geas. What exactly is it? And what would happen if I tried to break it?"

She heard the rush of an indrawn breath.

"Don't do anything rash, Justine. There are things you're not aware of."

"Obviously."

"You're a novice at spell-casting. If you tried to lift a geas, you could go from the frying pan right into the fire."

"Yeah, see, that's what I'm pissed about. Why are my only choices 'frying pan' or 'fire'? Why have you been keeping this from me? Didn't it occur to you that I had a right to know?"

"Where did you get this idea of a geas in the first place?"

Although Justine wanted to blurt out that she'd found out the truth from the Triodecad, she managed to hold her tongue.

The silence rode out until Sage asked, "Have you spoken with Marigold?"

Justine's eyes widened. "Does my mother know about this, too? Damn it, Sage, tell me what's going on!"

"Wait a moment. Rosemary has just come in from the garden."

Justine heard a muffled conference. She fidgeted and drummed her fingers on the desk. "Sage?" she asked impatiently, but there was no reply. She stood, pacing around the tiny office, the cell phone clamped to her ear.

Finally she heard Rosemary's voice. "Hello, Justine. I hear you're asking about a geas, of all things. What an upsetting word."

"It's more than a word, Rosemary. It's a *curse*."

"Not always."

"Are you saying a geas is a good thing?"

"No. But it's not necessarily a bad thing."

"Just tell me yes or no: Did someone bind a geas to me?"

"I can't confirm or deny anything until we can talk face-to-face."

"That means yes," Justine said bitterly. "It always means yes when someone won't confirm or deny something."

The revelation that Rosemary and Sage had both known about the geas hurt even more than Justine would have believed. All the times she had sat at their kitchen table and confided in them, told them how lonely she was, how much she longed to find love and was afraid it would never happen. And they had said *nothing*, even though they had known the truth: It was never going to happen because she'd been cursed.

"Come to the island and we'll talk," Rosemary said.

"Sure, I'll just drop everything. It's not like I have a business to run."

Rosemary's tone was reproachful. "Sarcasm doesn't become you, Justine."

"Neither does a lifelong curse." Yanking out her ponytail elastic, Justine scrubbed her fingers through her hair and pressed her palm against her tense forehead. "I'll come tomorrow morn-

76

ing after breakfast. It's supposed to be good weather—I'll take the kayak."

"We'll look forward to seeing you. We'll have lunch." A brittle pause. "You haven't . . . tried anything, have you?"

"What, like breaking the geas?" Justine asked with careful blandness. "Is there a spell that could do that?"

"It would be a difficult feat to accomplish on one's own. Especially for someone who hasn't practiced magic any more than you have. However, if someone did manage such a thing, the consequences could be severe. A geas is a powerful enchantment. Creating or breaking one exacts a heavy price."

"What do you mean?"

"We'll talk tomorrow," Rosemary said.

A defiant frown worked its way across Justine's face as the call ended.

It was one thing to pay a price for a mistake that she'd made on her own, but it was unbelievably unfair to have to pay a price for something that another person had done to her.

To Zoë's delight, Alex entered the inn's kitchen while she and Justine were preparing trays for afternoon tea. He was dressed casually in jeans and a T-shirt, his hiking boots coated with dried mud from having spent part of the day walking around the undeveloped Dream Lake property.

"My floor," Justine squeaked, seeing the track of footprints across the wood planks she had mopped that morning.

"Sorry." Alex had headed directly for Zoë, who was arranging plates of miniature fruit tarts on a silver tray. He hugged her from behind, one arm crossing high over her chest, the

77

other around her waist. "I'll clean it up before I leave," he told Justine over his shoulder, flashing an apologetic grin. Ducking his head, he kissed the side of Zoë's neck.

"Want a little tart?" Zoë asked, leaning back against him.

"Yes." Looking over her shoulder at the tray, he added, "I'll take one of those, too."

Zoë laughed and tried to swat him, and he crushed his mouth over hers in an ardent kiss. When she tried to end the kiss, he sank his hand into her blond curls, anchoring her in place as he sealed their mouths more tightly.

"Jeez," Justine said, "get a room." But she was pleased to see both of them so happy.

Alex had been known for the quality of his work, and for his ability to get a project done on time, but he'd also had a well-deserved reputation as a cynical and dissolute loner, a borderline alcoholic. It would not have been an exaggeration to call the change in him miraculous.

When the relationship had started, Justine had been honest with Zoë about her concerns, advising her not to try to save a man like Alex, who'd already been divorced once and appeared to be heading downhill. Zoë had agreed; you couldn't save a man like that. But you could be there for him if he was trying to save himself.

Only time would tell if Alex's transformation would hold. It was clear, however, that he was determined to be a good man for Zoë, the kind of man he thought she deserved.

"How did it go today?" Zoë asked breathlessly, when Alex took his mouth from hers.

He smiled down at her and lifted one of the tarts from the tray. "The deal looks good. I'm cautiously optimistic."

Justine knew that "cautiously optimistic" for Alex was the equivalent of wild enthusiasm for anyone else. "So what did you think about Jason Black and his entourage?" she asked.

"Kind of an odd group," Alex said. "All of them wound a little tight. Fast-talking and intense, and trying like hell to impress Jason." Alex devoured the tart in a single bite and paused to savor it, his eyes closing briefly. "God, that's good," he told Zoë.

Zoë smiled at him. "I'll get you some coffee."

"Thanks, sweetheart."

"And try one of those chocolate scones," Zoë added. "Usually I drizzle a glaze over them, but this time—"

"Stop feeding him," Justine commanded. "I want to hear more about Jason Black."

Alex picked up a chocolate scone, his gaze daring her to protest. "He's all business," he said. "Very smart, very direct. When he thinks an idea sucks, he lets you know. And when he makes a decision, that's it. No consensus-building, no compromise, just make it happen. Like most guys at his level, he's a control freak."

"Maybe you'll come to like him later," Zoë said, bringing him a cup of coffee.

Alex smiled at her optimism and took a swallow of coffee. "I like his project," he said, "and I like his money. That's not a bad start." He sent an amused glance to Justine, who was filling a stainless-steel samovar with water. "You may be interested to know that he wants the Dream Lake cottage."

"Wants to buy it?" Justine asked, her brows lifting.

Alex nodded. "We had the meeting there and had sandwiches brought in for lunch, and then he asked why the cottage isn't part of the Dream Lake parcel. So I told him it didn't belong to me, I was just renting it." Alex paused to finish the last bite of the chocolate scone, and washed it down with more coffee. "He asked me who owned it, at which point everyone pulled out their phones and tablets. Because whatever he wants, they all make sure he gets it."

A wide grin broke out on Justine's face. "What happened when you told him I'm the owner?"

"He looked at me like I'd just turned into a two-headed monkey. Your investment on that place is about to pay off big-time. Don't sell it for the first number they give you."

"I may not sell it at all," Justine said. "With that location, after the institute is built, I could charge a fortune for rent."

Alex grinned and told Zoë, "Looks like it's time for us to move."

Justine shook her head and laughed. "No, as long as Zoë wants to stay there, it's yours. But I figure you'll want to move eventually."

Catching hold of Zoë again, Alex ducked his dark head and said close to her ear, "You want me to build you a house? A little Victorian that looks like a wedding cake?"

Zoë turned to brush her lips against his and smiled as she picked up the tray. "For the next couple of years, you're going to be more than busy enough developing the Dream Lake property."

"Let me carry that for you," Alex said.

"No, just open the door. But please carry Justine's samovar; it's really heavy."

Quickly Alex moved to comply. As he came to take the water-filled container from Justine, she said, "Thanks, Alex."

He paused to rest the samovar on the counter and said, "About the cottage—don't hold back on selling it because of Zoë and me. We'll be happy wherever we live. And it would be a well-deserved windfall, after all you've done to help Zoë."

Justine smiled at him. "I'll think about it. I'm having dinner with Jason tonight. I'm sure he'll bring it up."

Surprise flickered in Alex's eyes. "He didn't mention that." After a brief hesitation, he added, "Be careful, Justine."

"Why?"

"After spending most of a day around Jason, I can guarantee you he's the type who arranges the game so he wins every time. I'm going ahead with the business deal, but if I thought about it too much, it would give me the yips."

"Me, too," Justine confessed sheepishly.

Alex glanced at her with an arched brow. He hefted the samovar. "Why are you having dinner with him, then?"

"He said he liked me."

"And?"

"The moment after he said it, I had this feeling that I sort of . . . almost . . . liked him, too."

"Women," Alex said feelingly, and carried the samovar from the kitchen.

Nine

....

Most of Jason's romantic relationships had evolved from situations of convenient proximity . . . a female executive he'd met at a game-developer conference, or a journalist who'd interviewed him, or a voice actress who'd had to do two hundred hours of recording for an Inari game.

He never let anyone set him up on a blind date, having learned long ago that it was the surest way to kill a friendship. In fact, Jason disliked the very premise of a date, which amounted to making the commitment of an entire evening with someone you didn't know and most likely wouldn't want to see again.

His relationships tended to be short-lived. He always ended them by giving the woman a piece of jewelry as a salve for hurt feelings, and it usually worked, except for a couple of times when a woman had told him that the parting gift felt like payment for services rendered. "A fuck-off bracelet," the last one had called it sourly, sliding the Tiffany diamond bangle onto her slender arm. But she hadn't given it back.

Justine Hoffman was the first woman he'd met in a long time who he suspected would probably tell him where to shove it, if he gave her a fuck-off present.

Maybe it was just that he'd become so accustomed to receiving admiring attention from women, from having his way too easily and too often, that it was a novelty to encounter a woman who had no desire to become involved with him. But he couldn't stop thinking about Justine. He kept remembering the way she laughed, throaty and natural, tapering down to a luminous grin. Irresistible.

Jason had already broken one of his personal rules: The woman always had to come to him. Since Justine clearly wasn't going to do that, he would have to do the pursuing. Another rule was that when he was interested in a woman, he would learn as much as possible about her while at the same time revealing as little as possible about himself. Justine would demand mutual risk, mutual honesty. He wasn't certain how much he could lower his guard, or to what extent he was capable of opening up to anyone. If he wanted her, however, he would have to try. He'd have to unlock doors that had been closed for so long, he would have trouble even finding the key.

It would be a hell of a lot easier just to walk away. He was good at walking away from things he wanted, ignoring temptation, letting the rational part of his brain override emotion. But once in a blue moon, he encountered something or someone he wanted too badly to deny.

Jason went to the doorstep of the cottage behind the inn at one minute before seven, and knocked.

Justine opened the door, all silk and slender curves. "Hi." Her smiling gaze ran over him. "Come in."

Jason obeyed, so mesmerized that he nearly tripped over the threshold. She was wearing a short halter dress made of a thin knit fabric, in a shade of peachy-beige that had given him a brief and startling impression of nudity. Her feet were bare, the toe-nails polished with pink sparkles. Her hair was pulled back in a simple ponytail with one lock wrapped around the fastener.

"I just need to put my shoes on," Justine said.

Still staring, Jason responded with a wordless nod as she went into an adjoining room. A miniature hook at the top of her dress zipper had been left undone. He couldn't help imagining pulling the zipper down, the slithering sound as the fabric opened and fell away from the smooth flesh of her back.

Trying to distract himself from erotic thoughts, he focused on his surroundings. The cottage was small and immaculate. The walls and furniture were painted in pastels, the plump sofa piled with oversized pillows covered in striped or flowered fabric, some trimmed with tassels. It was an unapologetically feminine room, but the distressed paint and touches of antique-shop finds made it comfortable and inviting.

Justine returned, wearing sandals with cobweb-fine straps and kitten heels.

"You look beautiful," Jason said.

"Thank you."

"I noticed—" He was forced to break off, the words sticking in his throat. "The hook at the back of your dress—if you'd like me to—" He paused again as he saw her blush. Not an ordinary blush, but a deep infusion of color that swept all the way from the bodice of her dress to her hairline. He wanted to follow that visible heat with his mouth and fingertips, kiss her everywhere.

"Yes, thanks," Justine said, trying to sound casual, not quite managing. "I couldn't reach it."

She turned away from him slowly, gathering the gleaming length of her ponytail over one shoulder. Jason's gaze passed over the fine musculature of her back, the tender nape of her neck with its nearly invisible dusting of down. She had the build of a dancer, slender and flexible.

The ties of the halter-neck bodice were done in a fragile bow. He hesitated, struggling for self-control. When he was able, he reached for the miniature hook-and-eye closure with the caution of a man defusing a bomb.

His knuckles brushed her silky back as he worked at the hook. He felt her stiffen, and excitement crackled through him like the pinging of metal that had heated too rapidly.

"Done," he said huskily.

She let her ponytail fall back into place. He wanted to grip the glossy length of it in handfuls, wind it around his palms.

Justine faced him, looking up at him with eyes the color of bittersweet chocolate. Heat underscored the silence in a dark, sweet pulse.

"Where are we going?" Justine asked.

It took him a moment to assemble thought into words. "The Coho Restaurant, if that's all right with you."

"Yes, it's one of my favorites."

The restaurant was in walking distance, only three blocks from the ferry dock. As Jason accompanied Justine along the quiet sidewalks, he matched his pace to hers, every stride relaxed and unhurried.

They entered the restaurant, a converted Craftsman house that seated only a handful of tables. Gentle flickers of candlelight dappled the white tablecloths. The servers achieved the perfect balance of attentiveness and restraint, appearing at the table when needed, becoming invisible for just the right amount of time.

"Did you have a good meeting with Alex?" Justine asked after the wine was poured.

Jason nodded. "He seems like the right guy for the job."

"Because . . . ?"

"It's obvious he cares about the details. His work is good, and he brings projects in on time. And he doesn't scare easily. We ended the day talking to the lawyers about adding a financial-risk transfer mechanism to the contract. If the project isn't finished by a specified date, we lose a million-dollar municipal tax credit, and Alex will be on the hook for it. He's fine with that. He knows he can get it done. I like that kind of confidence."

Justine looked perturbed. "But if something happens, Alex will be ruined. He wouldn't be able to come up with a million dollars."

Jason shrugged. "Big risk, big reward."

Picking up her wineglass, Justine said, "Well, then. Here's to obtaining your municipal tax credit."

Her expression was innocent, but Jason knew when he was being mocked.

"I would have suggested a more lyrical toast," he said.

"Feel free."

After a moment, he quoted, "'Every day is a journey, and the journey itself is home.'"

Justine gave him an arrested glance. "Who wrote that?"

"Matsuo. A Japanese poet."

"You read poetry?"

"Sometimes."

"I didn't know men did that."

"Being well read is one of the benefits of insomnia."

They touched glasses and drank, savoring the berry and smoke flavors of a Willamette pinot noir.

"Alex mentioned that you own the cottage at the end of Dream Lake Road," Jason said.

A glint of enjoyment appeared in Justine's eyes, as if she'd been waiting for such a remark. "Why, yes, I do."

"How did you end up owning it?"

"I never even knew about the cottage until this past summer. Zoë's grandmother Emma owned it, but no one had lived there for years. It was in terrible shape." She stared into her wineglass, swirling the bright liquid. "Emma had been diagnosed with vascular dementia, and she was going downhill fast. Zoë wanted to take care of her for the last few months of her life. So I offered to buy the cottage and renovate it, which gave Zoë and Emma some cash and also a rent-free place to stay."

"That was generous of you." From what he'd seen of Justine's finances in a background check, she wasn't exactly swimming in cash herself.

"It was no big deal," Justine said. "And Alex outdid himself with the renovations—he threw in a lot of custom stuff we didn't have to pay for." A quick smile crossed her face. "Somehow I think that had more to do with Zoë than with me."

"It doesn't sound like you have an emotional attachment to the place."

"I do now that I know you want it," Justine said demurely, sipping her wine.

Jason grinned and said idly, "I might have an interest in it."

Her slender fingers slid along the wineglass stem, and his gaze tracked the movement closely. "Does it bother you that there's one little piece of lakefront you won't own?"

"I don't like loose ends," he admitted. "Have you thought about pricing the house?"

"I haven't even thought about selling it."

"I'll give you a half million for it," he offered, enjoying the astonished look on her face.

"You're not serious." She saw that he was. "My God. *No.*"

Jason looked askance at her reaction. "It's a generous offer."

"It's a *stupid* offer. Why would you offer to pay so much more than it's worth?"

"Because I can. Why are you offended?"

Justine let out an exasperated breath. "Maybe because an offer like that could be construed as trying to buy someone."

That reached down to the cynicism that was never far beneath the surface, and Jason found himself saying, "You're not going to argue the fact that everyone has a price, I hope."

"No. But you can't afford my price."

"I have a lot of money," he countered.

"My price has nothing to do with money." She stared at him with a bruised gravity that touched him. "And don't do that."

"Don't do what?"

"Don't try to impress me with your oversized wallet. It's annoying. And it's not fair to either of us."

Jason gazed at her for a long moment. "I apologize," he said gently.

Her face relaxed. "It's okay."

Conversation paused as the server brought their entrées. They had both ordered halibut sheathed in potato crust and doused with chardonnay cream sauce, accented with the crackle of fried basil leaves.

As they enjoyed the fresh, perfectly prepared food, they turned the discussion to their families. They quickly found they had something in common: Neither of them had one. In response to Justine's tentative questions, Jason told her about the point in his life when everything had fallen apart, midway through his sophomore year at USC.

"It started when I realized I was never going to be more than competent at college ball," he said. "I didn't have the instinct that makes a competent player into a great one." He smiled wryly. "And on top of that, I'd become obsessed with game design. Whenever I was working out or going through conditioning drills, all I could think about was when I'd get a chance to hang out in the campus digital media lab." Catching the stem of his wineglass between his fingertips, Jason traced along it slowly, remembering. "So I went home at Christmas to tell my parents I was dropping out of the football program. I would pay my own way—I'd already written and sold a 2-D game, so I had a foot in the door. But the second I saw my mother, I forgot all about my personal crap. In two months, she'd turned into a skeleton."

"Why?" Justine asked softly.

"She'd been diagnosed with liver cancer. She hadn't told me. Refused treatment of any kind. That kind of cancer moves like a freight train. She died within a week of that visit."

College hadn't mattered after that. Nothing had mattered.

He'd left school and home and everything familiar, in the attempt to find meaning in something.

"I'm so sorry," Justine said.

He gave a quick shake of his head, not wanting sympathy. "It was a long time ago."

Her hand crept toward his. Jason let his hand open naturally, palm exposed. Her touch was tentative, warm.

"What about your dad?" Justine asked. "Do you see him at all now?"

Jason shook his head, still staring at their adjoined hands. "If I did, I might kill him."

Her fingers stilled against his palm. "He was a bad father?" she asked in a neutral tone.

Jason hesitated before answering. You could either describe a man like his father with a hundred thousand words, or one. "Violent."

As a residential plumber, Ray Black had had no shortage of work supplies to use in disciplining an unruly son: wrenches, pipes, brass chains, flexible plumbing line. Jason had endured more than a few emergency-room visits, joking with the nurses and doctors about what a clumsy teenager he was, always getting contusions and fractures. High school football injuries. Got his bell rung again, that was contact sports for you.

"Your father knows he went too far. He promised it won't happen again. Smile and say it was an accident."

And Jason had done what his mother asked, smiling and lying, knowing it was far from the last time. Knowing also that the way to be as different as possible from Ray was never to lose control.

"Before my mother died," he heard himself say, "she asked

90

me to forgive and forget. But so far I haven't managed to do either."

There were no reserves of forgiveness left in him. The details of his childhood were as indelible as headstone engravings. He remembered things he didn't want to remember. Although no one could understand him without knowing at least some of those details, he'd never brought himself to confide in anyone. His past was not something to be used as a bargaining chip to force someone's sympathy. And so far he hadn't seen any benefit in having someone understand him.

Justine's fingers slid across the inside of his wrist, rubbing lightly as if she could feel his heartbeat. "I haven't managed it, either," she said. "My mother and I are estranged. We blame each other. She can't forgive me for—" A helpless pause. "So many things. Mostly she can't forgive me for not wanting her life."

"Which is?"

"Oh . . ." Justine shrugged and looked away from him, her smile evasive. When her gaze cut back to his, she seemed to look at him through a hedge of secrets. "She's . . . different."

"Different how?"

"She's very committed to what you might call an alternative religion." Another weighted pause. "Nature based."

"She's Wiccan?"

"Sort of beyond that."

Jason stared at her alertly.

Her hand began to pull away, but Jason closed his fingers over hers in a gentle snare.

"I was raised pagan," she said. "Most of my childhood was spent at psychic festivals, spirit gatherings, magical arts meetings,

91

drum circles . . . I even marched in a couple of pagan pride parades. I'm sure it looked pretty crazy to outsiders. It looked crazy from the inside, too." Justine smiled and tried to sound light, but a vein showed on the porcelain surface of her forehead, a delicate blue longitude of tension. "I was always different," she said. "I hated it."

Jason wanted to touch her face, smooth away the signs of distress. Instead he let his thumb skim her knuckles in soothing strokes.

"At Halloween," Justine continued, "I never got to dress up in a costume and go trick-or-treating. Instead I had to go to a Samhain dinner and sit next to empty plates set for the spirits of deceased relatives."

His brows lifted slightly. "Did any of them show up?"

"I can't tell you, or you'd freak out and run away."

"Not before dessert." He paused. "I'm getting the impression that your paganism involved some elements of . . . witchcraft?"

She blanched and kept silent.

To her astonishment, his eyes contained a glint of irreverent humor. "So are you a good witch," he asked, "or a bad witch?"

Recognizing the quote from *The Wizard of Oz*, Justine tried to smile but couldn't. "I'd rather not be labeled."

She had told him too much. And even worse, it had all been true. What was it about him that turned her into such a blabbermouth? Feeling vaguely ill, she tried to pull her hand away again, but Jason wouldn't let her.

"Justine," he said quietly. "Wait. Can I just say something? . . . I've spent the past ten years creating complex fantasy worlds full of dragons and ogres. It's the kind of job that a normal person couldn't do. A couple of my closest friends, who both happen to work with me, have been known to wear pointy latex ears or hobbit feet to office meetings. And as I've already told you, I'm a pathological workaholic insomniac with no soul. So a little dabbling in the black arts during your spare time is hardly a problem for me."

Justine was afraid to believe him. But she stopped trying to pull away. And the sick feeling was fading. Her fingers were tucked firmly in his now; she wasn't going to let go.

Neither of them were.

Ten

For the rest of dinner, Justine felt way more intoxicated than two glasses of wine would have justified. The conversation had assumed its own momentum, flowing without effort. They had similar taste in music—Death Cab for Cutie, The Black Keys, Lenny Kravitz. Jason tried to explain Japanese anime as an art form, the stylistic exaggerations, the linear quality derived from Japanese calligraphy. She agreed to watch *Howl's Moving Castle* with an open mind.

Some men were so good-looking that they didn't have to be sexy. Some men were so sexy they didn't have to be good-looking. For this man to be both was proof that life was essentially unfair. He was one of nature's randomly created genetic lottery winners.

No one would blame me if I slept with him. That beautiful face, those hands . . . I wouldn't even blame me.

They shared a dish of orange-ginger sorbet, crisp and tart against her tongue. It dissolved instantly in her hot mouth.

I want to kiss him, she thought, staring helplessly at the firm contours of his lips.

Trying to distract herself, she asked more questions about his family, his mother, and he answered obligingly. Her name had been Amaya, which meant "night rain" in Japanese. She had been kind but cool-natured. She had kept the house clean and organized and there had always been cut flowers in a vase on the table.

I want to lie on a bed with him and feel his hands on me. I want to feel him everywhere. I want his breath on my skin.

"Were your parents ever in love?" she heard herself ask. "Did it at least start out that way?"

Jason shook his head. "My father had the idea that marrying a half-Japanese woman meant he would have an obedient wife. Instead he ended up with an unhappy one."

I want to feel him move inside me and see the pleasure on his face. I want him to tease me until I beg for more.

"Why did she marry him?"

"I think it came down to a question of timing. She was lonely, and he asked. So she settled."

"I would never do that," Justine said.

"You haven't been as lonely as she was. She was an outsider. Most of her family was in Japan—"

"I've been exactly that lonely. You're not connected to anything. Some nights it feels like you're dying by the hour. You're so desperate you can't even attract the kind of person you once swore you'd never settle for. So you stay busy working, and you take magazine personality quizzes, and you try not to hate couples who wear stupid coordinating shirts and look happy just to stand together in the checkout line—"

She stopped abruptly, blinking, as Jason took one of her hands in both of his. He stared at her steadily, his thumb circling into her palm, which had turned acutely sensitive, nerves prickling at the thin-skinned center.

Her voice had risen, she realized with a stab of sick horror. She'd been talking too loudly in this tiny restaurant. Ranting. About *loneliness*.

Spirits, please kill me now.

Humiliation like this could not be endured. She would have to leave the country and change her name. Self-deportation was the only answer.

"I usually do better than this on a first date," she whispered.

"It's okay," he said gently. "Whatever you do, or say, or feel. It's all okay."

Justine could only stare at him. Whatever she did was okay? What kind of man said something like that? Was there a chance he actually meant it?

Jason had already paid the check. Standing, he helped her up, pulling back her chair efficiently.

They went outside. The sky was cloudy and milk-pail gray, the air filled with mist that tasted like sea spray. The blare of the arriving ten o'clock ferry coursed along the street, reverberating against darkened shop doors and quiet buildings.

The serrated caw of a crow scraped along Justine's nerves. She saw the flap of raggedy black wings as the bird flew away from its perch on the restaurant roof. A bad omen.

Jason took her elbow and drew her to the side of the building, his movements slow and deliberate.

She drew in a quick breath as his arms went around her. Shadows surrounded them in stone-scented coolness, fine gravel excoriating the thin soles of her sandals. She was briefly disoriented by the darkness. One of his hands slid behind the nape of her neck in an electrifying grip. His other hand went to her back, pulling her against his unyielding body. The wool of his sports coat, the scent of his skin and plain white soap, mingled in a clean and intoxicating fragrance.

His head bent, his mouth finding hers with searing pressure. She gasped, and he went after the hushed sound as if he could taste it, his mouth stroking over hers. Kisses easy and slow, melting heat wrapped in coolness.

He stroked a wisp of hair that had slipped from her ponytail, gently tucking it behind her ear, and his mouth went to her exposed neck. So gentle, as if her skin were as delicate as jasmine petals. He found a tender pulse point, and she shivered and arched against him. Pleasure pooled low in her stomach and the tips of her breasts and between her thighs.

Shaking too hard to support her own weight, Justine leaned against him. His arm braced her back, reinforcing her balance. His lips shaped hers, pressing them apart. He tasted like oranges, sweetness on his tongue. Some of her breaths broke into moans, and she tried to swallow them back, tried to make herself be quiet.

Harder, deeper kisses, slowly ravishing until she couldn't breathe or think, all she could do was feel, her body absorbing sensation, brimming with it. She didn't know how many aching minutes had passed before Jason eased back. His mouth was slow to leave hers, stealing back for another brief nudge of a kiss, then grazing her cheek as if he couldn't stop tasting her.

The night had cooled, darkness falling like midnight flowers. Removing his coat, Jason settled it over her shoulders. Gratefully Justine pushed her arms through the silk-lined sleeves, his warmth and scent wrapped around her. He took her hand.

There was very little conversation as they walked back to the inn. So much had been said in the past few hours, so much privacy had been willingly discarded. Except that Justine couldn't think of what she would choose to take back. She tried to figure out the moment when the line had been crossed, when she had revealed too much. But there had been no line. There still wasn't a line.

As they followed a stone path that led around the back of the inn to her cottage, Justine felt her stomach lift and suspend, as if she were on a plummeting hot-air balloon. Everything was too acute, too sensitive.

Was this how it was supposed to feel, this wrenching attraction that stunned and scared and thrilled all at once? Maybe this was other people's normal.

God, how do they stand it?

As they approached the cottage, light from an inside lamp shone through a window and scattered in lemon rectangles on the ground. Justine turned to face him at the front threshold. Nervousness had turned her insides into a pinball machine, all rattles and bells and springs.

"What are you doing tomorrow?" she asked.

"I'll be up early for a boat checkout with a charter rep."

"What kind of boat are you leasing?"

"A twenty-two-foot Bayliner. I'm going to take a couple of the guys out for some fishing and touring."

"There's not a lot of fishing space on a boat that size."

"The way we fish," he said dryly, "it won't matter."

"There are some tricky shallows and rocks around here."

"I can read a chart."

"That's good." She wondered if she should say something about the kiss . . . kisses . . . outside the restaurant. Jason remained quiet. Fumbling for the doorknob, she opened the door a few inches and faced him again. "Thanks for dinner. I enjoyed it more than I expected to. That is . . . I had no expectations. I mean . . . I didn't think that you and I—"

"I understand," Jason said with a slight smile. "I'll see you tomorrow."

He wasn't going to make a move on her, then. Justine expected to feel relief. But there was only the deflating sense that she was facing yet another long empty night. "I'll be gone most of tomorrow," she told him. "I'm visiting a couple of friends on Cauldron Island. A pair of women who live in the old lighthouse."

"Are you taking a water taxi?"

"No, I have a kayak."

Jason's face changed, the amusement fading. "You're going alone?"

"It's not far. A couple of miles at most. And it's a familiar route. I can make it in an hour or less."

"You have a signaling kit?"

"And a repair kit."

"You still shouldn't go alone. I'll take you on the Bayliner."

She gave him a skeptical glance. "And then how would I get home?"

"I'll pick you up later. Or if you'd prefer, I'll send a water taxi."

"Thanks, but I don't like waiting to be picked up, or making someone else wait. Really, there's no need to worry. I like paddling to Cauldron Island. I've done it a lot, and I've never had any problems."

"Where are you launching from?"

"Roche Harbor."

"You'll be wearing a wet suit?"

His concern over her safety was both flattering and vaguely irritating. She wasn't used to answering to anyone for her decisions. "No, no one does for a short trip like this. Kayakers around here dress for the air temperature, unless they know they're going to be facing challenging conditions."

"You can't know for certain whether you're going to face challenging conditions or not. And you could capsize regardless. Wear a wet suit."

"Wear a wet suit?" Justine repeated. "We're back to giving orders again?"

Although she could tell that Jason wanted to argue further, he kept his mouth shut. Shoving his hands in his pockets, he turned to leave.

He was going to walk off without another word?

"I'll bring up your vodka in a few minutes," she said.

Jason paused. "Thanks, but I don't want it tonight," he said without turning around.

"It's no problem. And I'm not going to risk being bitch-slapped by Priscilla tomorrow for skipping her instructions."

Jason returned to her, looking annoyed. "You can skip the vodka if I tell you to skip it."

"I'll leave a tray outside your door. You can take it or leave it, but it's going to be there."

He gave her a cold stare. "Why would you insist on doing something I've just told you not to do? Especially when it's unnecessary work for you."

"You're not refusing the vodka to spare me unnecessary work," she shot back. "You're refusing it because you're pissed at me for taking my kayak out alone tomorrow."

Jason shouldered his way into the cottage, taking her with him. The jacket slid from her shoulders to the floor. He took her upper arms and hauled her upward until she was forced to stand on her toes. She was pressed all along him, the feel of him electrifying.

He bent over her so that she couldn't see his face. The low rasp of his voice raised every hair on her body.

"The reason I don't want you to bring anything to my room, Justine, is because there's only so much temptation I can handle. In case you haven't figured it out yet"—a hard, intimate nudge caused her to gasp—"I want you. Every time I looked at you in that damned dress tonight, I imagined you naked. I want to—" He broke off, holding her tightly, trying to regulate his breathing. "Do not come to me tonight," he said eventually, "or you'll end up in my bed, and I'll screw you to the Stone Age and back. That clear enough for you?"

Justine nodded in a daze. The thin layers of their clothing did nothing to conceal the shape of his aroused flesh, the aggressive hardness and heat. It felt so good, being caught tightly against him, that she was paralyzed. She could smell his skin, salt and amber and night air.

After a sweltering pause, Jason's chest rose and fell unsteadily.

"I have to let go of you," he said, seeming to speak more to himself than to her.

Justine clung to him. "You could stay," she managed to whisper.

"Not tonight."

"Why?"

"You're not ready."

"Make me ready."

His breath caught. His hand moved in a restless stroke up and down her spine. "Justine . . . have you ever had sex on the first date?"

"Yes," she said instantly.

Jason took her chin and forced her to look up at him. After trying to hold his gaze for a few seconds, Justine flushed. "No. But stay with me anyway."

He continued to stare into her eyes. The strong angles of his features were thrown into sharp relief by the lamplight, one side cast in shadow. "It's too soon," he said flatly. "Some people can hook up without feeling bad about it the morning after. You're not one of them. No matter how good it was, you would regret it tomorrow."

"I wouldn't," she protested.

"It's written all over you. So we're going to take it slow." As she opened her mouth to argue, he said, "Not for my sake. For yours."

Her body was a collection of hungering aches. She could hardly think past the desire that had turned her insides molten. A lifetime's worth of desire, leading to this man, this moment. "But I want you," she said, appalled by the plaintive note in her voice.

Something in his face gentled. He approached her slowly, reaching for her. His hands slid over her body, feeling her through the silky knit fabric, gently gripping the high curves of her hips. She lifted her face blindly as his mouth descended, her thoughts scattering in a rush of excitement. A moan stirred in her throat, and he licked deep as if he could taste the sound. His hand traveled from her midriff to her breast, cupping the firm curve while his thumb moved over the tip in teasing swirls. Perspiration bloomed on the surface of her skin until the synthetic fabric of her dress clung uncomfortably, and all she could think about was how much she wanted to strip it off.

Jason reached low behind her hips, grasping through the back of her skirt to curl his fingertips beneath the elastic strap of her thong. He exerted just enough light tension to pull the tiny crotch of the underwear taut between her thighs. Justine quivered as the scrap of silk cradled a hard, urgent throb.

"I can take care of you," Jason whispered.

"You . . . you changed your mind?" she asked, her lips feeling swollen.

Letting go of the thong strap, he tugged her skirt higher and slid his hand beneath. He caressed the sensitive curve of her hip. "No. But I'll make you feel good. Right here and now." His thumb slipped beneath the elastic strap of the thong. "All you have to do is hold on to me. Tell me you want it. Just tell me . . ."

As his hand slid over her bottom, Justine reached back and caught at his wrist. "Wait. We're not going to have sex, but you want to . . . go to casual third base?"

The phrase caused his lips to twitch. "I can't remember the specifics of casual third base," he said dryly. "But that sounds about right."

"But I would be the only one getting off?"

"Yes."

"*No.*" Scowling, Justine stepped back from him. "Condescending jerk. You turn me down for sex because you've decided that I'm too immature to—"

"Inexperienced."

"Same thing."

"No it's not."

"Too immature," she continued heatedly, "to be able to make decisions about what I want to do with my own body."

"It's not an insult when a man wants to take it slow with you."

"Then what is it?"

"A compliment."

"It doesn't feel like one." Somewhere inside she knew she should give him credit for trying to be a gentleman, but at the moment she was too sexually frustrated to care. Scowling, she went to the door and opened it. "*Go.* And don't bother asking me out again. I don't give second chances."

Jason grinned and obliged her, bending to pick up his jacket from the floor. Before leaving, he paused at the threshold and said, "You shouldn't rule out second chances. Sometimes they come with interesting bonus features."

After a broken night's sleep, Justine woke up early and began the day as usual, filling and starting the commercial coffee machine in the kitchen, setting the tables in the dining area, and preheating the ovens for Zoë.

When Zoë arrived, looking as fresh as sunshine and daisies, she took one look at Justine and asked, "What happened?"

"Nothing," Justine grumbled. She was sitting at the kitchen table, holding a mug of coffee with both hands. She lifted the mug to her lips and drained its contents without stopping.

After stirring cream and sugar into a fresh mug of coffee, Zoë brought it to her. "The date didn't go well?"

"The date was fantastic. Incredible food and wine, great conversation, with the most gorgeous guy I've ever met. By the end of dinner, I was ready to have sex with him on the hood of the nearest car."

"Then why . . . ?"

"He didn't want to. Something about 'too soon' and 'for my own good,' which everyone knows is guy-speak for 'you're not bangable.' And then he took off like he was heading out of the forest covered in bees."

"You're exaggerating," Zoë said, a tremor of laughter in her voice. "Is it possible that he respects you enough not to want to rush into anything?"

"Guys don't think like that. Their idea of a great first date is not, 'Wow, I'd really love to watch that woman eat and then go home by myself.'" She shook her head morosely. "It's all for the best. He's too rich. Too controlling. Too *everything*."

"What can I do?" Zoë asked, her eyes soft with concern.

"If you wouldn't mind keeping an eye on Annette and Nita while they work today? . . . I'm going to paddle out to Cauldron Island and visit Rosemary and Sage."

"Of course. I'm glad you're going to see them. It always seems to do you good."

It was nearly impossible to dress for a combination of seventy-five-degree air and fifty-degree water temperature. Kayak outfitting that provided a decent amount of warmth in the water would be unbearably hot and restrictive while paddling. Given such a choice, most kayakers decided to forgo wet suits and take their chances. Justine decided to compromise by wearing a short-sleeved Gore-Tex dry top, and neoprene knee-length pants. It wouldn't be as comfortable as a simple base layer tee and shorts, but if she capsized, she would need the extra protection.

Sudden immersion in cold water was dangerous even for experienced swimmers and kayakers. Justine had experienced it a couple of times in the past while taking a kayaking class. Even being prepared for it, the cold shock was nasty and overwhelming. It forced an involuntary gasping response, which was big trouble if your face was underwater. And even if your head was above water, your larynx could close up your airway, a form of death known as "dry drowning."

The day was overcast, the wind brisk, a light chop to the water. A low-pressure system was moving in, which might result in light rain and stronger winds. Having managed those conditions easily in the past, Justine wasn't worried.

"I wouldn't stay out for long, if I was you," a boater at the Roche Harbor dock said, while Justine folded up her kayak dolly and stowed it. The elderly man was standing with a cup of coffee in one hand and a doughnut in the other. "Front's coming in."

Justine gestured with her phone before zipping it into a dry bag. "My weather app says it's going to be okay."

"App," he scoffed, and ate another bite of his doughnut.

"Clouds yesterday looked like mackerel scales. That means a storm's coming. See those gulls coming in, flying low? See all the smelt feeding at the surface? All signs. Mother Nature's the app I've used for fifty years, and she's never wrong."

"Those smelt haven't checked the local Doppler," Justine said with a grin. "The forecast is fine."

He shook his head in the manner of a seasoned mariner who was rarely heeded by impudent youngsters. "Forecasts and dead fish: Both of 'em go bad quick."

After fastening her life jacket, Justine set out with efficient forward strokes of her paddle, pacing herself for the hour-long trip. The wind cut through the warmth of the day and kept her comfortable. Gripping her paddle, she concentrated on planting the blades behind each successive oncoming wave.

The wind changed, forcing Justine to zigzag from her original heading. Bending low to lessen the wind resistance, she grabbed and pulled water with the paddle. It was a high-intensity workout. Her momentum was broken by the constant bracing necessary to keep the kayak from broaching and turning parallel to the waves.

The wind gusts, now needled with rain, hit with escalating force. Quartering winds pushed her in one direction while the water pushed her in another. The fetch of the waves lengthened, energy rising in foamy liquid hills. Squinting at the sky, Justine was startled by how dark and thick the cloud cover had become, the leading edge thick and abnormally tall.

It was happening too fast. It didn't make sense.

This isn't natural, she thought with a stab of fear.

"Don't try to bluff fate," Rosemary had once warned her.

She had been paddling for at least an hour—she should have

reached Cauldron Island by now. As she tried to get a fix on her position, she was stunned to realize that the fifty-foot bluff of Cauldron Island was still at least a mile away, and the current had pushed her well off course. If she didn't make headway fast, she was going to find herself tossed like a child's toy in the rough-and-tumble of Haro Strait.

Waves broke hard over the bow, knocking out items she had tucked beneath the elastic deck line . . . a bottle of Gatorade, her signal kit.

Her heart was slamming with effort. If she'd had a free hand, she would have shaken a fist at the sky. Attacking the water with renewed fury, she muscled her way through roller-coaster swells. In a couple of minutes, better sense prevailed and she tried to spare her aching arms by keeping the paddle strokes low and using her trunk muscles. The only thoughts left were those connected to survival.

The entire world was water. Rain and ocean, above and below, spraying and roiling, pushing and tossing.

Billows shoved the kayak parallel and broadsided her. She leaned into each oncoming surge to keep from capsizing, and paddled to turn the bow of the kayak into the whitecaps. Another wave hit, but she couldn't react fast enough.

The kayak flipped.

Eleven

· ·

Burning-cold blackness. Pain everywhere, all at once, as if she'd been set on fire. She tried to complete an Eskimo roll, but the kayak had capsized toward her weaker rolling side, and she couldn't carry the movement through. Suspended upside down, disoriented by the cold shock, she grappled for the fastening loop of the waterproof spray skirt that held her into the cockpit of the kayak. The cold had already begun to mix her up; she couldn't find the loop and panic was taking over.

She managed to fight her way sideways until her face broke the surface for the split second necessary to drag in a quick breath. Going back under, she searched for the loop and found it. A frantic tug, and the spray skirt came off. She fought her way out of the kayak. Coming to the surface, she grabbed the overturned craft and filled her lungs before another wave broke.

It was unbelievably cold. Her skin and flesh were numb, her blood pressure ratcheting furiously. The kayak paddle bobbed a few feet away, still tethered to the bow on a leash fastened with nylon snap hooks. Panting, she maneuvered to the bow, gripping the elastic deck to maintain her hold on the kayak. Gripping the leash, she tugged until the paddle was in reach. It was hard to make her hand close around the handle.

She had to get out of the water. Her fine motor skills were gone. In about ten minutes, blood flow to nonessential muscles would shut off.

Reaching under the kayak, she found the foam paddle float stored beneath the bungee cord on the deck, and pulled it free. She needed the paddle float to climb back into the kayak. Her hands were as clumsy as if they were encased in pot holders. She worked to slide one end of her paddle into the nylon pocket on the back of the float.

Before she had finished, a wave slammed into her. It was like running into a concrete wall, the impact nearly knocking her out. Wheezing, choking, she saw that the foam paddle float had been carried away. Her fist gripped the paddle handle, its leash still fastened to the kayak.

She made her way back to the kayak, grateful for the buoyancy of her life jacket.

With the paddle float gone, the only option was to flip the kayak right side up and try to climb onto the stern in a ladder-crawl maneuver. As she grappled for the deck line, however, she found she barely had any grip strength left.

It was happening too fast. The cold knifed deeper, her muscles stiffening as if she were turning to stone. She was scared, but that was a good sign; it was when you stopped feeling scared, when you stopped caring, that you were in the worst danger.

She tried to think of a spell, a prayer, anything that made

sense, but words floated at the top of her head like the letters in a bowl of alphabet soup.

The yellow plastic surface of the kayak bumped against her head, galvanizing her.

The choice was simple: Get back in, and live. Stay in the water, and die.

Panting, grunting with effort, she flipped the kayak over and worked her way to the stern. The water shunted her in violent surges, up, down, sideways.

Every movement required intense will and focus. She knew what to do: Stow the paddle in the rigging. Push the stern down with your body weight. Kick your feet to launch yourself onto the stern decking. Crawl to the cockpit.

But Justine wasn't sure if she was actually doing those things or merely thinking them. No, she was still in the water. The bow of the kayak had risen; she must have pushed the stern down. She couldn't tell if her legs were moving, if she would be able to execute a strong enough kick to launch herself onto the craft. If she screwed up, there wouldn't be another chance.

In a moment she found herself sprawled on the stern, her legs straddled on either side of the kayak. *Thank you, spirits.* Fighting to keep the craft balanced, she began to crawl toward the center.

But another wave was coming. A five-foot wall of water rolled directly toward the side of the kayak. Justine watched it approach with a strange sense of resignation, understanding that she was going to capsize again. It was over. She closed her eyes and held her breath as the world spun. The kayak and the paddle were ripped away from her, and she was submerged in a hell of churning coldness. The life jacket buoyed her to the milk-froth surface.

111

She could barely see or hear in the chaos, but a thunderous roar descended as if the entire sky were caving in. Shuddering, she turned to see a massive white shape upwind of her, rising and falling on the tumult. It took a long time for her disoriented brain to register that it was a boat. She was at the point of not caring about anything at all, not even whether she was rescued.

Someone was shouting. She couldn't make out the words, but from the sound of his voice, he was probably cursing a blue streak. She felt another wave strike. Coughing up a mouthful of salt water, she tried to push a wet curtain of hair out of her eyes, but there was no feeling left in her hands. More shouting. A bright orange bag with a loop landed directly in front of her.

Her thought process had been dismantled. She stared at it dumbly, her brain slow to process what her reaction should be, her limbs and torso shuddering violently.

Furious commands shot through the air, willing her into action. She knew the sounds were words, but they made no sense. Although she didn't understand what she was supposed to do, her body took over. She found herself making clumsy pounces for the bag, like a puppy playing with a ball. The second time she tried, she managed to close her arms around the orange foam shape. She held it to her chest. Immediately she was towed through the punishing water.

Her thoughts kept disintegrating before she could attach meaning to them. It didn't matter, although some distant part of her brain knew that it should matter. The whole world was water, above and below, water dragging at her feet, urging her to sink into the feeling and go to sleep where it was dark and calm, far beneath the waves.

Instead, she was hauled upward with stunning force. Consciousness jolted through her as she was dumped onto a padded bench in the back of the boat. Shivering too hard to speak or think, she lay on a bench, looking up at a man whose face was familiar but whose name she couldn't recall. He stripped off his Windbreaker and wrapped it around her. Lightning split the sky with long branches as the man went to the helm station.

It was a recreational boat with a removable bow cover, unsuited to heavy open seas. The outboard engine snarled as the man threw it into gear. Since the waves were too high to put the boat into planing mode, he was forced to go slowly.

Jason. The recognition curled through the vapor of exhaustion, and with it, she felt the faintest flicker of emotion. She couldn't fathom how he had come to be there. No sane person would put his life at risk for a woman he barely knew.

He worked methodically at the helm, taking ninety-degree turns, fighting waves that attacked the boat from all sides. It took experience and skill to do what he was doing, riding each crest at an angle, reducing power on each downward slope to keep from burying the bow. The boat rolled up and down, yawing, while the water's energy threatened to push the stern sideways. Justine expected the boat to capsize in a trough at any moment.

She huddled inside the thin carapace of the waterproof jacket while her circulation made a cautious attempt to restore itself. Continuous full-body shivers made her teeth clack until her skull vibrated. Stiffening against the tremors could make them stop for a second, but they resumed instantly. Time faltered like a badly edited video. Her hands were entirely numb but she felt tack-hammer pulses at the insides of her elbows.

Justine closed her eyes, steeling herself to endure every upswing and dizzying descent, every smack of cold water coming over the side. Although she wasn't watching Jason, she was aware of his struggle against every shift and jolt of the boat to adjust their course.

Eventually it seemed that the waves weren't as rough. The engine was running slower. Raising her head, Justine cast a bleary glance toward the bow and recognized the lighthouse on its familiar bluff. He had gotten them to Cauldron Island. She couldn't believe it.

Jason flipped the boat's starboard bumpers to the outside of the hull. They approached the dock at an angle with the engine in neutral. As soon as the boat lined up, he shifted the engine in reverse, causing the stern to swing neatly toward the dock.

After cutting the engine, he proceeded to tie the lines. Seeing Justine struggling to sit upward, he pointed a finger at her and snarled a couple of words. Although she couldn't hear him over the storm, it was clear that he didn't want her to move yet. With despair, she saw the towering line of narrow stairs leading to the top of the bluff. The climb was a challenge even on good days. She wasn't going to be able to make it.

When Jason had finished tying the lines to the dock cleats, he reached down into the boat for Justine. She gave him her stiff white hand and did her best to help as he pulled her out. As soon as her feet touched the dock, she found herself being lifted over Jason's shoulder. Her body collapsed like a folding chair. He carried her fireman-style up the steps, one arm locked behind her knees, the other gripping the stair railing at intervals.

She tried to stiffen against the shivering, knowing the involuntary movements weren't helping. But Jason's hold on her was hard and secure. He ascended with astonishing ease, taking some of the stairs two at a time. As they reached the top, his breathing was labored but steady. He could have carried her twice as far without stopping.

Taking Justine to the front door of the limestone house, Jason banged on it with the side of his fist.

In a matter of seconds, the door opened. Justine heard anxious cries from both Rosemary and Sage . . . "Mother of Earth!" and "For Hades' sake . . ."

Jason didn't stop to ask or answer questions. He carried Justine into the main living area and started to issue commands before he had even deposited her on the sofa.

"Get blankets. Start a bath. Warm, not hot. And make some tea with sugar or honey."

"What happened?" Rosemary asked, opening the storage ottoman beside the sofa and pulling out quilted blankets.

"Kayak capsized," Jason said brusquely, bending over Justine's shuddering form. He tugged off her wet neoprene boots. His voice was low and ferocious as he continued. "Did it occur to you to take five fucking minutes to listen to the weather radio, Justine? Ever hear of a small-craft advisory?"

Stung, she tried to explain that no advisories had been in effect when she'd set out, but she could only manage a few incoherent sounds through the chattering of her teeth.

"Shut up," he told her roughly, and yanked off her socks.

Rosemary, who wasn't generally fond of men to begin with, shot him an affronted glance.

Sage laid a gently restraining hand on her arm. "Start the bathwater. I'll make tea."

"Did you hear the way he—"

"He's just a bit frazzled," Sage murmured. "Let it be."

Jason wasn't frazzled, Justine wanted to tell her. He was furious, and sky-high on adrenaline. And she didn't especially want to be left alone with him in this mood.

As both women exited the room, Jason began the difficult task of removing Justine's neoprene pants. The insulated fabric clung stubbornly to her legs despite the nylon facing inside. Jason's breath came in harsh bursts as he pulled the pants free, the neoprene actually ripping in his brutal grip. Justine lay with her fists clenched, her body shaking until it felt as if the flesh were about to rattle loose from her bones.

Tossing the pants aside, Jason reached for her base-layer capris. Realizing that he intended to strip her naked, Justine began to protest.

"Quiet," Jason said roughly, pushing her hands aside. "You can't do this by yourself."

Her dry-top and tee were next, joining the pants in a soggy heap on the floor. Her wet bra and panties were removed efficiently. The tremors running through her limbs were so violent that she couldn't even cover herself. Justine blinked her burning lids against a rush of tears. She felt like a miserable half-dead sea creature, like some unwanted catch that had been dragged up in a fisherman's net.

Standing over her, Jason grasped the hem of his damp T-shirt. Justine's eyes widened as he stripped it off in an efficient movement. He was powerfully built, all tough, defined muscle with no hint of softness. His skin was smooth and honey colored, with a dusting of dark hair trailing down from his navel and disappearing into the top of his board shorts.

Kicking off his boat shoes, Jason lay beside Justine. He pulled her naked torso against his and arranged quilts around them both.

"It's the best way to warm you," she heard him say gruffly.

Justine nodded against his shoulder to let him know that she understood.

He tightened his arms, his shoulders hunching in the effort to surround her with himself. He was inhumanly hot, or it must have seemed that way because she was half frozen. The sensation made her frantic to have more. As another attack of bone-jarring shudders went through her, she struggled to get closer.

"I've got you. Try to relax." He was still breathing fast from exertion, searing strikes of air against her neck. His hair-roughened legs tangled with hers, the solid muscles of his thighs clamping to keep her still.

She wouldn't have survived without this, his body heat feeding into her, penetrating down to the lurking coldness. He was all around her, his breath mixing with hers, his skin salty with sweat and ocean water. She could feel his pulse points, the flex of muscles, the movement of his throat when he swallowed. At some point in the near future, she was going to be humiliated by the memory of this, but at the moment, she was too desperate to care.

She was overtaken by another paroxysm of shuddering, and another, while he murmured to her, gripping her close. Gradually her skin began to prickle with the return of sensation. Her hands hurt, palms needling until her fingers opened and closed convulsively. Wordlessly Jason reached for her hands and pressed them flat against his sides.

"Sorry," she croaked, knowing her touch was icy.

"Everything's fine," he said gruffly. "Relax."

"You're angry."

He didn't bother to deny it. "When I saw your kayak floating

117

upside down—" He paused and took a short breath. "I knew that even if I managed to find you, you were going to be in bad shape." A savage note entered his voice. "Do you know what would have happened if I'd taken a few minutes longer, you reckless idiot?"

"I wasn't reckless," Justine burst out. "The weather wasn't that bad when I—" She was forced to stop as a cough tore through her salt-scoured throat.

"You were stubborn," he insisted. "Pigheaded."

That's just great, coming from you, she wanted to say, but she stayed silent, her chest heaving. Every time she tried to breathe, a sob escaped.

She felt Jason's hand pass gently over the tangled wet mass of her hair. "Don't cry," he said, his tone softening. "I won't say anything else. You've had enough for now, poor baby. It's all right. You're safe."

She struggled to hold back the humiliating tears and pushed at him.

"Let me hold you," he said. "I'm an asshole, but I'm warm. And you need me." He sat up and lifted her into his lap, and wrapped the quilt around both of them. "You scared the hell out of me," he murmured. "When I pulled you out of the water, you were only half conscious and you were turning blue." He used a fold of the quilt to blot her wet cheeks. "If this is an example of how you look after yourself, I swear I'm going to take on the job. Because someone has to take care of you." He rocked her as if she were a child, murmuring roughly into her hair. "Someone has to keep you safe."

Justine's sobs eased into sniffles. His arms were solid around her, his heartbeat strong beneath her ear. She had never felt so dependent on someone in her adult life. The surprise was that it wasn't altogether unpleasant. The gentle rocking motion lulled her, and she wanted to sleep, but Jason kept asking questions . . . whether she felt cramps in her legs, and what day of the week it was, and what she remembered from being out on the ocean.

"I'm tired," she told him at one point, her head slumped on his chest. "I don't want to talk."

"I know, baby. But I can't let you sleep yet." His lips brushed the rim of her ear. "What was your favorite toy when you were a little girl?"

A few last shivers ran through her, and his warm hands chased them. "Stuffed animal."

"What kind?"

"A puppy. The kind with black-and-white spots."

"Dalmation?"

Justine nodded. "I kept trying to invent spells to make him real."

"What was his name?"

"Didn't have one." She licked at the film of salt on her dry lips. "I knew I couldn't keep him. Never kept any of my toys. We moved too often. Better not to care." She made a protesting sound as he eased her upward to a sitting position. "No—"

"Your friend is here with some tea. Lift your head. No, I'm not giving you a choice, you're going to drink some."

Justine opened her mouth reluctantly as he pressed the rim of the mug to her lips. She took a tentative swallow. The liquid was warm and heavily sweetened, the honey soothing her throat. She felt its progress all the way into her chest, softening the innermost chill. "Another," Jason prompted, and she obeyed, her hands lifting to cradle the sides of the mug.

119

The more she drank, the warmer she felt. With startling rapidity, the temperature under the quilt blazed into a bonfire. She felt as if she'd been sunburned from head to toe. Gasping, she tried to dislodge the quilt to let some cool air inside.

"Stay still," Jason told her.

"I'm too hot."

"Your temperature gauge is off. You're not warm enough by a long shot. Drink more tea and stay under the blanket."

"For how long?"

"Until you start sweating."

"I am sweating." She could feel the dampness between them.

His hand swept along her naked thigh, resting at her hip. "I'm the one who's sweating," he told her. "You're as dry as a bone."

As Justine tried to argue, he held the mug against her lips and forced her to drink again.

After bundling Justine more firmly in his lap, Jason turned his attention to Sage and Rosemary, who had both come to occupy the chairs near the sofa. Justine could only imagine what they were making of the situation.

Sage filled the petite upholstered Queen Anne chair like a nesting hummingbird. She was diminutive and pink-cheeked, her white hair framing her face in spun-sugar waves. She beamed at Jason with sky-blue eyes, clearly one blink away from infatuation.

Rosemary's attitude was far more equivocal. She sat in the chair matching Sage's and stared at Jason with a narrowed gaze. Whereas Sage was adorable and apple-cheeked, Rosemary was tall, angular, regally beautiful, a lioness in her later years.

In response to their questions, Jason explained that he had

taken the boat out with the charter company captain in the morning, when the weather had been overcast but still relatively calm. After a couple of hours of assessment, they had returned to the marina to go over the paperwork. By the time the charter process was completed, the storm surge had started to move in and a weather advisory had been in effect. Priscilla had called Jason before he had left the marina, to tell him that Zoë was concerned about Justine's safety.

Justine only half listened to the conversation, feeling as if she were on the brink of heatstroke. She was roasting beneath the blanket, held firmly against Jason's bare chest. When she finished the tea, Jason took the empty mug and leaned forward to set it on the coffee table. The movement drew a stifled gasp from her. Now that she was thawing out, the heat and proximity of him was nearly overwhelming. The thin synthetic layer of his board shorts was all that separated them, making it impossible to ignore the hard masculine contours of his body.

She was acutely aware of her nakedness beneath the blanket, the intimacy of being pressed against him. She didn't like feeling so vulnerable. Her tense weight settled deeper into his lap, and unnerving darts of pleasure went up her spine. No matter how she tried, she couldn't keep from squirming. Beneath the quilt, his hand clamped on her hip, holding her immobile. Steaming, trembling, she turned her face against the hot skin of his shoulder.

"Zoë called us when she saw the storm gathering," Rosemary was saying, "and when I told her that Justine hadn't arrived yet, we were all very worried."

Jason explained that he had taken the Bayliner out to look for Justine, and the storm's escalation had made what should have been a short trip into a prolonged struggle to keep the boat on course. He had eventually seen the bright yellow flash of Justine's kayak amid the swells, and had gone to pull her out of the water.

"We can never thank you enough," Sage told him earnestly. "Justine is like a niece to us. We would be devastated if any harm came to her."

"So would I," Jason said.

Justine lifted her head to look at him in surprise.

He smiled slightly and touched her face, his thumb stroking over a film of perspiration that had gathered on her cheek. "I think she's warm enough now," he said to Rosemary. "I'll carry her to the bathtub, if you'll show me the way."

"I can walk," Justine said.

Jason shook his head, stroking back a lock of salt-stiffened hair from her face. "I don't want you to move any more than necessary. There can be an afterdrop with hypothermia, when your core temperature keeps going down."

"Really, I'm—" Justine began to argue, but he ignored her, lifting her against his chest as if she weighed nothing.

"It seems you'll be staying with us for the night, Mr. Black," Sage said. "According to the latest report, the storm isn't likely to end until tomorrow."

"I'm sorry to impose on you."

"It's not an imposition in the least. There's a pot of soup on the stove, and two loaves of Dark Mother bread in the oven."

"Dark Mother?" Jason repeated with polite interest.

"A reference to Hecate. We're nearing the autumn equinox, or what we call Mabon, which is the modern word for the celebration of—"

"Sage," Justine protested, her voice muffled against Jason's shoulder. "He doesn't want to hear about that."

"I do, as a matter of fact," Jason said to Sage. "Maybe later this afternoon?"

Sage smiled at him. "Yes, I'll show you our harvest altar. I think it turned out especially nice this year . . ." Still chattering happily, Sage headed to the kitchen.

Jason followed Rosemary through the lighthouse, into the master bedroom and connecting bathroom. The storm pummeled the stalwart limestone and wood-shingled lighthouse, rain hitting the multipaned windows like the sound of marbles being dropped onto the floor. The lighthouse, having withstood a thousand squalls and tempests, creaked as it settled in patiently for a long, wet night.

"I need to make a couple of calls," Jason said to Rosemary.

"I've already phoned the inn to let them know that you brought Justine here safely. You probably won't get a cell signal out here, but you're welcome to use our landline in the kitchen."

"Thank you." Jason carried Justine into the bathroom. He lowered her feet to the floor, wrapped a towel around her, and lifted the toilet lid. "The kidneys go into overdrive when you've been exposed to extreme cold," he said in a pragmatic tone.

Justine gave him an affronted glance. He was right, of course. But the way he was standing there seemed to indicate an intention to remain during the process. "I'd like some privacy, please."

To her disgruntled surprise, Jason shook his head. "Someone should stay with you in case there's a problem."

"I will, of course," Rosemary said from the doorway.

"Don't leave her alone even for a minute."

"I don't intend to," the older woman replied, her dark brows drawing together. "There's another bathroom in the lighthouse tower bedroom—you may shower there."

"Thank you," Jason said, "but right now I have to go back to cover the boat and pump excess water from the bilge. It may take a while."

"No," Justine said in concern, not wanting Jason to go out alone in the storm. He had to be tired after all he'd done, rescuing her from the ocean, carrying her up all those stairs from the dock. "You should rest first."

"I'll be fine." Jason paused at the door, keeping his gaze averted from her as he continued. "After your bath, go straight to bed."

"You're ordering me around again," Justine said, although her tone was wry rather than accusatory.

Jason still didn't look at her, but she saw the flicker of a smile at the corner of his mouth. "Get used to it," he said. "Now that I've saved your life, I'm responsible for you."

He left the bathroom, and Rosemary stared after the extraordinary stranger with a stunned expression.

After Justine had settled carefully into the warm comfort of the bath, Rosemary dropped an herb-filled sachet into the water. "This will help with muscle soreness," she said. "And the tea Sage brewed for you was a special medicinal blend. You'll be back to your usual self soon."

"I thought she must have put something in it," Justine said. "I felt much warmer right after I drank it."

The other woman's tone was gently astringent. "I suspect

sharing a quilt with Mr. Black might have helped the warming process considerably."

"Rosemary," Justine protested with a discomfited laugh.

"How long have you been involved with him?"

"We're not involved." Justine stared at the surface of the water, which quivered from the infinitesimal trembling of her legs. "We've gone out once for dinner, that's all."

"What happened to the last boyfriend? What was his name . . . ?"

"Duane."

"I rather liked him."

"So did I. But I messed it up. We were having an argument about something stupid—I don't even remember what it was—and I got so angry, I—" Breaking off, Justine sloshed her hand through the water, sending ripples across the surface. "The headlight on his motorcycle exploded. I tried to come up with an excuse for it, but Duane knew I caused it. Now every time he sees me in town, he makes the sign of the cross and takes off at a dead run."

Rosemary looked at her sharply. "Why didn't you tell me?"

"I just did." Justine felt a riff of unease as she heard the consternation in the other woman's voice. "I don't want to bother you with every twist and turn of my love life, and besides—"

"Not Duane," Rosemary interrupted. "I meant about the bulb exploding."

"Oh. Well . . . it's not all that unusual, right? I've seen you and Sage and a couple of the other coveners do tricks like that."

"After years of training. But never as a novice." Rosemary's expression made Justine sorry she had mentioned anything about the lightbulb. "It's not a trick, Justine, it's a dangerous ability. Especially if you haven't acquired the techniques for focusing and grounding. And it should *never* happen as a result of temper."

"I won't do it again," Justine said. "I wasn't even trying to do it in the first place."

Rosemary picked up a hand towel from the edge of the sink and refolded it needlessly. "Was that the only time it's happened?"

"Yes," Justine said at once.

Rosemary's brows lifted.

"No," Justine admitted. She tried to sound casual. "I may have tripped a circuit breaker once."

"What?"

"I dropped a can of floor wax on my foot," Justine said defensively. "I was hopping around the room and swearing, and the next thing I knew, the circuit blew and I had to go trip the breaker switch in the basement."

"You're sure that you caused it? It wasn't a coincidence?"

Justine shook her head. "I felt a weird kind of energy running under my skin."

"Depolarization." The hand towel was shaken out and refolded again. "All living cells generate natural electric charges. But a few individuals are able to build a charge imbalance until a current releases. Like an electric eel."

"Can any crafter do it?"

"No. Only natural-born witches, and very few of those."

Deciding to make light of it, Justine waggled her fingers in the air. "So how much power do you think I've got in these things?"

"Equal to the amount of your average defibrillator," Rosemary said with quiet asperity.

Blinking, Justine lowered her hands.

"There is no choice, Justine: You must have instruction. A covener—Violet or Ebony would be best—will help you learn how to manage this. Otherwise you'll be a danger to yourself and others."

Justine groaned, knowing that the more she had to do with any of the coveners, the more they would pressure her to join. "I'll manage it on my own. It's not going to happen again."

"Because you've decided so?" Rosemary asked caustically.

"Yes."

That earned her a stern glance. "You can't control your power, Justine. You're like a six-year-old at the wheel of a car. Sage will discuss it with you later. I'm sure she'll persuade you to see reason."

Justine lifted her gaze heavenward, and began to nudge the floating bath sachet with her toes. She played idly with the chain around her neck, following it down to the small copper key that dangled between her breasts. Lifting the key, she tapped it absently against her lips. A storm gust hit the bathroom window with startling force, the wind shrieking as it rampaged from the roiling sea.

Hearing the hiss of a quick indrawn breath, Justine glanced at Rosemary.

The older woman's gaze left the window and went to the copper key in Justine's hand, and flicked back to the window again. "You've broken the geas," she said dazedly. "Haven't you? The spirits are in turmoil."

"I—" Justine began, but the words died away as she saw the expression on Rosemary's face, one she had never seen before.

Fear.

"Oh, Justine," Rosemary said eventually. "What have you done?"

Before Justine had admitted to anything, she had insisted on an explanation about what Rosemary and Sage knew about the geas, and why they had never mentioned it to her. That had led to an impasse. "We'll deal with it later," Rosemary had finally said, "when you're not exhausted."

And when Sage is here to keep it from turning into a brawl, Justine thought darkly.

Rosemary helped her from the bath and gave her a white flannel nightshirt to wear. "You'll nap on our bed for the afternoon," she told Justine. "Tonight you can stay in the tower bedroom." She paused diplomatically. "Will Mr. Black be sleeping with you, or will he take the sofa down here?"

"The sofa, I think." Justine sighed in comfort as she settled onto the old four-poster bed with its deep cushiony mattress. Rosemary propped some pillows behind her and covered her with a quilt made up of random patches of silk, velvet, brocade, with a backing of sugar-sack fabric.

The storm had thickened, the afternoon sky the color of wet newspaper. A crack of lightning caused Justine to jump. As far as Justine was concerned, Jason couldn't return a moment too soon. She wanted him safely back inside.

Sitting beside Justine, Rosemary began to braid her damp, freshly washed hair.

The feel of the older woman's hands in her hair reminded Justine of all the times Rosemary had done the same thing for her when she was a little girl. In the endless whirlwind of being raised by Marigold, Justine had savored their visits to the light-house, where life had been calm and quiet and Sage had played old-fashioned songs on the piano, and Rosemary had taken her to the top of the tower to help clean the crystal Fresnel lens. Justine had thrived on their unconditional affection.

Impulsively she snuggled close to Rosemary.

A gentle hand came to her cheek.

Sage came into the room, humming "Pennies from Heaven." She carried a stack of tissue-wrapped clothing, which she laid carefully on the bed.

"What is all that?" Rosemary asked, resuming her work on Justine's hair.

"Mr. Black will need something to wear. I opened the cedar trunk and found some of Neil's old clothes. They'll suit him nicely."

Justine bit back a grin as she saw how much Sage was enjoying the situation, having a man in the house.

"Heavens to Hades," Rosemary said with annoyance, "those garments are from the sixties."

"They're still in perfect condition," Sage said placidly, un-wrapping the tissue. "And vintage style is so fashionable these days." She held up a cream-colored linen shirt with a plain point collar. "Perfect. And these—" She shook out a pair of slim-cut casual trousers, tan with a subtle windowpane check.

"They won't even reach Mr. Black's ankles," Rosemary said sourly. "Neil was hardly bigger than you, Sage."

Sage laid out the garments and ran an assessing glance over them. "I'll have to make some alterations, of course." She said a few words beneath her breath and waved a small, pudgy hand. "How tall would you say Mr. Black is, Justine?"

"About six feet," Justine said.

Sage tugged at the hem of one of the trouser legs. With each little pull, the fabric extended until she had added a good six inches to the inseam. The magic was accomplished with an ease that Justine admired. "A wonderful-looking man, isn't he?" Sage asked of no one in particular. "And so well endowed."

"Sage," Justine protested.

"I was not referring to the fruit of his loom, dear. I meant endowed with looks and intelligence. Although . . ." Sage proceeded to lengthen the crotch of the pants. She held them up and asked Justine, "What do you think? Have I allowed enough room in the rise?"

"I think you're a little too interested in what he's packing."

Rosemary gave a little snort. "Sage is trying to find out in her usual circuitous way whether you've slept with him, Justine."

"No," Justine replied with a sputtering laugh. "I haven't, and I don't intend to."

"That's probably for the best," Sage said.

"I agree," Rosemary added promptly.

Sage smiled at her partner. "You noticed, then." She began to work on the linen shirt, adding inches to the sleeves.

"Of course." Rosemary finished Justine's braid and fastened an elastic band around it.

Justine's puzzled gaze swept across them both. "Noticed what? What are you talking about?"

Sage replied with equanimity. "Mr. Black has no soul, dear."

Twelve

. . . .

"What does that mean?" Justine demanded, her eyes widening. "Jason told me the same thing a couple of nights ago."

"He's aware of it, then?" Sage asked, folding the trousers neatly. "How fascinating. Usually they have no idea." She slid a significant glance to Rosemary.

"Someone explain it to me," Justine said urgently. "Are you saying he's a clinical sociopath or something?"

"Oh, not at all." Sage chuckled and leaned over to pat Justine's knee through the quilts. "I've met some perfectly lovely people with no souls. It's nothing to criticize, and it certainly can't be helped; it just *is*."

"How did you know about it? What tipped you off?"

"Hereditary witches usually have the knack of sensing when someone is soulless. Didn't you feel it when you first met Mr. Black?"

After considering the question, Justine replied slowly. "For a second I sort of wanted to step back from him. I wasn't sure why."

"Exactly. You'll experience that from time to time when you meet someone new. But of course you must never say anything about it. Most of the soulless aren't aware of what they lack, and they would never want to know."

Justine was unaccountably upset. "I don't get this. Any of it."

"Even without a soul," Rosemary explained, "you would still have emotions, thoughts, and memories. You would still be you. But you wouldn't have . . . transcendence. There would be nothing left after the body dies."

"No heaven or hell," Justine said slowly, "no Valhalla, Summerland, or underworld . . . just 'poof' and you're gone for good?"

"Exactly."

"I've always wondered if they don't sense it deep down," Sage mused aloud. "People without souls rarely seem to reach old age, and they tend to live so very intensely. As if they're aware of how limited their time is."

"It reminds me of that little poem you've always liked, Sage. The one about the candle."

"Edna St. Vincent Millay." Sage smiled as she recited, "'My candle burns at both ends; / It will not last the night; / But ah, my foes, and oh my friends— / It gives a lovely light!'"

"That describes the soulless perfectly," Rosemary told Justine. "They are driven to experience everything they can before the ultimate demise. Voracious appetites. But no matter how much success they achieve, it's never enough . . . and they never understand why."

"How does someone end up without a soul?" Justine asked in a hushed voice.

"Some people simply aren't born with one. It's a trait just like eye color or the size of one's feet."

"But that's so unfair."

"Yes. Life is often unfair."

"How can this be fixed?" Justine asked. "How could a person manage to get a soul if he doesn't have one?"

"He can't," Rosemary replied. "It's not possible. Or at least I've never heard of such a thing happening."

"But if they realize they are soulless," Sage said, "that's when things become precarious. Every living creature is compelled to preserve its own existence. Is there anything a man like Jason wouldn't do for a chance at eternity?"

No. He would stop at nothing.

Justine's hand crept to the center of her chest, where the little copper key was hidden beneath the bodice of the nightgown.

Rosemary glanced at her with compassion. "I see that you understand now. Associating with a man like Jason Black could turn out to be a dance with the devil."

"Could Jason ever love someone if he has no soul?"

"Of course," Sage said. "He still has a heart, after all. What he doesn't have is time."

After seeing to the boat, Jason made the long, slow climb back to the lighthouse. The ancient stone steps had settled badly, some of them diagonally slanted, many of them cracked. The center of each step had been worn into hammock shapes by the tread of countless shoes. Rain had made all of them perilously slick. Wind gusts struck from different directions, challenging his balance. He still didn't know how he'd managed to carry Justine up the stairs without falling; he'd been too jacked with adrenaline to think about it at the time.

He doubted he would ever recover from the sight of Justine struggling in the ocean, her face gray with the resignation of someone who was on her way to dying. He would have done anything for her, risked anything, without question. He would have given her his life, fed his own blood directly into her veins, if that would have saved her. And to say the least, self-sacrifice was a new concept for him.

The strangest part was that he wasn't trying to reason himself out of it; he didn't even want to. The way he felt about Justine was something he had no choice in, just as he had no choice about whether he wanted to breathe or sleep or eat. It was too soon to be this certain. But that didn't matter, either.

His past relationships had ended when they became inconvenient or stale. And each time Jason had gone on his way with the arrogant conviction that love would never get the better of him.

What an idiot he'd been.

Now he knew that it was only love when you knew there could be no end to it. When it was as inevitable as gravity. Falling in love, a helpless descent in which the only way to avoid being hurt was to keep going. Keep falling.

As he neared the top of the stairs, he took a good look at the lighthouse. It was a turn-of-the-century design, constructed of limestone and wood shingles, with surrounding porches braced by wood columns. The octagonal tower, integrated with the keeper's cottage, overlooked the steeply pitched and gabled roof.

134

Passing a fog bell mounted on the front porch, Jason shouldered his way past the door and closed it against the storm. He removed his jacket and hung it on a hook, and took off his sodden boat shoes. His T-shirt, which he'd put back on before going down to the dock, was cold and clammy. His board shorts had dried, but he felt sticky and sea-brined. The smell of baking bread filled the house, making his mouth water. He was starving.

"Mr. Black." Sage hurried to him with an armload of white towels, her silver curls dancing like butterfly antennae. "Here you are," she said brightly.

"Thank you. Please call me Jason." He scrubbed the towel roughly over his hair and the back of his neck. "How is Justine?"

"She is sleeping comfortably in our bedroom. Rosemary is watching over her."

"Maybe I should check on her," Jason said, trying to contend with a tight feeling in his chest, iron bands around his heart. Worry. Another new feature on his emotional landscape.

"Justine is a healthy young woman," Sage said gently. "A little rest, and she'll bounce back to her usual self." She gave him an arrested glance, as if something in his face had surprised her. "You were very brave to do what you did today. I understand what it means for a man in your position to take such a risk."

A man in his position? Jason held her gaze, wondering exactly what she had meant.

"Let me show you to the guest bathroom," Sage said. "You can take a nice hot shower, and put on some dry clothes."

He grimaced. "Unfortunately I don't have a spare shirt or—"

"Not to worry, dear boy, I have set out some things that belonged to my late husband. He would be delighted for someone to get some use out of them."

"I wouldn't want to . . ." Jason began, uncomfortable at the prospect of wearing old clothes that had belonged to a dead man, but his attention was seized by the phrase "late husband." "You were married?"

"Yes, Neil was the lightkeeper here. After he passed, I assumed his post. Follow me to the guest room—we'll take a roundabout path so you can see the house along the way."

"The lighthouse isn't active now, is it?"

"No, after it was decommissioned in the early seventies, the Coast Guard sold it to me for practically nothing. And in return for maintaining the house, I've been awarded a life pension from a private historic preservation foundation. Later you'll have to go up to the top of the tower—the original Fresnel lens is still there. It's made of French crystal. Very beautiful, like an Art Deco sculpture."

The rooms were painted in delicate shades of robin's-egg blue and sea green, and filled with cozy upholstered furniture and polished woodwork. The main room opened into a large kitchen, and a smaller room that served as a multipurpose area. "This is called the keeping room," Sage said. "Most of the time we use it for craft projects, but when we have guests, such as tonight, we put an extra leaf in the table and make it into a dining room."

Jason went to the corner of the room, where an antique bronze diving helmet had been set on a built-in shelf. The helmet had a glass front door, a dumbbell lock with a chain and pin, and a leather gasket. "This is like something out of a Jules Verne novel. How old is it?"

"It was made in nineteen-eighteen, or thereabouts." Sage gave a wondering laugh. "Neil said the same thing when he bought it—it reminded him of Jules Verne. Have you read any of his novels?"

"Most of them." Jason smiled. "Jules Verne managed to predict a lot of inventions that eventually came true. Submarines, videoconferencing, spaceships . . . I've never been able to decide if it was genius or magic."

She seemed to like that. "Perhaps a little of both."

Sage showed him to the guest room at the lower level of the tower. It was a fairy-tale room, octagonal with bay windows and upholstered benches set in nearly every wall. The only furnishings were a spacious iron-framed bed placed in the center of the room and a tiny painted wooden table next to it. Although the room would be cold at night, the bed was layered with ivory quilts and pillows piled three deep. A simple button-down shirt and a pair of trousers had been laid out. "I'm afraid we have no socks that will fit you," Sage said regretfully. "Until your shoes dry out, you'll have to go barefoot."

"I went barefoot all the time in my grandmother's home in Japan," Jason said.

"You're part Japanese? . . . Ah, that explains those cheekbones and lovely dark eyes."

He laughed quietly. "You're a flirt, Sage."

"At my age, I can flirt all I please and it causes no trouble."

"I think you could cause plenty of trouble if you wanted to."

Sage chuckled. "Now who's the flirt?" She gestured to a small bathroom with an old-fashioned shower. "The guest toiletries are in the basket under the sink. There's more than enough time for a nap—you may rest up here, and no one will bother you."

"Thanks, but I don't usually take naps."

"You should try. You must be tired after your heroics today."

"I wasn't heroic," Jason said, uncomfortable with the praise. "I just did what was necessary."

She smiled at him. "Isn't that the definition of a hero?"

Thirteen

Jason went downstairs three hours later. He had showered and shaved, and had taken Sage's advice about trying to rest. Although he had always found it nearly impossible to nap, he had fallen asleep within a couple of minutes after lying down. It was something about the tower room, he decided. Sleeping in a place so high and isolated, surrounded by storm and ocean, had allowed him to relax as deeply as if he'd spent hours in meditation.

The clothes Sage had set out for him were soft and comfortable, with none of the mustiness or discoloration he would have expected. A crisp scent of cedar permeated the fabric. He owned handmade shirts from London and Hong Kong that didn't fit him this smoothly. These could have been made specifically according to his measurements. Which didn't strike him as coincidence.

So far, Jason thought wryly, he was enjoying the company of witches far more than he would have expected.

He reached the bottom floor and found the main room empty. Appetizing smells hung in the air. The sound of voices and clanking utensils resonated from the kitchen. Pausing at the threshold of the keeping room, he saw that the table was covered in white linen and set with flatware and sparkling glassware.

Justine was lighting candles, her back turned to him. A thin blue sweater and a long flowered skirt followed the slender lines of her body before flaring gently. She was barefoot, sexy, her hair loose and rippling. Still unaware of his presence, she clicked a long-necked butane lighter repeatedly but couldn't get a flame started. The shoulder of the sweater sagged away from an ivory shoulder, and she hitched it up impatiently. Setting aside the lighter, she snapped her fingers in front of each candlewick. A succession of brilliant flames appeared.

More witchery. Although Jason didn't react outwardly, he was startled by the sight of Justine creating sparks with her fingertips. *Jesus Tap-dancing Christ.* What else was she capable of? Staring at her, he slid his hands in his pockets and leaned casually against the side of the doorjamb.

At the sound of the floor creaking beneath his feet, Justine started and whirled to face him.

She turned white and then flushed, her velvet-brown eyes wide. "Oh. I . . ." One hand made a fluttering gesture to the table behind her. "Trick candles."

His mouth twitched. "How do you feel?"

"Fine. Great." Justine sounded breathless. Her gaze took a swift, nervous inventory of him. "How about you?"

"Hungry."

She motioned in the direction of the kitchen, nearly knocking over a candlestick. "Dinner's almost ready. Those clothes are great on you." She hitched up the side of the sweater again.

"How do you feel?"

"Better since you put me on a defrost cycle." Her color deepened. "Thank you."

"I didn't mind thawing you out," Jason said, reaching out to stroke his fingers through a few of the wavy, shiny locks of her hair. Gently he tugged the sweater down her shoulder, caressing the silky exposed curve with his palm. He heard her breath change. He thought about the things he wanted to do to her, all the ways he wanted to penetrate, pleasure, possess her. And he forced himself to let go of her while he was still able. Justine wandered into the kitchen, seeming dazed, while Jason went to the front door and opened it.

Standing in a blast of cold air, he tried to create a peaceful scene in his mind . . . an Alaskan glacier, a snow-topped mountain. When that didn't work, he thought about foreign debt crises. Piranhas. Oompa-Loompas. When that didn't work, he began to list prime numbers in his head, backward from one thousand. By the time he reached 613, he was able to return to the keeping room.

Justine was setting bowls of vegetable soup on the table. She glanced at him, her cheeks pink.

"Can I do something?" he asked.

Rosemary replied as she carried baskets of bread from the kitchen. "All taken care of. Have a seat, please."

He went to help Rosemary and Sage into their chairs, and took a seat next to Justine.

Rosemary blessed the meal, praising the earth for growing the food they were about to enjoy, thanking the sun for nourishing it, the rain for quenching its thirst, and so forth.

"Jason," Sage invited when the blessing was finished, "tell us about your foreign relatives. I find that so intriguing. Were both your grandparents Japanese?"

"No, my grandfather was an American serviceman, stationed at Naha Port—a logistical base in Okinawa—during Vietnam. He married my grandmother against her family's wishes. Not long afterward he was killed in action, but by then my grandmother was pregnant with my mother."

Justine passed a basket of bread to him. "How did your mother end up in America?"

"She visited Sacramento when she was a teenager, to get to know some of her American relatives. She ended up staying here for good."

"Why didn't she go back?"

"I think she wanted the chance to live independently for a while. In Okinawa, her family had kept a close eye on her, and they all lived under one roof: my grandmother and assorted aunts, uncles, and cousins."

"Heavens to Hecate," Rosemary exclaimed, "how large was the house?"

"About three thousand square feet. But it allowed a lot more room than the American equivalent. Not much furniture, and no clutter. The interior could be made into different rooms with all these sliding paper doors. So when it was time to go to sleep, everyone laid their futons on the floor and pulled the doors shut."

"How could you stand the lack of privacy?" Justine asked.

"I learned that a sense of privacy doesn't have to depend on walls and doors. At least not external ones. Two people could sit in a room and read or work separately without ever breaking the silence. It's an ability to put up walls in your mind, so no one can get through."

"And you're good at that, aren't you?" Justine asked.

Relishing the challenge she presented, he gave her a level stare. "Aren't you?" he countered.

Her gaze was the first to fall.

Jason turned the conversation to Sage, asking what life had been like on Cauldron Island when she'd first moved there. She described the years she had been employed as the island school-teacher, with approximately a half dozen students. They had all met every morning at a one-room schoolhouse at Crystal Cove, not far from the lighthouse. Now the only families who lived there were retirees or part-timers, so the school had been closed.

"We still use the schoolhouse from time to time," Sage volunteered. "The building is in perfect condition."

"What do you use it for?" Jason asked, and felt Justine's toes in a warning nudge against his ankle.

"Social gatherings," Rosemary said briskly. "Are you enjoying your dinner, Jason?"

"It's terrific," he said. The soup was hearty and fresh-tasting, made with potatoes, kale, corn, tomatoes, and herbs. Honey-sweetened Dark Mother bread was served with homemade apple butter and slabs of local white cheese.

Dessert consisted of an eggless breadcrumb cake sweetened with molasses and dried fruit. According to Sage, the recipe was from the Depression era, a time when eggs and milk hadn't always been available.

The elderly women were like an old married couple, reminiscing about their life on the island. They told stories about Justine as a child, such as the time she had been so determined to have a surprise birthday party for herself that she had planned it out and given Rosemary and Sage meticulous instructions. They had thrown it for her, of course, and had called it Justine's unsurprise party.

And during one winter visit, Justine had complained about their pagan Yule traditions because she had wanted a Christmas tree.

"I explained to Justine," Rosemary said, "that our tradition was to put a straw Yule goat out in the yard. She asked what tradition we would have if it weren't for the goat, and I said I wasn't certain. And the next morning"—she paused as Sage chuckled and Justine buried her head in her hands—"I looked out the window to discover that the Yule goat was gone. There was only a smoldering pile of ashes on the ground. Justine denied all responsibility, of course, but she said with great enthusiasm, '*Now* we can have a tree.'"

"You burned the Yule goat?" Jason asked Justine, amused.

She explained with chagrin, "It was a ritual sacrifice. He had to go."

"We've had a Christmas tree every year since," Sage said. "Even when Justine wasn't with us."

Justine reached out and put her hand on Sage's shoulder. "I visited every holiday I possibly could," she said. "We haven't missed one for a while, have we?"

Sage smiled at her. "No, indeed."

After dinner they went into the main room to sit by the fire and relax with glasses of elderberry wine. Eventually Sage and

Rosemary sat side by side at the piano and played a showy duet of "Stardust," embellished with arpeggios and glissandi.

Justine curled up in the corner of the sofa, gathering up her knees beneath the long flowered skirt and hooking an arm around them. She smiled at Jason as he settled next to her. "They like you," she said in an undertone.

"How can you tell?"

"'Stardust' is their best piece. They only play it for people they like."

"Are they . . . together?" he asked tactfully.

"Yes. They don't usually talk about their relationship. The only thing Sage has ever said to me about it is that no matter how old you get, you're always capable of surprising yourself."

Jason watched Justine's expression as the melancholy notes of "Autumn Leaves" filled the air. It was the kind of song that didn't need words, emotions balanced on every lonely note. Firelight played over Justine's porcelain skin and the wistful curve of her mouth. Delicate shadows smudged her eyes. She was tired. He wanted to hold her while she slept, her body tranquil and dream-heavy in his arms.

Lightning shot through the sky, accompanied by an earsplitting crack that caused Justine to start. "It feels like the storm will go on forever," she said.

"I think it will die down enough for you to leave tomorrow," Sage said, still playing the piano. "Of course, we'll have to work up a good strong protection spell before you go."

Justine's expression tautened, and she gave Jason a wary glance.

"Protection from what?" he asked, his voice pitched so the other women couldn't hear. "The storm?"

145

"Sort of." Justine's fingers harrowed the folds of her skirt, plucking and smoothing.

His hand covered hers, subduing the restive movements. "Can I help?"

The question nudged a brief smile to her lips. "Saving my life was more than enough."

As Sage finished the song, Rosemary turned on the bench to face Justine. "We have something important to discuss," she said.

Even though he knew it was none of his business, Jason couldn't stop himself from saying, "It would be better to wait until the morning." Justine was still fragile from the day's events, not entirely in control of herself. At the moment, the only likely result of a discussion, or argument, was mutual frustration.

Justine frowned, pulling her hand from his. "It's something I have to talk to them about," she told him. "I wouldn't be able to sleep otherwise. It's why I came to visit in the first place." Her mouth pulled into an apologetic little grimace. "I don't mean to be rude, but . . . could you go to the guest room for a little while?"

"Of course." Standing, Jason went to the built-in bookshelf near the fireplace. "I'll grab a couple of books to take with me. I've been wanting to catch up on my reading." He pulled a couple of random volumes from the shelf. "Especially . . ." He paused to glance at the top title in the stack. "*Mushrooms of the Pacific Northwest*. And *The History of Marine Propellers and Propulsion*."

"You'll love that one," Justine told him.

He gave her a sardonic glance. "Don't spoil the ending for me."

Jason had insisted on carrying the dishes into the kitchen before going upstairs to the tower bedroom. It had pleased and surprised Justine to discover that a man of his position would help with housework. And it amused her to see how much Rosemary liked him in spite of herself.

"It's not that I dislike men," Rosemary said defensively, after Justine had made a comment to that effect. "It's just that I dislike so many of them."

That remark, and her sour expression, caused both Justine and Sage to crack up as they rinsed and stacked dishes at the sink.

Rosemary wiped the countertop with great dignity. "I will admit," she said after a moment, "that Jason is a charming and well-spoken man. Not to mention intelligent. I can hardly credit that he once played football."

Justine affected a tone of grave concern. "I hope he hasn't ruined any stereotypes for you, Rosemary."

"I don't stereotype. I generalize."

"Is there a difference?" Justine asked with a grin. "You have to explain it to me, because I don't see one."

"I'll explain it," Sage interceded. "If Rosemary were to say that *all* men are insensitive brutes who love football and drink beer, that would be stereotyping. However, if Rosemary said that *most* men are insensitive brutes who love football and drink beer, she would be generalizing."

Justine listened with a dubious expression. "Neither version gives men much credit."

"That's because none of them deserve it," Rosemary said.

Sage said to Justine sotto voce, "*That* is stereotyping."

The three of them worked companionably in the kitchen,

rinsing dishes and loading the dishwasher until it was full. Justine volunteered to wash the large soup pot in the sink. As she plunged her hands into hot soapy water and scrubbed the pot, she pondered how best to open the subject of the curse, when Sage did it for her.

"Justine, darling . . . Rosemary seems to believe that you have somehow managed to break the geas. Which I told her couldn't be true, since it would be nearly impossible for you to accomplish such a thing on your own."

Justine didn't pause in her scrubbing. "So you admit there was a geas?"

A nerve-grating silence greeted her question.

Justine was astonished that they were trying to keep secrets from her, even when those secrets had a profound impact on her life. After Zoë, there was no one Justine had ever trusted more than these two women. To be deceived by them hurt her on as deep a level as Marigold had ever reached.

"There was a geas," Rosemary admitted quietly. "Let's return to the main room and sit together while we—"

"Not yet. Still working on this pot." Justine scoured the stainless steel with frantic intensity. She needed an activity—if she had to sit still with nothing to occupy her, she felt as if she might explode.

"Very well." The two women sat on wooden stools at the small kitchen island table.

Sage's voice again: "Justine, will you tell us how you found out? And what you've done about it?"

"Yes. But first I'm going to tell you *why* I did it. Although you already know."

"You wanted love" came the quiet reply. Justine wasn't even certain which one of them had said it.

"I wanted at least a chance at it." Justine drained the soapy pot and began to rinse it industriously. She tried to speak calmly, but her voice had tightened like a windup mechanism until it threatened to break. "How many times have I sat in this kitchen and bitched and cried and told you that I *knew* something was wrong with me? I even asked you once if it might have something to do with magic, and you both said no. You said things like, 'It'll happen someday, Justine. Just be patient, Justine.' But you were lying. You knew there was no freaking chance I'd ever have anyone. That I would always be alone. How could you do that to me?"

"One can be alone," Rosemary said, "without being lonely. And lonely without being alone."

Infuriated, Justine set the pot on the counter with unnecessary force. "I don't need fortune-cookie wisdom. I need answers."

Sage spoke gently. "Justine, you were going to tell us how you found out about the geas."

Still facing away from them, Justine braced her wet hands on the sink. "The Triodecad," she muttered. "Page thirteen."

Her shoulders stiffened as she heard audible gasps.

"Jumping Jupiter on a pogo stick," Rosemary said.

"Oh, Justine," Sage faltered, "you were told never to do that."

"I was told about a lot of things. Unfortunately the geas was not one of them. So I had to find out from the Triodecad." Justine turned to face them defiantly. "It's my spellbook, and my decision to make."

Rosemary sounded more bewildered than accusatory. "You

aren't nearly so naïve as to think you can break one of the rules of magic without causing consequences for everyone in the coven."

"I'm not a covener. So it's my business and no one else's. I opened the Triodecad to page thirteen, and it gave me the spell to break a geas, and I followed the instructions." She gave them both a rebellious glance. "Now I've got some questions: Who cast a curse on me, and why? Does my mother know about it? Why hasn't anyone ever told me? Because I can't imagine what I've ever done to make someone hate me that much."

Neither of them wanted to reply. As Justine looked from one face to another, she had a bad feeling, a standing-on-the-train-tracks feeling.

"It wasn't done out of hatred," Sage said carefully. "It was done out of love, dear."

"*Who the hell was it?*"

"It was Marigold," Rosemary said in a quiet voice. "She did it to protect you."

Justine was stunned, suspended in ice. It made no sense. "Protect me from what?" she managed to ask, although it hurt to force the words from her throat.

"Marigold barely survived losing your father," Sage said. "She wasn't . . . herself for a long time afterward."

"She wasn't sane," Rosemary said. "She was in the kind of pain that leaves no room for anything else. And even after she recovered, she was never the same. She came to us when you were still an infant, and said she had decided that her only child must never endure such agony. She wanted to bind a geas to you, so that you would be protected from loss forever."

"Protect me from loss," Justine said in a hollow voice, "by making certain I'd never have anything to lose." She wrapped

150

her arms around herself, an instinctive effort to keep from falling to pieces. Emotions flooded into the blankness like watercolors bleeding across wet paper.

". . . disagreed with her," Sage was saying. "But she was your mother. A mother has the right to make decisions for her child."

"Not that kind of decision," Justine said fiercely. "Some decisions even a mother doesn't get to make." It infuriated her further to read from their expressions that she had scored a point. "Why didn't you stop her?"

"We assisted her, Justine," Rosemary said. "The entire coven did. The geas was too powerful a spell to accomplish on her own."

Justine could hardly breathe. "You all helped her?"

"Marigold was one of the coven. We were bound to help her. It was a collective choice."

"But . . . *I* never got a choice."

They had betrayed her, all of them.

It seemed as if everything in the universe were a lie. Justine felt like a wounded wild thing, ready to attack, wanting to hurt someone, including herself.

"It was for your safety." She heard Rosemary's voice through the pounding blood in her ears.

"Marigold didn't want me to be safe," Justine cried. "She wanted me to be in a prison she'd made. I would be alone, and then what choice would I have except to copy her life exactly? I would have to join the coven and follow her plan, and she would oversee everything I did and I would be *just like her*. She didn't want a daughter. She wanted a clone."

"She loved you," Sage said. "I know that she still does."

It outraged Justine more than anything else that Sage could

look at what had been done to her and call it love. "*How* do you know that? Because she said so? Don't you understand the difference between love and control?"

"Justine, please try to understand—"

"I understand," she said, thrilling with anger so intense it felt like panic. "You're the ones who don't understand. You want to believe every mother wants the best for her child. But some don't."

"She didn't mean to hurt you, Justine—"

"She meant to do exactly what she did."

"She may not have been a perfect mother, but—"

"Don't try to tell me what kind of mother Marigold was. I'm the only person in the world who knows what it was like to be raised by her. A mother is supposed to want her child to have an education and a stable home. Instead I was dragged around like a cheap suitcase. My mother never stayed anywhere or stuck with anything unless it was 'fun.' And whenever parenting wasn't fun, which was most of the time, I had to fend for myself. Because I was inconvenient."

It was the truth. But neither of them wanted to hear it, like most people faced with uncomfortable truths. Their relationships with Marigold and Justine, their culpability in the geas, their trust in the coven's collective wisdom, all of it was suddenly precarious. And Justine knew exactly how they were going to handle it. They would blame her for being rebellious and difficult. It was easier to blame the troublemaker, the unhappy victim, rather than look inward.

"Of course you're upset," Sage said. "You need time to adjust to this, but there isn't time. We must do something now, darling, because in changing your fate, you've managed to—"

152

"I didn't change my fate," Justine snapped, "I changed it *back*." Energy smoldered beneath her skin, racing from cell to cell.

Rosemary was staring at her oddly, her face drawn. "Justine," she said carefully, "you can't ever change things back to exactly what they were before. Your fate has been shaped by every action you've ever taken. For every action there is a reaction. And in breaking the geas, you've upset the balance between the spiritual realm and the physical world. You've created a storm in more ways than one."

As far as Justine was concerned, the last straw was having to endure a lecture from a woman who had helped to place a lifelong curse on her. "Then you shouldn't have helped to curse me in the first place!" The energy released in a volatile and undirected snap, flooding the light fixture on the ceiling. A trio of bulbs exploded, glass raining and glittering in the remaining glow from the corner lamp.

"Justine," Rosemary said sharply, *"calm down."*

Flatware rattled and jumped beside the sink. Justine's mouth was filled with the taste of ashes. The rage and hurt cut through her like blades.

Sage was white with astonished concern. "We only want to help you—"

"I don't need your kind of help!" A paring knife and a few stray pieces of magnetized flatware shot across a counter and stuck to the side of the stainless-steel refrigerator. Justine was half blind with fury. Nothing was the way she'd thought it was; nothing was real or true. She heard them calling her name, Rosemary's voice angry, Sage's pleading.

Amid the turmoil, she was aware that Jason had come into

the room. Rosemary told him harshly to stay back, that Justine was out of control and would hurt him. Somewhere beneath the rage, Justine was terrified that Rosemary was right.

Ignoring the warnings, Jason reached Justine in a couple of ground-eating strides and pulled her close. He took her head in his hands, forcing her to look up at him. "Justine," he said, his voice low and urgent, "look at me. It's okay, baby. Remember what I told you? . . . Whatever you do or say or feel. Look at me."

Gasping, crying, Justine dragged her unfocused gaze to his. She was held by those midnight eyes, by the way he stared at her as if he knew her inside and out. He was calm and steady, compelling her to be there with him. Guiding her out of a storm, once again. "Are you hurt?" He smoothed her hair back. "Did you step on any glass?"

"I don't th-think so." She felt the white-hot energy draining away. But the anger, and the anguish, were still raging. She couldn't look at either Rosemary or Sage. "This is why," she told Jason, trembling and laughing, tears leaking from her eyes. "The truth or dare question, remember? Why I broke up with my boyfriend. He was afraid of me. You should be, too. You should—"

Jason hushed her, kissing her forehead, stroking back a lock of hair that had stuck to her wet cheek. He reached for a nearby roll of paper towels and tore one off. After blotting Justine's eyes, he held the paper towel to her nose, and she blew obediently.

Sage sighed as she saw that the tempest had passed. "We'll take care of this," she said to Jason as he glanced over the mess in the kitchen. "Thank you, Jason. We'll finish talking to Justine, now that she's—"

"No." He was staring at the flatware and the knife stuck against the refrigerator. "I'm taking her upstairs."

Justine stiffened as she followed Jason's gaze. He should run from her, like Duane would have. Instead he put a hard, bracing arm around her shoulders. "Careful where you step," he said. "I'm good with hypothermia, but I'm damned if I can do stitches."

"She has more ability than we thought," Rosemary said to no one in particular. "Possibly more than I've ever seen in one individual. And she can't control it at all."

Exhausted and sullen, Justine remained silent. Her jaw trembled as she stiffened it against more crying.

"I think we'll call it a night," Jason said in a deliberately pleasant tone, guiding Justine from the room.

"There is something both of you must know," Rosemary said.

"It can wait until later," Jason replied.

"No it can't. You see—"

"Rosemary," Jason interrupted firmly, "with all due respect . . . it's time to shut up now."

The older woman opened her mouth to disagree, then closed it and glanced at Sage, looking rueful. "Perhaps it is."

Fourteen

· ·

Consciousness came to Justine by degrees. The sound of rain . . .
the bruised soreness in all her limbs . . . the scent and softness of
clean cotton sheets. The bleak gray light of morning slipped
beneath her eyelids, and she closed them more tightly. The air in
the tower bedroom was cold, but it was warm all along her
back and bottom and legs, as warm as sunlight. Jason was with
her. He had slept in his clothes, on top of the sheets and blankets, using one of the quilts to cover himself. Justine was in her
nightgown, cocooned deep under the covers.

Memories of the previous night came to her. She had talked
without stopping, although it must have been difficult for Jason
to make sense of the words wedged between hiccuping sobs. He
had held her and listened patiently while she had told him
things she never told anyone in her life. Whether Jason believed
in anything she had said or not, he had held and comforted her

when she had needed it most, and she would always be grateful for that.

Even now she still couldn't believe that her own mother had cursed her. A controlling act disguised as love. It was impossible to accept the contradiction of that; there seemed no way to make sense of it.

"It will never make sense," Jason had told her, "because it doesn't."

He had sounded so certain that Justine had almost believed him. "Are you sure?" she had whispered, resting in the crook of his shoulder. "Rosemary and Sage believe it was for my own good. Does that put me in the wrong? Do I get to be angry about it?"

As he had replied, his hand played with her hair, gathering the long wild locks into a single stream. "Justine, whenever someone says 'this is for your own good,' it's a guarantee they're about to cause you some kind of damage."

"You sound like you know what you're talking about."

"My father used to pound the hell out of me," he had said. "With plumber's line, lengths of chain, anything he could get his hands on. But the screwjob wasn't the beating. The screwjob was when he said it was because he loved me. I always wondered how love could translate into an emergency room visit."

Justine had put her arms around him and stroked his hair.

After a moment Jason had said, "My point is, when someone is hurting you, they can call it whatever the hell they want. They can even call it love. But words lie, actions don't."

There had been a measure of relief in hearing the truth, no matter how painful.

157

"You're not in the wrong," Jason had murmured. "And you do get to be angry about it. Tomorrow. But for tonight, sleep."

Now she lay quietly while fretful wind gusts wrapped around the tower. It had been a long time since Justine had woken up with someone in her bed. Even through the layers of quilts that separated them, Jason radiated heat. A cozy shiver ran through her, and she inched back to fit more snugly against him.

Jason stirred, his breathing slow and even. His hand came to rest at the side of her rib cage in a reflexive gesture. Ticklish pleasure awakened all along her back and spine.

It occurred to Justine that this was the first time she had ever slept with a man without having had sex with him first. Jason could have taken advantage of her last night, while she was distraught. But he hadn't. He'd been a gentleman. She wondered what it would take to make him lose that iron self-control. As she began to roll toward him, the underside of her breast nudged against his hand. The sensation went to the pit of her stomach.

Jason stretched and moved, sliding his arm more comfortably over her. She felt his breath against the back of her neck, lightly stirring the fine hairs. Was he awake? Should she say something? His hand drifted along her side, fingers cupping beneath her breast. Definitely awake. Excitement pulsed through her as she felt him begin to unbutton the long placket of the nightgown, every movement easy and deliberate.

His fingers slid beneath the thin white flannel. So gentle . . . such a contrast to the brutal strength of his grip on her yesterday. Her heart quickened, each heavy thump rolling forward into the next. He cupped her breast, lifting the soft weight, rubbing his thumb over the tip until it gathered into a tight peak. The subtle stimulation pulled up rich throbs from inside.

"Jason—"

His forefinger went to her mouth, resting briefly on her lips.

She felt an openmouthed kiss at the back of her neck, the tip of his tongue touching her skin . . . tasting her . . . as if she were some exotic delicacy. He reached into the welter of the white sheets and quilts, grasped a fold of her nightgown, and tugged it up to her waist. Gooseflesh rose on her legs as they were exposed to the cool air. His warm hand slid over her taut stomach, a fingertip tracing the rim of her navel.

Desperately Justine reached down to grasp his wrist.

"Patience," he said against her hair.

"I can't just l-lie here like a statue—"

"Maguro," he said near her ear, his lips grazing the delicate edge.

"What?" she asked in bewilderment.

"The Japanese word for a woman who lies still in bed." The pitch of his voice was low and morning-roughed. His hand returned to her stomach, rubbing a soothing circle. She felt the shape of his smile against her neck. "Also the word for tuna."

"Tuna?" she echoed indignantly, trying to turn over.

Jason held her in place. Amusement rustled through his voice. "Sushi grade. An expensive delicacy in Japan. Something to savor."

"They . . . they *want* a woman not to move?"

Jason pulled away the quilt. "Sexual passivity is considered feminine." Drawing back the bedclothes, he lay behind Justine, close enough that she could feel the hard muscles of his body beneath the linen shirt and pants. "There's always a passive partner and an active partner."

Her stomach contracted with a sharp pang of anticipation as

she felt the jutting pressure of his erection against her bottom. His thigh pressed between hers, holding them open.

"And the man is always the active partner?" she managed to ask.

"Of course." He nuzzled at the side of her neck, while his hand slid into the wild mass of her hair.

"That's sexist." She gasped as his hand gripped the hair close to her scalp, exerting a light but riveting tension. "What are you—"

"Quiet." The heat of his breath collected in the shell of her ear. "Don't ask anything. Don't move unless I tell you to." Bringing his lips close to her ear, he whispered, "Be a good girl for me."

No one had ever spoken to her that way. Justine would never have expected herself to tolerate it. But she was caught firmly, with his fingers in her hair and his leg holding hers open. She couldn't seem to breathe fast enough, deep enough. Her muscles went lax, as if she'd been drugged. All she could do was wait, helpless with anticipation and need.

His hand slid from her hair. He pulled her top leg back, widening the flection of her thighs, and his fingers slid over the tender furrow. Gently he separated the fullness, teasing the swollen center. The sensation was so sweetly excruciating that she moaned in surprise. He found an intimate seep of moisture and stroked through it.

Her thigh muscles tightened and loosened in a rhythm she couldn't control. A sound of frustration trembled in her throat as his hand pulled away and his thigh withdrew.

Desperately she twisted to reach for him. "Jason—"

His fingers touched her lips, a wordless imperative. A light saline perfume rose to her nostrils, the intimate scent of her own body. She fell silent, trembling with confusion and heat, her inner muscles clasping on emptiness.

"On your back," he said quietly.

She obeyed, gasping as he pulled at the open neckline of her gown until her breasts were uncovered and the tight fabric trapped her arms.

His fully clothed body lowered between her naked thighs. She felt a soft touch on her breast . . . his mouth . . . surrounded by the electrifying roughness of morning bristle. He covered the tip and tugged lightly, and stroked with his tongue. She gritted her teeth to hold back the plangent sounds rising in her throat.

"Open for me," he said against her breast.

Her legs parted, revealing a slow leak of wetness.

"Wider."

She obeyed, burning with embarrassment, aroused beyond anything she had ever thought possible. His thumb came to rest at the center of sensation, stroking and tickling with butterfly lightness. Craving more pressure, dying for it, she hitched upward against his hand.

Instantly his touch was withdrawn.

She sobbed his name, her hips lowering, her hands clenching at her sides. Jason waited, his discipline absolute. The silence was punctured only by the agitated gusts of her breathing. Pleading words hovered at her lips . . . *Do something. Anything.* After what felt like an eternity, he touched her again, parting the fervid flesh, massaging gently. Tension gathered like folds of silk, layering until it accumulated in the weight of pleasure.

He slid two fingers in her, his touch gentle but insistent. She felt him stretching her. Another finger, the inner pressure uncomfortable. She began to protest, but he wouldn't stop, thrusting slowly as he told her that she would take everything he gave her, and then he slid lower on her body, licking and nibbling. She was lost, her breath coming in sobs and gasps.

His mouth closed over her tender flesh in a long sucking kiss. She cried out and shuddered, unable to stop the rush, unable to control anything. More visceral sensation, and more, until she thought she would pass out, but instead she was pushed into a lush, hot, briary release that bore no resemblance to the weak spasms she'd felt in the past.

The feeling came from all directions, coursing wildly through her. Gradually it broke into slow-ebbing ripples. His tongue rested on her, soothing every intimate quiver and twitch. His fingers flexed inside her. Justine moaned, her body replete.

But he wasn't finished. He pressed deeper, more of a pulse than a thrust, over and over. Using his mouth, he built the sensations with fiendish patience, staying with her, not letting her twist away. Unbelievably, the heat was flooding her again. "No," she whispered, certain that she couldn't survive it again, but he wouldn't stop, only drove her ruthlessly into another climax. By the time he had finished, she was limp and half conscious.

Pressing a kiss to the skin of her inner thigh, Jason left the bed and went into the bathroom.

As she heard the shower running, Justine sat up, blinking and rubbing her eyes. "What about your turn?" she asked dazedly, but he didn't hear her over the running water.

Standing on unsteady legs, Justine went to the bathroom and opened the glass stall. She flinched as a mist of cold water hit her face. He was taking a cold shower, his body facing away from her to allow the spray to hit his chest and run downward over his aroused body. He was a magnificent sight, his skin honey colored under a shimmer of water, his shoulders and back and buttocks a mass of bulging muscle.

"Jason," she said, bewildered, "why are you doing that? Come back to bed. Please—"

He glanced at her over his shoulder. "We don't have condoms."

Justine steeled herself against the chilling spray and reached into the stall to turn up the water temperature. When it had warmed sufficiently, she stepped into the shower with him. She embraced him from behind, pressing her cheek on his smooth back. "We don't need condoms," she said. "I'm on birth control."

His tone was vaguely apologetic. "I always use them. A personal rule."

"Oh. Okay." Flattening herself against his back, she savored the heat of the water rushing over them both, as if they were one being instead of two. Her hands slid slowly around his middle, palms riding the unsettled pattern of his breathing. Carefully her fingers investigated the subtle depressions between the sturdy framework of his ribs.

Her blind exploration progressed to the coarse silk of body hair, a fine pathway leading to a denser, thicker patch. He tensed in every muscle as her hand closed around hard, distended flesh. She caressed him up and down, gripping at intervals.

A harsh gasp escaped him, and another, and he turned in the slender compass of her arms to grip her body high and tight against his. She was lifted nearly off her toes, her weight pitched forward. He ground against her abdomen in water-slicked thrusts, and in a matter of seconds he muffled a low growl into the wet ribbons of her hair. Pleasure unraveled in the heat of constant rushing water, rushing and receding, leaving them entangled and spent.

Eventually Justine thought that she should unwrap herself from around him, but Jason seemed in no hurry to let go. And she wasn't certain where to start anyway . . . there seemed no way to separate out which limbs and hands and heartbeats belonged to whom.

Mercifully, breakfast was not a long sit-down meal. Instead Rosemary had set out food on the kitchen counter: fig muffins, sliced fruit, and plain yogurt made at a local dairy. Although Justine was tempted to maintain an injured silence, she found herself joining in the casual conversation, all of them covering the underlying tension as if with a tarpaulin.

She had been deceived by Rosemary and Sage, but that didn't negate all the good things they had done for her in the past. She loved them. She wasn't sure how her trust in them could be restored. But love was not something that could be thrown away easily. Even imperfect love.

Besides, it was awfully hard to act cool and resentful when she was basking in an afterglow that wouldn't quit, her nerve endings glowing like fiber-optic filaments. She kept glancing at Jason, who looked athletic and sexy in the T-shirt and board shorts that Sage had washed for him. Every now and then he sent her a brief, private smile that made her light-headed. *This is what it's supposed to feel like,* her senses told her. *This is what you were missing.* And she wanted more.

Only one thing nagged at the edge of her afterglow: the question of where all this was leading. She didn't want to think about that, since the obvious answer was . . . nowhere. They had met at the intersection of two divergent paths. Jason's fast-paced lifestyle held absolutely no appeal for Justine. And whenever she tried to imagine a place for him in the low-key pattern of her days, she couldn't fathom it.

So the question wasn't whether the relationship would last. Clearly they weren't destined for a happily-ever-after. But Justine wouldn't mind dragging out the "happily" part for as long as possible. The strange thing was, even knowing they could never be together couldn't stop her from feeling connected to him on a level that had nothing to do with reason. Almost as if they were soul mates.

But how could you be soul mates with a man who had no soul?

"The storm surge has died down," Jason said after breakfast. "There's some chop to the water, but nothing the Bayliner can't handle. It's your call, Justine. If you want to leave later in the day, that's fine."

"No, I need to get back to the inn," Justine said, although her stomach turned over at the thought of getting back onto a boat and heading out across that rough water.

Jason stared at her for a long moment. "It'll be fine," he said gently. "You don't think I'd let anything happen to you, do you?"

Surprised that he could read her thoughts so easily, Justine gave him a round-eyed glance and shook her head.

"Justine," Sage said quietly. "Before you leave, we have something for you."

Following her to the sofa, Justine sat with her, while Rosemary stood at the threshold. Jason remained at the window, his arms folded negligently across his chest.

"We went to Crystal Cove at sunrise," Sage told Justine, "to cast a protection spell. It's not permanent, and we don't know how much it will help, but it certainly won't hurt. Wear this to strengthen its effects." She gave Justine a bracelet made of chunks of pink translucent stone strung together in a glittering circle.

"Rose quartz?" Justine slid the bracelet over her wrist, holding it up to admire the beauty of the crystals.

"A balancing stone," Rosemary said from the doorway. "It will help to harmonize the spirits and protect you from negative energy. Wear it as often as possible."

"Thank you," Justine managed to say, although she was strongly tempted to point out that she wouldn't have needed protective spells or crystals if they hadn't helped create the geas in the first place.

"Wear it for Jason's benefit, as well," Sage said, with a nod in his direction. "We tried to extend the spell to him."

"Why would Jason need protection?" Justine asked warily. "He had nothing to do with breaking the geas."

"There is one more thing you haven't been told about," Sage said. "There wasn't a need before now. But since the geas has been broken, there is a particular danger that you must be made aware of."

"I don't care if I'm in danger. Don't tell me."

"You're not the one in danger," Rosemary informed her. "He is."

Justine glanced at Jason's expressionless face. She looked back at the elderly women, feeling sick inside.

"I'll explain," Rosemary said. "As you already know, Justine, the universe demands balance. For the power that a hereditary witch enjoys, a price must be paid."

"I don't enjoy it," Justine said. "I'd give it away if I could."

"You can't. It's part of you. And like the rest of us, you will pay a forfeit."

"What forfeit?"

"Any man a witch truly loves is fated to die. The Tradition calls it the witch's bane."

"*What?* Why?"

"Being born to the craft is a calling," Sage said. "A commitment to serving others, not unlike the vocation of a nun. I don't know when or how the bane originated, but I've always thought that it was to ensure that we would not be distracted by the demands of husbands and families."

It was too much to take in, especially after the other revelations of the past twenty-four hours. Justine drew up her knees and rested her head on them, and closed her eyes. "Because it's not at all distracting to have the man you love die," she muttered.

"Marigold wanted to spare you that suffering," Sage said. "And it's the reason that I, perhaps wrongly, helped with the geas. I thought it would be easier for you to be relieved of such a burden. Never to know the pain of lost love."

Jason had been listening with a wry twist to his lips. "Everyone's fated to die, sooner or later," he said.

"In your case," Rosemary replied, "probably sooner. You'll be fine for a time. No one can predict how long. But one day the misfortunes will begin . . . you'll fall ill, or there'll be an accident. And if you manage to survive that, something will happen the next day, and the next, until finally it's something that you won't survive."

"Only if I fall in love with him," Justine said hastily, not looking at Jason. "And I haven't. I *won't.*" She paused. "Is there an escape clause? A loophole? Some kind of banishing spell or rite or—"

"Nothing, I'm afraid."

"What if I don't believe in it?" Jason asked.

"My Neil didn't," Sage replied regretfully. "Neither did Justine's father. It doesn't matter what you believe, dear boy."

The words made Justine cold all the way through. She found herself anxiously taking inventory of her emotions. It wasn't too late. She didn't love Jason. She would never let herself love anyone if it would turn him into a victim of some supernatural penalty.

Occupied with her thoughts, she didn't notice Jason's approach until she felt his warm hand on her back.

"Justine—"

"Don't," she said, stiffening, shrugging off his hand.

"Don't what?"

Don't touch me. Don't make me love you.

"I don't want to talk about this anymore," she said in a monotone, averting her gaze. "I want to go home. And then I'm going to do my best to stay away from you."

Fifteen

. . . .

The ride to Roche Harbor was lightly choppy, a few cloud breaks revealing flashes of porcelain-blue sky. Jason navigated with care, mindful of the rocks and islets rising through the water. Many of them had been designated as bird refuges for gulls, auklets, oystercatchers, and cormorants. An eagle surveyed the ocean from its perch on a bone-clean tree snag. As the harbor came into view, a wedge of whistling swans crossed in front of the Bayliner, headed to California for the winter.

Jason glanced at Justine, who barely seemed to notice the scenery. She played with the rose quartz bracelet around her wrist, her mouth set and moody. Ever since they had left the lighthouse, she had been remote, as if even the attempt to make conversation might pose a mortal danger to Jason.

They docked in the slip, and two of the red-shirted marina staff came to grab the lines and take care of the boat's mainte-nance. Jason helped Justine from the boat and walked with her along the wooden dock. He slung an arm around her shoulders, and felt her tense.

"Sorry about your kayak," he said. "Maybe it'll turn up somewhere."

"It's probably at the bottom of the ocean." Letting out a quick breath, Justine tried to sound cheerful. "But at least I'm not in it, thanks to you."

"Can I offer to buy you a new one while at the same time making it clear that I'm not trying to impress you with my oversized wallet?"

Justine shook her head, a reluctant smile appearing. "Thank you. But no."

"So what now?" he asked.

Her mouth turned wistful. "We go back to the inn," she said. "You go to work, and so do I. And . . . that's it."

Jason stopped with her at the end of the dock, his hands gripping either side of the rail as she backed against it. Their bodies weren't touching, but he knew how she would feel against him, his body remembered the soft radiant heat of hers.

He stared into her troubled brown eyes. "We have unfinished business."

She understood what he meant. "I—I can't do that with you."

"You were willing this morning."

"I wasn't thinking straight." A blush covered her face. "But now I am."

"You're afraid you might start to care about me." He let a trace of sarcasm enter his tone. "And that will somehow put me in danger. Is that it?"

"No. Yes. Look, no rational person would claim that you and I should be together anyway. I mean, would *you* pick me for you?"

"I just did."

She tried to move out of the enclosure of his arms, but he wouldn't let her. "It's not worth it," she said, facing away from him. "Jason, I know what happens when a person without a soul dies. That's *it*. There's nothing left of you. Your time is limited enough as it is."

"How I spend it is my choice."

"But if I hurt you in any way, I'm the one who has to live with it." Her face contorted, and she struggled with a sudden urge to cry. "And I couldn't," she said thickly. "I couldn't stand it."

"Justine." He pulled her closer, and she twisted away, and ended up with his arms wrapped around her front. His head bent until his mouth was near her ear. "It's a risk I'm willing to take. This happens once in a lifetime. You meet someone and have this crazy reaction . . . you touch her skin and it's the best skin you've ever felt, and no perfume on earth could be better than her smell, and you know you could never be bored with her because she's interesting even when she's doing nothing. Even without knowing everything about her, you get her. You know who she is, and it works for you on every level." His arms tightened. "I've spent the past ten years being with one wrong person after another—which qualifies me to know when I've found the right one." He kissed the little space behind her earlobe. "You feel it, too. You know we're supposed to be together."

Justine shook her head. Incredulously, she felt him smile against her ear.

"I'll make you admit it," he said. "Tonight."

"No."

Jason turned her to face him. "Find a spell, then," he said in a low voice. "Find a way for us."

Justine bit her lip and shook her head. "I've already racked my brain. The only thing I could come up with is a longevity spell, and I can't do that."

His gaze sharpened. "Why not?"

"It's in the area of high magick. Anything that messes with life or death is forbidden—those kinds of spells are dangerous even in the hands of the most experienced crafters. And if a longevity spell worked, it would be terrible. People usually think of longevity as a blessing, but in just about every grimoire you look in, it's classified as a curse. It's a cruel fate to live beyond the natural order of things . . . you would outlive everyone you care about, and your body and mind would decay, but no matter how much pain or loneliness or sorrow you felt, you would keep living. You would end up begging for an end to your suffering because death would be a mercy."

"What if I still wanted you to try? What if I said it's worth it to be with you?"

She shook her head. "I wouldn't do that to you. And even if I were willing, and I cast the spell correctly, it still wouldn't work out for us. We're too different. I would hate your life; I could never be part of it. And I can't see you giving up everything you've worked for to live on a quiet little island. Eventually you'd be unhappy. You'd blame me." Justine turned to face him, her face hidden. "It's no good," she said in a muffled voice. "We're better off apart. It's fate."

Jason wrapped his arms around her and held her for a long time, oblivious of strangers who passed them on the dock. It seemed as if he had resigned himself to the inevitable.

Except that when he finally spoke, he sounded anything but resigned. "The only kind of fate I believe in, Justine, is what

172

happens when you don't make a choice. I want you. And I'll be damned if I let anything get in the way of that."

Jason's return to Artist's Point was greeted with relief by the Inari group, which consisted of Gil Summers, a college friend who now ran the company's development shop . . . Lars Arendt, his lawyer . . . Mike Tierney, an accounting and acquisitions manager . . . and Todd Winslow, the architect for the Inari building in San Francisco.

"Didn't think you could survive without a cell signal," Gil had said with mock concern.

"I enjoyed the break," Jason had told them pointedly. "I can handle being unplugged."

Mike had looked dubious. "You once told me that if heaven and hell existed, they would both be small Midwestern towns except that hell would be the town with no Internet."

"My guess is," Todd had said with a sly grin, "Jason didn't mind the lack of wireless access because he was getting some client-server action from a long-legged brunette."

Jason had sent him a warning glance, and although Todd had grinned unrepentantly, he hadn't said anything further. There were lines of privacy that everyone, even Jason's close friends, knew not to cross.

Priscilla, on the other hand, dared to broach subjects that no one else would. A year earlier Jason had interviewed and hired her from a pool of interns as his own assistant, after one of his managers had narrowed the field down to three candidates. With her country-fried accent and unconventional background, Priscilla had been an offbeat choice. However, her intelligence and competence had already made her a standout among the other interns.

What had clinched the deal, however, had been her comment near the end of the interview, when Jason had asked if there was any information about herself that she might want him to know. "I reckon there is," she had said. "I couldn't help noticing that you don't have a soul." As he had stared at her, she had added, "Maybe I could help you with that."

There was no way Priscilla could have known. He had pressed her to explain, and she had said she could sense it. He had hired her with the expectation that more revelations would come later, and they had. Eventually she had admitted to Jason that she was a natural-born witch.

"You could say me and my kin are the rough end of the Fiveash line," Priscilla had told Jason. "We got witch blood, but no one in this branch of the family ever did anything with it. But one night back in '52, my granny Fiveash made the moon fall from the sky. Bounced on the horizon and went right back up again. Ten minutes from start to finish. Whenever Granny talked about how she'd drawn down the moon, my mama always told me it was really just a pilot balloon from the Weather Bureau. But I knew Granny was telling the truth."

According to Priscilla, her mother hadn't wanted her to know the truth about their family's magical legacy. It would have caused them to be expelled from their God-fearing Ozark community. So Priscilla had covertly tried to learn what she could from her grandmother and her great-aunt, both of them crafters who had secretly practiced magic.

After coming to work for Jason, Priscilla had researched the histories of a handful of ancient grimoires. The Triodecad had been listed among them. Following the descendants of the Triodecad's previous owners, Priscilla had finally identified Justine Hoffman as the last one in the lineage. She was almost certainly in possession of the grimoire by now. And if any book on earth contained secrets that might help Jason, it would be the legendary Triodecad. By a stroke of either coincidence or fate, it had turned out that Justine lived on the island where Jason had already considered buying property.

Jason was grateful to Priscilla for leading him to this place. And he had come to like her as much as he could like anyone who could reminisce fondly about pimento cheese and white bread sandwiches, or grape jelly meatballs, or who thought that the pinnacle of Clint Eastwood's career had been the movie with the orangutan.

Assuming the role of mentor, Jason had tried to make Priscilla understand the values of subtlety and moderation. You didn't need to use a sledgehammer to kill a fly. Gradually she was learning that the skills that had helped you climb out of the gutter were not necessarily ones you wanted to hang on to once you were out.

"How is Justine?" Priscilla asked, sitting at the table in Jason's room and flipping open her laptop.

Jason sat on the edge of the bed. "She's fine."

"Did you—"

He stopped her with a brief gesture. "Let's clear away the business first."

Priscilla tucked a front lock of straight coppery hair behind one ear and opened a file on her screen. "Only a couple of things you need to answer. You've been invited to do the keynote at QuakeCon in Dallas next summer."

That one was easy. "No."

"Will you at least do a panel talk? For an hour?"

Jason shook his head. "I'm going to Cal-Con next week. One conference a year is all I can handle." He had agreed to host a private party to fund-raise for a cancer charity, but it would be a low-profile event. A few other pieces of business were discussed—the latest round of bug fixes for Skyrebels, including a logic error with loading screens from add-ons, and a few new memory and stability optimizations.

Priscilla closed the laptop and gave Jason an expectant glance. "What happened?" she asked. "With you and Justine."

Jason paused, uncertain how to answer. A basic recounting of facts wouldn't convey the truth of what had happened, what was still happening. It was impossible to quantify what he wanted or how he felt.

"Ever heard of something called a geas?" he asked.

Priscilla shook her head.

As he explained, Priscilla listened in the way she always did when her brain was filing away information for future use. Unlike Justine, she was not at all conflicted about the use of magic. She wanted to learn as much as possible. The pitfalls didn't matter to her. Yet.

Someday they would.

"Poor thing," she commented, looking genuinely sympathetic. "I can't imagine being cursed by one of my kin."

"Justine is taking it hard," Jason said. "And it didn't help to find out that Rosemary and Sage were part of it. They're like family to her. She was devastated."

"Lucky for her you were there to help her through it." Something in Priscilla's tone turned the comment into a light barb.

"I was there for her as a friend," Jason said curtly.

"A friend wouldn't scheme to steal her spellbook."

"I'm not going to steal anything. I'm going to return the book after I get the information I need."

"Why don't you ask Justine to loan it to you?"

"She'd refuse."

"How come? If she's a friend . . ."

"It's complicated."

Priscilla regarded him with unblinking blue eyes. "I found the spellbook while you were gone," she said eventually. "Under Justine's bed in her cottage out back. The book is locked."

"I know where the key is. Justine wears it on a chain around her neck."

"Even if you get the key from her, the book is protected by something a lot stronger than a copper lock. You'd never make it past the front door."

Jason shook his head slightly.

Seeing his incomprehension, Priscilla explained. "A grimoire is held to its owner by a whole lot of binding spells. If you try to pull it away, it resists. Like a magnet."

"How do I get past that?"

"My best guess is, you get Justine to trust you. Care about you." Priscilla looked troubled. "The agreement we shook on . . . you're gonna hold to it? You won't hurt Justine by taking away her spellbook for good?"

"I've already said I'm going to give it back. I have no intention of hurting Justine or making an enemy of her. Just the opposite, in fact."

Priscilla looked vaguely startled. "You're not planning on trying to stay friends with her after this, are you?"

"That's my business."

Priscilla studied his impassive face. "Remember what I told you: Never ever get involved with a witch. If she falls in love with you, you're doomed. Even the nicest of us are man-killers. We can't help it. Every man in my family died before his time, including my daddy. You don't want to have anything to do with this. You can't win against it."

"You just told me to make Justine care about me."

"Care, yes. Not love. After you get what you want, leave Justine as fast as possible, and don't look back."

"You're sure you're all right?" Zoë asked again, stocking ingredients in the pantry.

"Everything's great," Justine exclaimed as she cleaned the commercial coffee machine. "I'm fine, other than losing my kayak. But it's replaceable. I guess my pride's a little wounded—I felt like an idiot, getting caught in that storm."

"You must have been relieved when Jason appeared."

"Beyond relieved," Justine said, deciding there was no need to worry Zoë by explaining that she'd been half dead at the time.

After returning to the inn, Justine had been gratified to learn that everything had gone smoothly at the inn during her brief absence. Annette and Nita had cleaned the rooms and common areas, and Zoë had taken care of the kitchen. No complaints from the guests—they had been happy to lounge in the reading room by the fireplace during the storm, while Zoë had brought in trays of refreshments.

Zoë seemed to sense that Justine wasn't telling her everything

178

about the experience on Cauldron Island. After listening to Justine's expurgated version of the night at the lighthouse, she asked skeptically, "*Nothing* happened between you and Jason?"

An image appeared in Justine's mind, of being held against Jason's muscular body . . . that skin as golden and hot as sunlight . . . and she felt herself flush. "I guess I wouldn't be human if I didn't have a little crush on him." She tried to look nonchalant.

"What about Jason?" Zoë asked, bringing a roll of paper towels for Justine to use on the coffee machine. "Does he feel something for you, too?"

"Well . . . that doesn't matter."

"Why not?"

"He's my total opposite, Zo. He's a one-percenter. He has a company plane. He has three houses and doesn't spend time in any of them. I can't be with someone like that."

Zoë gave her a look of fond exasperation. "Is he kind to you? Does he make you laugh? Do you enjoy talking to him?" After Justine nodded in answer to all three questions, Zoë said, "Maybe those are the only things you need to focus on."

"It's not that simple."

"I think it is that simple. People use complications as an excuse to give up too soon." Zoë helped Justine to push the heavy coffee machine back into place. "A group of the girls want to get together this weekend. Are you up for a movie night?"

"Sure. But do me a favor—warn them beforehand not to ask me anything about Jason."

"You're going to have to come up with some PR version to tell them," Zoë said. "Otherwise, they won't stop pestering you."

"PR as in 'public relations'? Or do you mean 'pointless rambling'?"

"Provocatively risqué," Zoë suggested with a twinkle in her eyes.

Justine smiled and went to one of the tall kitchen cabinets and opened the door. "Where is the little marble mortar and pestle you use for grinding herbs?"

"I'll get it for you." Zoë went to open one of the upper cabinets. Pulling out the white mortar and pestle, she brought them to Justine. "Can I help with something?"

"No, I was thinking about trying out a recipe for an oatmeal and honey mask."

"Add a squeeze of lemon juice," Zoë suggested, reaching for the fruit bowl. "It'll brighten your complexion." She picked up a ripe lemon and handed it to Justine. "As for what we were talking about . . . try to stay open-minded, Justine. Sometimes love happens in unexpected places."

Justine gave her a dark glance. "So do weeds."

Zoë smiled. "All right, I'm going."

After Zoë left, Justine went to her cottage, retrieved the spellbook from under her bed, and brought it to the kitchen. Leafing through the section on potions, tonics, and tinctures, she found the recipe she wanted. A discouragement potion, one guaranteed to break the bonds of any romantic attachment or attraction. If given to Jason by her hand, he would lose all interest in her.

Since he could not be expected to drink the potion voluntarily, Justine would have to find a way to slip it to him without his knowledge. She felt more than a little guilty about that, but there was no other choice. It was for his own good, after all. She was trying to save his life.

She winced, however, as she remembered him telling her, "*Whenever someone says 'this is for your own good,' it's a guarantee they're about to cause you some kind of damage.*"

Wasn't there a word for when you had to choose between two equally unpleasant options? "Screwed," she decided ruefully.

She went out to her herb garden to gather fresh licorice root, mint, cilantro, and marjoram. Returning to the kitchen with fragrant handfuls of green, she locked both doors. It was important to follow the recipe to the letter—she wasn't going to risk interruptions.

She ground the herbs with the mortar and pestle, scraped the pungent green mash into a copper saucepan, and added water. After setting the pan to simmer on the stove, Justine went into the pantry to retrieve a cardboard box from the top shelf. It contained a few basic magic supplies, including small glass jars and bottles and packets of resins. Crushing a small lump of myrrh and a pinch of dragontree resin into powder, she added them to the contents of the saucepan.

As the mixture boiled, Justine lit a white sage smudge stick and waved it around the kitchen in a negativity-cleansing ritual. When the herbs were sufficiently steeped, Justine strained the brew into a small bowl. She cleaned up the kitchen and returned to the table to finish the potion. She flipped back to the formula, which called for "Maiden's Tears."

"Great," Justine said to the book sardonically. "I'm pretty sure I don't count as a maiden." In the absence of readily available weeping virgins, however, her own tears would have to do.

But how was she supposed to make herself cry?

Heading into the pantry, she found the wire bin where Zoë kept onions. "This better be worth it," she muttered, setting a fat yellow onion onto a cutting board. She sliced it in half. Cringing, she lowered her face over the caustic fumes, forcing her eyes to stay open. They began to sting and water instantly. "Oh, *jeez*," she gasped, fumbling for a tiny glass bottle. Somehow she managed to capture a couple of teardrops. After blotting her eyes with paper napkins, she took the bottle to the table and used a medicine dropper to fill it with herbal solution.

Now all she had to do was recite the spell, and the discouragement potion would be complete.

But as she reached for the Triodecad, the pages riffled and the book slammed shut.

"Hey," Justine protested, "quit playing around and let me finish this." She forced the book open and found the spell again. Quickly she recited the words, using her forearms to pin the book down as it strained to close itself.

Passion evermore proscribed
when maiden's tears imbibed
Elixir, cool his heart within
discourage love ere it begin.

Breathing with effort, Justine closed the Triodecad and screwed the dropper top onto the little bottle. "All done," she said aloud. "One drop of this, and Jason won't be able to run far or fast enough from me."

Her eyes stung again. "Stupid onion," she said, reaching for another napkin.

Even though the sliced onion was on the other side of the room.

At nine P.M. sharp, Justine knocked on Jason's door. She gripped the silver tray more tightly than necessary. The vodka shots and ice rattled in her hands.

The door opened.

Jason's unnerving gaze swept over her. It started a carousel of emotions spinning inside her, warmth, desire, infatuation.

He urged her inside the room and took the tray from her, setting it on the table.

I'm not in love with him, she told herself as he reached for her. Even though she was intoxicated with the clean sea-salt fragrance of his skin and the comforting feel of him all around her. Even though her throat had gone tight as if she were going to cry.

"You're leaving the day after tomorrow," she found herself saying awkwardly.

"And?"

"This will be over."

"Nothing will be over," he said. "We've just started."

"Any other woman would be better for you. You know I don't fit in your life."

Jason bent to kiss her neck. His hands slid to her hips. His whisper curled softly against her skin. "I think you'll fit me perfectly. Let's try you on."

Wicked, wicked man. Her face was burning. She could hardly stay still, every nerve in her body twitching with hunger. She couldn't help imagining it, just for a moment . . . the feel of him inside her.

"I brought your vodka," she said, pulling away from him. All nerves and twitches, she scrubbed her hair into a wild flurry and tugged at the hem of her T-shirt. "You should have a shot. It'll help you relax."

"An entire fifth of vodka wouldn't do that," he said behind her.

Wrapping her arms around her middle, Justine wandered to the window and looked at the outline of her cottage, the night rustling cool and dark around the inn. The little door lamp was haloed like the painted gold circles around the figures in medieval icons.

"What if I agreed to sell you my Dream Lake house?" she asked without looking at him. "At a fair price. That way you could stay there whenever you need to check on the progress of the construction site. You wouldn't have to come to Artist's Point again."

"You're trying to bribe me to stay away from you?"

The hair on the back of Justine's neck prickled as she heard the sounds of ice jangling in the tray. He had picked up one of the vodka glasses.

"Not bribing," she said. "I just want to arrange the situation so we can avoid future problems."

"You can't avoid future problems," he said. "Even if you find a way not to care about me, or even talk to me, there'll be other problems. Because that's what life is. One problem after another. You can't control any of it. All you can do is reach out for something good whenever you can. And hold on no matter what."

"I can't," she said fiercely. "Because I'm trying to save you."

A long pause. She heard the clink of a glass being set on the table. "Don't try to save me. Just try to love me."

"That would be *easy*." Anguish shredded her voice. "So ridiculously easy to love you." She kept facing away from him. "My God, I wish I'd never broken the geas. They were right—I was better off before. And so were you."

"You weren't—"

He stopped. He drew in a long, rough breath.

Turning, Justine saw Jason with his hands braced on the table, his head lowered over the empty shot glass. His back tensed until she could see the delineation of muscle even through the knit fabric of his polo shirt.

"Justine." His voice sounded odd.

He had taken the discouragement potion. Was it working? Had she made a mistake? He wasn't breathing well. *Hades' bones*. Had she made him sick?

"Yes?" she asked, approaching him warily.

"What did you put in the vodka?" His voice was deceptively mild.

"Maybe a little drop of something herbal. Sort of a . . . um, health tonic. How do you feel?"

He was breathing and swallowing, his skin infused with a darkening flush. "Like a racehorse on steroids."

Justine shook her head in consternation. That didn't sound good. Something had gone wrong.

Jason looked at her then, his eyes dilated into pools of molten black. "Justine," he muttered, "what the hell have you done to me?"

185

Sixteen

· ·

"You should sit down," Justine said anxiously. "I'll get you some water. You're—" She broke off in surprise. One glance along his body revealed that he was aroused. *Really* aroused. Definitely not the side effect of a discouragement potion. Astonished, she reached for the second shot of vodka and took an experimental sip, barely wetting her lips.

A flash of heat covered her from head to toe all at once, taking her breath away. She felt fire racing through her veins. And between her thighs, a hard intimate throb. She could hardly think through the haze of lust and confusion. All from a single taste of the vodka.

And Jason had taken an entire shot.

"This is the *opposite* of what I wanted," she exclaimed in frustration. "What could have gone wrong?"

Jason took a fistful of ice chips from the tray and held them against the back of his neck. The ice melted as if it had been dropped into a hot skillet. Glittering rivulets snaked around his throat and into the fabric of his T-shirt. He was breathing through his teeth, gasping, shivering.

"I'm so sorry," Justine told him miserably, reaching out to touch him, then snatching her hands back as he gave her a baleful sideways glance. "I never meant to . . . I shouldn't have . . . What would help? More ice? Should I start a cold shower?"

Jason didn't seem to have heard. He rubbed his chilled wet hands over his face and lower jaw. The crests of his high cheekbones were bright with color, his long black lashes water-spiked. Stripping off his polo shirt, he wadded it up and blotted his damp neck and shoulders. For a moment Justine could only stare at him.

"I'm sorry," she said again. "I keep making everything worse."

The long muscles of his back flinched as she touched him, as if even the lightest touch were torture. She pressed her cheek remorsefully to his blazing skin.

Jason turned slowly, as if a sudden move would break the tenuous thread of his self-control. He took her against him. She felt the hard, hungry tension of a leopard ready to spring.

"I followed the formula exactly," she managed to say. "It should be working."

Jason dragged his mouth down to the joint of her neck and shoulder, nuzzling roughly. "Paradoxical reaction," he said.

"You mean like when an antidepressant causes suicidal thoughts in some people, or—" She started as she felt his hands go to the fastenings of her jeans, the top button popping free, the zipper hissing. "Or when pain medication gives someone a headache—" A gasp was torn from her throat as his hand slid into the back of her jeans, beneath her underwear.

"I want you," he muttered against her skin. "And I hope the feeling's mutual . . ."

"Yes, but I—"

". . . because there's no chance in hell that you're leaving this room without getting laid."

Justine's eyes widened. She couldn't think straight with the way he was rubbing her against him, his mouth and hands navigating her body with urgent demand. She was shocked by the things he was saying between each ragged breath . . . he wanted to kiss and touch and own every part of her, make her beg, make her come so hard she would think she'd been turned inside out. "And I wanted all that, damn you," he muttered, "even before you slipped me a roofie."

"It wasn't a roofie," she protested. "I mixed up a discouragement potion to . . . to make you not want me."

He crushed his lips to her throat, the kiss strong and gnawing. "Does this feel discouraged to you?" he demanded, shoving her jeans down her hips, gripping her bottom with both hands.

Her eyes half closed and her head tipped back as he brought her against the thick, enticing pressure of his erection. "No," she managed to say weakly. "If you want, I could go look up an antidote."

"I already have one in mind." He tugged her shirt over her head and reached for the back fastenings of her bra. She felt her jeans slip to the floor, and she stepped out of them clumsily. After her underwear was flung aside, Jason shed his own jeans, his gaze locked on her as if he half expected her to bolt and run. They were not going to talk first, turn down the lamp, close the window, lay their discarded clothes on a chair. There was a strong possibility that they weren't even going to make it to the bed.

188

He pulled her against him, front to front, kissing her endlessly, his mouth gentle and savage by turns. The heat of him was unbearable, the skin of his stomach and chest and groin blistering. Justine pulled her lips from his, panting. The air was sauna-hot, scorching the insides of her lungs. Jason reached to the table behind her, fumbling with the crushed ice. He cupped some of it against her breasts, drew an icy handful along her torso. Justine shivered and gasped in relief. The water trickled over her skin, raising gooseflesh. His mouth caught at a budded nipple, sucked the moisture from it. He reached behind her for more ice, spread it over his own chest and down the front of his body, and cupped some to his mouth.

Burning and disoriented, Justine gripped the edge of the table behind her as Jason lowered to his haunches. She bent her head, her hair falling in streamers around her face. She felt his cold hands high on her thighs, thumbs stroking upward to where the skin was thin and excruciatingly sensitive. The blushing folds were parted, held open. She jerked with an incoherent sound as she felt the startling chill of his mouth, his tongue against her tender flesh, stroking cool circles around the swelling peak. She sobbed with every breath, struggling to keep quiet, but it was impossible. She covered her mouth with one hand to smother a low cry, and pushed frantically at his dark head.

A slow, shameless lick across the delicate full ache . . . a hoarse murmur . . . and then he stood. He nudged her toward the bed, but her legs were too stiff to walk. Picking her up with astonishing ease, he carried her to the mattress and lowered her onto her back.

Her thighs opened in a wanton sprawl, her arms half curled and defenseless above her head. She was on the edge of climax, red-faced and dazed. Reaching up for him, she drew him fully over her and pulled his head down. He kissed her, sending his tongue deep, and it felt so good that she moaned into his mouth. Widening her thighs with his knees, he entered her in a demanding thrust. Her knees drew up, her body buckling into the delicious masculine weight of him.

A sheen of sweat gave his skin a metallic luster, light gilding the paths of veins on his arms and neck. His eyes had closed, his brows drawing together as if he were in pain. He drove inside her with a fast, vehement rhythm, not holding back, and she didn't want him to. She pushed back at him, lifting and lifting, her flesh ratcheting tighter around the thickness of him until both of them groaned and shuddered in pleasure, shocks searing through every nerve. Jason shoved deep and held, and she could feel the heat of his release inside her.

Eventually Jason rolled to his side, bringing her with him. His breathing had slowed, the movements of his chest steady and even. They were still locked together, the pulses and tremors of his flesh secreted deep inside her.

She was going to regret this later . . . but at the moment she couldn't bring herself to care. She gasped as he withdrew from her. "Oh. You're still . . ."

"Yes." His tone was dry. "I've never taken Viagra, but as far as I can tell, you've managed to whip up one hell of a substitute."

"I'm so sorry. I really, truly didn't mean to do that to you." At his silence, she asked tentatively, "Are you mad at me?"

"Yes. But it's hard to focus on that when I'm drowning in endorphins."

She smiled slightly and relaxed against him.

Idly he let the backs of his fingers slide over the upper slope of her breast. "You're still on birth control?"

She nodded. "We broke your rule about condoms. I'm so s—"

"You don't have to keep apologizing." He caught the tip of her breast with his knuckles and tugged softly.

No one had ever held her for so long after sex, nor had she ever wanted anyone to. But Jason's hands were gentle as he coaxed delight to uncurl softly inside her, blooms and blooms of it.

"This is okay as long as I don't fall in love with you," she heard herself say.

"But you will."

That was enough to jolt her out of the euphoria. Pushing up on her elbow, Justine frowned at him. "No I won't. The only reason I'm in bed with you is because you're suffering from one of those four-hour emergencies they're always mentioning on TV."

"Caused by you," he pointed out.

"Yes, and I'm trying to help. But I'd appreciate it if you wouldn't try to make this into something romantic or meaningful."

His reply was gently arid. "What would you like me to do?"

Justine thought for a moment. "Tell me the worst things about yourself. Make yourself so unappealing that there's no way I could fall for you."

He gave her a dubious glance and pulled her from the bed.

Justine followed him to the bathroom. "Tell me some of your bad habits," she persisted. "Do you leave wet towels on the bed? Clip your fingernails in the living room?"

"No." Jason stepped into the shower and gestured for her to join him.

"Then what?" She stood beside him, shivering in comfort as

the hot water streamed over her. "You're not perfect. There has to be something."

Picking up a bar of soap, Jason lathered his hands. "When I get sick," he ventured, "I have the personality of a rabid bull terrier." He began to wash her, his big, soap-slick hands moving over her body. "During a movie, I always point out plot holes while everyone else is trying to watch." Noticing the growing smile on Justine's face, he bent his head to steal a kiss. "Sometimes during an argument, I'll pull out my cell phone to look up information to prove I'm right, and break back into the conversation when it's no longer relevant." He paused. "I leave empty containers in the fridge. Whenever there's a dish of mixed nuts around, I eat all the almonds and cashews and leave the peanuts for everyone else. And sometimes when I can't sleep at night, I randomly correct other people's Wikipedia pages." His mouth swiped over hers, absorbing the sounds of her laughter as if he could taste it. "Tell me yours."

She went behind him and began to soap up his back, admiring the powerful contours. "I whistle while I'm mopping floors or vacuuming. Usually the beginning of that Black Keys song on the commercials. One day I whistled it so much that Zoë actually came after me with a spatula." She paused as she heard him chuckle. "When I'm bored," she continued, "I shop for stuff I don't need on the Internet. And I can stop playing a game, any kind of game, right in the middle, and never go back to it."

"Really? How can you do that?" Jason sounded genuinely mystified.

"Short attention span. I also love to give advice to people who haven't asked for it." She reached around him, her soapy hands coasting over his groin to grip the taut, heavy shaft. "And as you've recently discovered, I give aphrodisiacs to unsuspecting guests at my inn."

He was fully erect, his breathing sharp-edged. "You make a habit of it?" he managed to ask.

"You're the first, actually."

"I'll be the last."

Her fingers tightened and slid along the length of him. "How should I do it?" she whispered against his wet back. "Like this? . . . Or that?"

"That's . . ." He was forced to take an extra breath. "God. Yes. *That.*" Lowering his head, he braced his hands against the wall, his chest heaving.

Justine curved herself to his back and caressed him while water rushed over them both and white steam curled through the air. He muttered a few words, endearments, curses, and she drank in the sounds of his excitement. Her hold on him became urgent, her hand pumping and priming the sensation, the heat gathering hard and fast. He came with a low, helpless sound, and she crooned and pulled the pleasure from him, relishing his rough masculine shudders.

Jason turned off the shower and dried them both with a thick white towel. "Now you."

She shook her head. "I don't need anything."

Jason gripped the nape of her neck carefully, and bent his mouth to her ear. "You need what I'm about to give you," he whispered, and every hair on her body lifted. Taking her back to bed, he pulled the covers down and stretched her out on the sheets.

He loomed over her, drawing his fingertips over her body, mapping the most sensitive nerves. She writhed and whispered

193

for him to go faster. But it would be done at his pace, slow as summer twilight. He persisted until she was still and quiet, breathing deeply. Heat danced up to the surface of her skin wherever his lips touched, wherever his body pressed her.

He had already learned too much about her, and he was using it, playing her. Moving down between her thighs, he licked between the lips of her sex, tugging at the soft flange, and when the desire turned too raw, she whimpered and pushed at his head. But he grabbed her hands and held them tightly, and made her hold still, made her take it. The sensation went right to the top of her skull. She jolted with every melting stroke, the pleasure racing through her veins, sparks snapping and colliding. Her legs spread and her toes curled as she felt the beginnings of release, but he stopped and lifted his head.

Deliberately he pinned her with his weight, entering her with a low, heavy slide. He trapped her arms over her head and stared down at her with those intent dark eyes, while he circled his hips in a deliberate grind, teasing unmercifully. She thrashed and squirmed in an agony of tension, gasping out incoherent words . . . *oh please now please* . . . and she heard his quiet laugh as he made love to her with wrenching slowness, sending her into helpless spasms.

Later in the night she awakened with his hands on her again, his mouth at her breast. She moaned as he slid inside her, her head rolling back against his supportive arm. Sensation rippled through her, and the ripples became waves, and the waves surged without stopping.

The hours blended into a long, dark fantasy. She had never suspected that pleasure could be so varied, so dazzling. And then there were the drowsy conversations in between, when they lay together and savored words as if they were kisses.

"What was it like in the monastery?" Justine whispered, wanting to know more about an experience that was completely alien to her. "Did you like staying there?"

His hand stroked slowly over her back. "No. But I needed it."

"Why?"

"I was tired of feeling like nothing mattered. Of going through the motions. Zen teaches you that everything is important. Even a task like washing a bowl is worth doing well. It helps you to be aware, so that entire days and weeks of your life don't slip away."

Justine rested her head on his shoulder, her hand splayed gently over his heartbeat. "Did you have to do a lot of meditation?"

"In the evenings. The day started at four in the morning with a communal lecture. After that we had breakfast followed by work like weeding the garden or chopping wood. In the afternoon each disciple would have a private meeting with the temple master, the Roshi. And then meditation was after dinner. The Roshi assigned a question to each of us. While you meditate on it, you try to quiet your mind and understand its meaning. Some people struggle for years to find the answer."

His fingertips discovered the fine chain around her neck, tracing over it gently as he continued. "One night I had a vision while I was meditating. I was in a temple, walking toward a shadow that was shaped exactly like me. I realized that I was the temple—and the shadow was the empty space where a soul should have been."

Justine felt a chill of uneasiness mingled with sympathy. "Did you tell the Roshi about it?"

Jason nodded. "He didn't think the lack of a soul was anything to worry about. He advised me to accept it. Emptiness is a key concept in Buddhist philosophy. Part of the path to enlightenment." Jason's voice turned wry. "Unfortunately I turned out to be a lousy Buddhist."

"I'd make a worse Buddhist than you. I hate questions with no clear answers." Justine raised her head to look at him. "So you never came to accept it? Not having a soul?"

"Would you?" he asked wryly.

She hesitated and shook her head. No. She would probably be exactly like him . . . trying to fill the soul-shaped void inside.

The morning after was wretched, of course.

Justine awakened early by force of habit, and managed to dress and sneak out before Jason had opened his eyes. She was sore, and clumsy from exhaustion, and nearly sick with worry. Swearing and stumbling, she went to her cottage and took the hottest shower she could stand.

An inspection in the mirror revealed that her eyes were dark-circled and bloodshot. A faint whisker burn was emblazoned on her throat. Groaning, she pulled her hair back in a high, tight ponytail and covered her face with tinted moisturizer.

After downing a cup of coffee along with a couple of ibuprofens, she picked up her phone and dialed Sage. There were few people she would have called at this hour, but Sage was a habitually early riser.

"Good morning," Sage said in her usual sprightly tone. "How are you, Justine?"

"Okay. How about you?"

"Splendid. We spent yesterday picking elderberries. The next time you visit, we'll have pancakes with elderberry syrup."

"Sounds nice." Justine rubbed her forehead wearily. "Sorry to bother you so early, but . . ."

"Oh, no bother at all."

". . . I have a question I was hoping you could help me with. Yesterday I brewed a potion that didn't work, and I need to figure out why."

"Tell me all about it." Alchemy was Sage's specialty—she loved nothing more than brewing and mixing magical formularies. In the past, she had taught classes on oils, powders, elixirs, salves, and washes. She was knowledgeable about which ingredients might be substituted, or which ones could be added to augment a potion's power.

"It was a discouragement potion," Justine said. "I decided to give it to Jason yesterday."

"What a good idea."

"I thought so, too. But it didn't work."

"Are you sure? You should allow sufficient time for it to take effect."

"I'm pretty sure," Justine said, squirming a little as she recalled the sexual gymnastics of the previous night.

"Are you confident in the quality of the ingredients you used? Did you ritually cleanse the workspace first?"

"Yes." Justine described exactly what process she had used, and listed the elements of the formula. "Is it because I gave it to Jason in a shot of vodka? Would alcohol ruin it?"

"No," Sage said thoughtfully, "that shouldn't have made any difference."

"Maybe it's because I'm not a maiden . . . ?"

Blank silence.

"It called for maiden's tears," Justine said, "but I didn't think it would make that much of a difference if I wasn't, you know . . . *innocent,* so I—"

"Justine: Are you saying you put literal tears into the potion? You made yourself cry?"

"Well . . . yes. I've seen weirder ingredients in potions. I didn't think much about it."

Sage's tone was gently acerbic. "Maiden's tears is a plant, dear."

"A plant?"

"A weed also known as bladder campion. It's listed in the book on herbology I gave to you. You promised you would read all of it."

"I skimmed parts," Justine admitted. "It's hard to stay awake when I'm reading about plants."

"If you intend to practice magic even at the most basic level, Justine, you must study and prepare thoroughly. No skimming. No dabbling. The potion didn't result in adverse effects for Jason, I hope?"

Justine was too tired to put it delicately. "Other than making him as randy as a three-balled tomcat, you mean?"

"Oh, dear." A disconcerted pause. "Are you going to brew another batch?"

"No, Jason's leaving tomorrow morning."

"Praise Hecate" came Sage's immediate response.

"Yes. I should never have broken the geas, Sage. I had no idea I would be opening a Pandora's box."

"It wasn't your fault. After some soul-searching, I've come to regret the decision we made on your behalf so long ago. It was

198

a mistake—done with the best of intentions—but still a mistake."
Ruefully Sage added, "The Circle of Crystal Cove is a talented
coven, but I wouldn't say that the study of magical ethics has
ever been our strong suit."

"You've always said magic is fine as long as it doesn't hurt
anyone. You told me that's why so many spells end with 'An
harm ye none.'"

"Yes. But how are we to know when a spell will harm someone or not? We can never be certain of all the repercussions.
That was the dilemma we faced when Marigold asked us to bind
a geas to you. But she persuaded us that it would spare you suffering."

"She may have been right," Justine said mournfully.

Sage let out a slow sigh. "Oh, Justine. All day yesterday I kept
remembering how it felt to lose Neil. Even now, there are times
when it takes my breath away to remember that he's gone. But
there are gifts that we receive only through grief."

"I don't want to think about the possible benefits of grief,"
Justine said. "All I want is for Jason to be safe."

"Will he be?"

Justine knew that what Sage really meant was, *Are you in
love with him?* "I don't know." She gripped the phone tightly.
"I'm scared. I'm not sure how far it's gone. I keep telling myself
that it can't happen this fast. I mean, I can't fall in love with
someone I've only just met."

"Of course you can," Sage said gently. "Some people's hearts
are very efficient that way."

Justine's throat clenched. "If I've put him in danger, I have to
fix it," she said. "There must be an answer in the Triodecad.
There has to be something I can do."

"My poor darling girl, don't you think I tried anything and everything to save my Neil? Don't you think your mother sought to have your father spared? Whatever you do will only make things worse. The nature of the bane is sacrificial."

A human sacrifice. Was that the price of love for someone like her?

"You once told me that nothing is impossible in magic, only improbable."

"Yes. But I also told you that we must never attempt the improbable. No meddling with matters of life or death. That is the spiritual realm of high magick, which is beyond our power. It's trying to assume a godlike role for human purposes. And that will *never* end well."

· ·

Seventeen

Jason spent the better part of the day sitting at a table with Alex Nolan, the two of them signing reams of documents while lawyers and Realtor supervised. A preliminary design-build agreement, letters of intent concerning purchase and sale, qualifying language, timing of events and obligations and ownership transfer. Jason signed each efficiently and without hesitation.

He had wanted to establish a learning institute ever since his first big success at Inari, understanding that he had to do something good in the world before he left it. He saw no point in accumulating wealth for its own sake. Better to use the money to create a place where people could find connection and community, and learn things that would make their lives better.

The decision to establish the institute on San Juan Island was made all the easier by the fact that he would be closer to Justine. Thoughts of her lingered in his mind like a soft autumnal perfume, earth and leaves and rain. He and she were right for each other in the same way darkness was complemented by light, night by day. *Inyodo* was the Japanese word for it. If Justine were willing to make a place for him in her life, he would stop at nothing to be with her.

As the day progressed, Jason was disgruntled but not surprised to discover that Justine wasn't returning his calls. According to Zoë, Justine had gone for the day. Jason knew exactly why Justine didn't want to face him yet. She was trying to come to terms with what had happened—and no doubt figuring out a strategy to deal with him.

Reining in his impatience, he packed for the morning's departure. As evening approached and there was still no sign of Justine, Jason went out to dinner with the rest of the Inari group. Alex and his fiancée, Zoë, had agreed to join them in celebrating the preliminary signing for the Dream Lake development.

"I haven't heard from Justine today," Jason said casually to Zoë during dinner. "I hope everything's okay."

"Yes, she's fine," Zoë said, a blush infusing her porcelain skin. "She was busy with errands."

"All day?" Jason couldn't resist asking.

Zoë looked flustered and vaguely apologetic. She replied in an undertone that no one else at the table could hear. "Justine said she needed some time alone."

"What kind of mood was she in?"

"She was . . . quiet." Zoë hesitated before adding, "She said that having a wish come true was one of the worst things that had ever happened to her."

Jason gave her a puzzled glance. "What did she wish for?"

After a long hesitation, Zoë replied without looking at him. "I think it was you."

The lights in Justine's cottage were on when Jason returned to the inn after dinner. He waited until the inn was settled and still before walking across the lawn. The night was clear, stars blinking as if to semaphore-coded messages. The scythe-shaped moon was angled to cut a swath through the dark sky. A nightjar cried in a low churr as it chased moths into the shadows.

Jason knocked at the front door. His stomach had contracted into a tight knot. He was accustomed to taking risks. In the past he'd agreed to business deals involving unthinkable sums of money, and launched games that would bury the company if they flopped. He'd handled it all without flinching. But nothing had ever unnerved him like the prospect of losing Justine.

The door opened slowly to reveal Justine with her hair pulled back in a ponytail and her face clean-scrubbed. There was something damaged in her posture, a slump like a broken flower stem. He was filled with the desire to comfort her, give her respite and pleasure and ease.

"I missed you today," he said.

She swallowed audibly. "I had errands."

Jason lifted a hand to her tense jaw, gently tilting her face upward to stare into her tired eyes. "Talk to me for five minutes. Please. I can't leave tomorrow morning without us settling a couple of things."

Justine started to shake her head before he had finished the sentence. "There's nothing to settle."

Jason stared at her, considering his options. Charm. Seduction. Bribery. Begging was not out of the question. "There's at least one thing."

"What?"

He said in a businesslike tone, "I'm here to complain about my room."

Her eyes slitted open. "What's wrong with it?"

"The bed is too hard. And the sheets are scratchy." Seeing that Justine was going to argue with this assessment of her luxurious guest accommodations, he added, "And my orchid's wilting."

"Try putting water on it."

"My bed?"

Justine tried to look severe. "Your orchid. I can't do anything about the bed. Besides, you're an insomniac, so you don't sleep anyway."

"I want to hold you tonight," he said. "No sex. I just want to lie next to you while you sleep."

Her expression didn't change, but he thought he saw a spark of amusement in her eyes. "Like hell."

"Okay, I want sex," he admitted. "But after that, I would let you sleep."

The hint of a smile faded. "I can't be with you again. And don't make me explain, because you know why."

Jason reached out for her, unable to hold back any longer. "It's not all your decision. It's mine, too."

"There's nothing you can say—"

"Tell me what you want, Justine. Not what you're afraid of, not what you've already decided. Just what's in here." He slid one hand to the center of her chest and flattened his palm over her rapidly beating heart.

She shook her head, looking unsettled but stubborn.

"You're not going to admit it?" he asked, tenderly mocking. "What a little coward. I'll say it for you, then: You want me.

You're in love with me. Which means that I'm already living on borrowed time."

"Don't say that," Justine snapped, trying to push away from him, but he wouldn't let her. He hugged her close, surrounding her with his warmth.

"I'm a dead man walking," he said, his voice muffled in her hair. "A goner. My goose is cooked. My number's up. I'm Screwdini."

"Stop it!" she cried. "How can you joke about this?"

His arms tightened. "One of the few advantages of not having a soul is that you have no choice except to live in the moment. And any moment that I have you in my arms is a good one." He kissed her hair. "Let me in, Justine. It's lonely out here."

Justine went still. She took a long, broken breath. When she looked up at him, her eyes glittered with some strong emotion. "Just for a few minutes," she said, and stepped back as he crossed the threshold.

As soon as she closed the door, he hauled her close until they were pressed front to front. He took Justine's wrists and pulled them around his neck. Her breath was fast and anxious against his skin.

"Help me do what's right," she begged.

"This is what's right." Jason cupped his fingers around the back of her skull, guiding her head to his shoulder. It felt insanely good to hold her, the embers of last night dancing into fresh flame. "I'm leaving tomorrow," he said, "but I'm coming back in a week or less. I just have to make some arrangements."

"Arrangements for what?"

"Restructuring. There's no reason I can't delegate some of my

205

responsibilities at Inari. The stuff that only I can do, I'll either handle remotely or it can wait until I make it back to the office."

Justine sounded dazed. "What are you trying to say?"

Jason traced the delicate rim of her ear with his thumb, and kissed her earlobe. "I want to be part of your life. I have to be. Since you have to stay at the inn to do your job, I'll come to the island as often as I can."

"Where . . . where are you planning on staying?"

"That depends on you."

"I want you to go away. For good."

"Because you don't care about me? Or because you do?"

Justine didn't respond, didn't look at him. He continued to hold her, trying to interpret her silence.

"I lose everyone I care about," she eventually said. "I lost my father before I ever got to know him. I lost my mother because I couldn't be what she wanted. I lost Duane because he couldn't handle what I am. Now you're asking me to care about you, knowing I'm going to lose you, too. Well, I can't." Defeat gave each word the weight of a brick, to be used in the wall she was building between them. Wriggling out of his arms, she turned away.

He would have her, and damn anything that got in the way. God knew he'd never been a man to back down from a fight.

"Are you worried about the possibility that I might die?" he asked. "Or the chance that I might not?"

Justine whirled to face him, her face reddening as the implication sank in. "You *asshole*!" she exclaimed.

"What if I don't?" he persisted, turning ruthless. "What if I stick around long enough for you to have to deal with a real relationship? Compromise, intimacy, forgiveness, sacrifice . . . could you handle all that? You don't know."

Justine glared at him. "You won't be here long enough for me to find out."

"Everyone's got an expiration date," he said. "When you love someone, you take your chances."

Justine covered her face with her hands, clearly not above a touch of drama. "I'm trying to do what's best for you, you obnoxious bonehead."

He gripped her against him, letting her feel his strength, his steady determination. "You're what's best for me. And I'm not going to turn tail and run because of some crazy superstition."

"It's not a superstition, it's . . . it's supernatural causality. It's going to happen. And don't try to claim you don't believe in the paranormal, Mr. I-don't-have-a-soul."

Jason smiled. "As a Buddhist, I don't have to be consistent."

Justine made an infuriated sound and tried to push him away, but he kept her against him easily. He bent to kiss her, opening her mouth with his. Justine quivered and went pliant against him, her hands groping over his back. He could feel a subtle vibration running through her, fervency barely contained in stillness. He wanted to be inside that energy, driving it higher, hotter.

Breaking the kiss, he breathed in the soft fragrance of her neck, letting it tease his senses. "Let me stay with you tonight."

Her voice was muffled. "No way in hell."

"Give me one night. If you tell me tomorrow morning that you still want me to leave you, I will."

"You're lying."

"I swear I won't come back unless you ask me to."

She maneuvered in his arms until she could see his face. "What are you planning?" she asked warily. "Why do you think one night will make a difference?"

Eighteen

. . . .

The way Jason stared at her made her uneasy. She didn't trust the glint in his eyes. "I already know you're good in bed," she continued. "There's nothing left to prove in that department."

"I want to try something with you," he said. "It's a kind of . . . ritual."

"Ritual," she repeated, narrowing her eyes in suspicion.

"It's called *Kinbaku.*"

The foreignness of the word, three distinct and precise syllables, tapped delicately on her eardrums and made her shiver.

"Is that something sexual?"

"Something physical. It doesn't have to be sexual, if you don't want it to be."

Mystified, Justine chewed on the insides of her lips. "What does that word mean?"

A faint smile touched his lips. "It's translated as 'the beauty of tight binding.' Do you have any cord or thin rope?"

"Yes, I keep some in my closet for—" Justine stopped, her eyes turning huge. "Are we talking about *bondage*? No. No, I don't have any rope."

"You just said you did."

"Not for that. I don't like pain."

"There's no pain involved. It's . . ." He paused, clearly considering how to convey the meaning of a Japanese word when there was nothing in English to approximate it. "It's artistic. Ropework shaping the body into a living sculpture. The basic form is *Shibari,* but it becomes *Kinbaku* when emotion is involved."

Justine wasn't buying it. "That sounds like a sophisticated way of saying you want to truss me up like a rotisserie chicken at the grocery store deli. And I don't see the point."

"It's like trying to explain the point of skydiving or skiing to someone who's never done it. You have to experience it to understand."

"Have you ever done it before?"

His face was inscrutable. "I was involved with a woman in Japan who introduced me to it. There are shows where *Shibari* is performed as an art form, not to mention seminars—"

"What kind of woman?" Justine asked, surprised by the bitter tang of jealousy. "Like an escort service woman or—"

"No, not at all. She was an executive at a software company. Smart, successful, and very beautiful."

That hardly eased her jealousy. "If she was so great, why did she let you do that to her? Wasn't she—" Justine broke off and swallowed audibly. "Ashamed?"

"There's no shame in a willing exchange of power. The ropes are an extension of the dominant partner . . . he uses them to hold a woman, focus on her . . . guide her into deeper layers of surrender. My partner said that when she was restrained on the outside, it allowed her to be unrestrained on the inside. It revealed things she'd never known about herself."

Their gazes held, the silence charged and impellent.

Justine didn't know what to say. She was amazed by her own reaction, the darts of heat that went through her. She had to admit that she was intrigued. It didn't seem like the kind of thing that would end well. But she couldn't quite bring herself to refuse.

"I can do that for you," Jason said, "if you're willing to trust me."

Her lips had gone dry. "Should I?"

"I hope you will."

"That's not a yes."

"It's not a no."

Justine let out an uneven laugh. "Damn you. Why don't you just say yes?"

"Because trust is not something I can talk you into. It's your choice. What does your gut tell you?"

"I don't trust my gut, either."

Jason was silent, waiting patiently.

She didn't understand herself, why she was even considering it. The rational side of her brain was aware that he was tempting her into some kind of novelty sex. But her intuition pulled toward a different understanding. As she stared into his midnight eyes, a word came to mind . . . "charmer." Not the modern definition of the word, but the ancient biblical meaning: a worker of spells, binding blessings or curses to an object using knotted cord.

One night, and then he would leave.

"Promise you wouldn't trick or hurt me," she said suddenly.

"I guarantee it."

Flutters awakened inside her as he fitted his hands at her waist. "What if I don't like it? What if I want you to stop?"

"You'll have a safe word. The second you say it, I'll stop."

"What if I forget my safe word?"

His lips twitched. "All you have to do is answer a security question, and I'll send you an e-mail to reset it."

Justine smiled uncertainly and took a nervous breath. There was no compelling reason to trust him; in the most objective terms, they hardly knew each other. And yet somehow he seemed to understand her better than any man ever had.

"Okay," she managed to say. "You can spend the night with me. And in the morning, you're out of here. Deal?"

"Deal."

She led the way to her bedroom, excruciatingly aware of his footsteps behind her. She turned on the bedside lamp and opened the closet door.

"Cinnamon," Jason said, as a whoosh of spiced air was pushed outward by the motion of the door.

"It's a clothes sachet." Actually the fragrance was from the besom broom she kept at the back of the closet, the rushes heavily anointed with cinnamon oil. However, she wasn't about to start displaying all her craft-related accessories—not her broom, candles, or crystals, and especially not her spellbook. Standing on her toes, she reached up to the top shelf and pulled down a bundle of soft red hemp rope, no more than five millimeters in diameter. Hesitantly she gave the little bundle to Jason.

After running his fingers along the fibers to make certain they were soft, Jason glanced at Justine quizzically. "What do you use this for?"

"Spell-casting circles."

"It's perfect. Do you have any more?"

Hesitantly she retrieved two more bundles. As Jason took the rope, Justine thought there was something interesting in the idea of using rope from her rituals for a ritual of his. She watched him unroll one of the lengths of hemp. "You're not planning to mummify me, right?"

He shook his head. "I only know a few basics. But a *Shibari* master would need more rope for complex patterns and suspensions."

"Suspensions?" she asked with vague alarm. "Hanging in the air? Like a Christmas ornament?"

Jason grinned briefly. "Don't worry. You're staying on the ground."

She let him draw her to the bed. His manner was relaxed, deliberate. A ritual, he'd said. She understood the value of rituals, designed to provide structure and meaning. But sex as a ritual was a new concept. How had Jason guessed at something she had never known about herself? . . . That her innermost desires might extend to something like this. What had been the giveaway? What had she said or done?

She remained standing as he sat on the edge of the mattress. He pulled her between his spread knees. "What if I like this?" she asked anxiously. "What does that mean?"

He understood what was worrying her. "Everyone has secrets. Twists and kinks they wouldn't necessarily want other people to know about. There's nothing wrong with having fantasies."

His fingers went to the fastenings of her jeans and worked at them deftly. Justine kicked off her sandals and held on to his shoulders, feeling bewildered and scared and excited as she lifted one leg out of her jeans, then the other. Jason pushed up the hem of her knit shirt, and she pulled it over her head. Seeing the tiny copper key dangling from the chain around her neck, he asked, "Would you mind if we took that off?"

Justine hesitated before lifting the long chain over her head and setting it on the nightstand.

Jason touched her breast over the unlined bra, stroking the curve with the pads of his fingers and then the backs of his knuckles. Leaning forward, he pressed his parted lips against the deep curve. She felt him breathing hotly, sucking through the fabric until it was wet and her nipple jutted into the delicious ache.

"What's your safe word?" he whispered.

"Chicken."

He smiled and unfastened her bra, drawing it from her shoulders. Pulling her to sit next to him, he made a soothing sound as he felt her trembling. "You don't have to be scared. I'm not going to hurt you."

"I'm not afraid of that. I'm afraid I'll feel silly."

He considered that. "Sex with dignity is never really an option."

"Yes, but—" She gasped as he hooked a finger into the side of her panties and eased them down.

"Relax."

"I'm not good at relaxing."

"I know," Jason said kindly, tugging at the other side of her panties. "That's why I'm going to tie you up."

Her breath caught as he slipped her panties off. She clamped her inner thighs into a prim, tight seam, acutely aware of his every movement. She watched as Jason tied a simple knot with a loop at the end. Lifting her ponytail, he laid a length of the rope around the back of her neck. "I'll start with a lightning harness," he said, threading a section of cord through the loop. "It won't restrain you in any way."

"Why is it called a lightning harness?"

"It makes a zigzag pattern."

Justine stared at him fixedly as he knotted the cord at the high center of her chest. Now that he had begun, he had the intent look of someone trying to solve a complex puzzle, or someone absorbed in a fascinating hobby.

Jason leaned forward, clamping the loop with his teeth to hold it in place while he reached around her back with both arms and rigged the rope across. Justine jumped a little, feeling his mouth so close to her skin, the searing rush of his breath. He drew his head back, created another loop, and repeated the process. Each time he wrapped the rope around her back, he used his teeth to hold the front loop in place. With each new loop added, he moved lower and lower on her body. The rope began to form a zigzagged web across her torso.

"Most of these are slipknots," Jason said. "Any time you want to stop, I can have you out of this right away."

Justine didn't want him to stop. It felt unexpectedly pleasant, this slow and meticulous binding. She spoke like someone in a trance. "Can I talk while you're doing this?"

He threaded another loop. "Talk the whole time if you want."

"This is like a new sport: extreme macramé."

"Are you uncomfortable?"

She shook her head. It was strange to feel snug and so exposed at the same time. Her breasts protruded between the lines

214

of rope in a way that made them feel larger, fuller. The harness had formed a light corset that seemed to contain and concentrate all the sensation in her body. Justine could feel her heartbeat between her thighs and at the insides of her elbows and the tips of her breasts. When the last loop had been threaded at her navel, Jason tied it with a hitch knot. His hands moved over the web of cord on her torso, his palms warm and soothing.

"More?" Jason asked, looking into her eyes.

Justine nodded.

His voice was soft. "Stand up, honey."

She complied, her heart beginning to pound as he drew the rope between her thighs and up behind her to loop around one of the back cords. Another pass between her thighs, so that now a cord lay on either side of her vulva. This was more directly intimate, more erotic. Justine cleared her throat and said shakily, "That could turn into one heck of a wedgie."

"I'll keep it loose." He ran a finger beneath the cord. She gasped a little as his fingertip brushed the verge of soft, sparse curls. "Does this feel okay?"

Justine could hardly speak. "Yes."

A finger slipped gently beneath the other side, his touch wicked and knowing. "Not too tight?"

She shook her head.

With his finger still hooked beneath the cord, he slid his knuckle to the shadowed channel between her thighs, and circled gently at the top of it. Her knees went weak, and she gripped his shoulders to keep from falling.

Jason lowered her to her back with infinite care. Her limbs were loose and splayed, her breasts plumped high between the bands of rope. He reached for more of the hemp and bound her

215

hands together, attaching them to a cord at her waist. Every movement was measured, the rigging progressing in a fluid and soothing rhythm. He kept glancing at Justine's face, sensitive to every nuance of her expression.

She had begun to breathe deeply, mesmerized by the sensation of being constricted by degrees, her body seeming to swell against the web of rope. Bound. Spellbound. There was no room to be embarrassed, no room for words or even thought.

Moving behind her on the bed, Jason gently turned her head to the side and unfastened her hair. The loose waves cascaded over his hands. His strong fingers curved beneath her head to lift it slightly, massaging her scalp. Justine moaned in pleasure and relaxed as he cradled the weight of her head. One of his hands worked down to her nape, gripping the tight muscles with delicious squeezes until they loosened.

Jason bent over her, his lips grazing hers in an upside-down kiss. "More?" he whispered.

"Yes. Yes." She lifted her face, her tongue touching the edge of his mouth where the masculine texture of shaven bristle met the silk of his lips. She felt the shape of his smile, smelled the hot mint of his breath. His fingers stroked her throat and face tenderly. She was lost, floating, her blood humming.

Keeping her eyes shut, Justine waited as he moved to the other side of the mattress and grasped one of her ankles. He took her foot in both his hands, warming her sole, her toes, his thumbs massaging into the sensitive arch. She writhed, delight unfolding like a multifoliate flower. His lips brushed her heel before his teeth dug in lightly. The little nip caused her to twitch in surprise, runners of heat going through her, a bloom of intimate moisture between her thighs. A nibble at her toes, a ticklish kiss, and then Jason began to wrap her ankle. His hands were gentle and clever, bending her leg until her heel nearly touched her bottom, winding the thin, soft rope in a spiral toward her knee.

Justine opened her heavy-lidded eyes to watch Jason's dark silhouetted form. He knew what he was doing. Every tug of the cord tightened the urgency inside, hunger and confusion knotting exquisitely until she writhed from the inner pressure. A large, warm hand came to rest on her stomach.

Jason was looming over her, hooking a muscular arm around her bent knee. "Beautiful," she heard him say softly. "The patterns on your body. Red cord and ivory skin. Like an image from a *shunga* print." He kissed the inside of her knee. "If I had a soul, I'd have sold it for a chance to see you like this."

How peculiar it was that she could feel naked and secure all at once, all her protections gone. She was nothing but a bundle of bare flesh tied in red cord, her nerves charged with need. Jason worked carefully, purposefully, tying and threading rope to shape her body as he wanted. Her knees were drawn upward and secured so that she was held defenseless and exposed. She was throbbing everywhere, her sex full, the air wafting coolly against a slick of moisture.

Jason drew his hands over her legs, tracing the pattern of the cord. The air was filled with the mingled rhythms of their breathing. Even with her eyes closed, Justine could feel the intensity of Jason's concentration on her. It gave her a disembodied feeling, being held and stroked and restrained, no choice except to submit.

Jason reached down to the ropes on either side of her groin and readjusted them, gently stretching each cord between the outer folds of her sex so that she was spread open. She began to tremble and strain, her insides pulsing and closing on emptiness.

Another whisper. "More?"

"Yes," she said on a sob of breath.

Seconds passed while she writhed in the restraints, her bound wrists flexing, her toes curling. His hands gripped her bottom, forcing her to hold still. His mouth descended, covering her with slippery heat and sinuous flicking. She gasped, struggling against the ropes. Slowly his thumb worked inside her, rubbing deep circles while her muscles clutched helplessly at the new invasion. Her spine turned molten, and she dissolved in the heat, coming so hard she couldn't draw breath to scream.

His thumb withdrew, his mouth playing on her, easing her into softness. Wordless minutes passed, while he cradled her trussed body as if she were a vessel he drank from. The lamplight slid over the dark head between her thighs, the layers of his hair touched with gold. She whimpered in surprise as the need built again, her swollen flesh tightening and twitching.

She felt the caress of his breath as he spoke hoarsely. "Use the safe word, Justine, or I'm going to take you while you're tied. Do you understand, honey? Tell me to stop before it's too late."

"Don't stop," she managed to say, the words sweet and raw in her throat.

He pressed a rough kiss at the entrance of her body and stood to undress. His body was sleek and powerful, shadows cutting across his golden skin like tiger stripes. Standing at the edge of the bed, he gripped the harness of ropes and pulled Justine to him. He was astonishingly strong, lifting her without effort. She was helpless to move or participate, her body so neatly restrained that he could manipulate her like a toy.

Reaching down, Jason positioned himself and entered her in a wet, skewering thrust. His mouth came to hers, absorbing her pleasured groans. He continued to kiss her as he gripped the ropes, using them to lift and rock her against him. It was like riding on waves, a steady undulation while the cords held her open, exposing her sensitive flesh to each lubricious plunge. His mouth covered hers, his tongue filling her, while his hands gripped the ropes to make her ride every hard thrust. She bounced helplessly, weightless, sightless, washed in the heat of a climax so prolonged that it had no definite beginning or end.

She had never surrendered herself so fully, had never imagined it possible, and yet it was what she had always craved, to be sublimated in pure feeling. To hear her name in Jason's voice, his body shuddering against hers, the thick pulse of him buried within her. To feel his arms go around her, his face nuzzling hard into her neck.

When the final tremors dissipated, Jason eased her back and worked at the knots, untying them slowly, smoothly, pausing only to caress a private curve, a damp hollow. Each length of red hemp was deftly coiled and set aside. Dazed and dreamy, Justine lay in a passive sprawl while he rubbed and kissed the faint cord marks on her body. Her limbs were heavy, her heartbeat unhurried. Every nerve was alert to the pleasure of Jason's hands on her, the intimate energy that flowed back and forth between them.

"What's a *shunga* print?" she asked eventually, her voice blurred as if she'd just come out of a deep sleep.

"Ancient erotic art." Jason wrapped a blanket around her and held her against his chest. "Hand-painted images showing couples in sexual positions." His hand played gently in her hair. "To make it as stimulating as possible, the men are usually shown with exaggerated genitalia."

"In your case, that would be accurate."

She felt Jason smile against her head. But a second later, he eased her head back to look down at her with a flicker of concern. "Did I hurt you?"

"No." She traced the edge of his upper lip with her fingertip. "I just meant that you're very . . . satisfying." Yawning, she leaned her head back against his chest. "And you were right."

"About what, baby?" he whispered.

"Being tied. I feel a little different, somehow. I feel . . ." She groped for words. "There was a moment when I was open and feeling everything and taking everything, and even though you were the one in charge, I felt like . . ." She hesitated, unwilling to say it.

"You owned me," Jason said quietly. "You knew I was yours."

Justine couldn't reply, even though it was true. Especially because it was true. Settling deeper in his arms, she became aware of a slight soreness here and there, subtle reminders of ropes and flesh and pleasure.

After a while, she was dimly aware that Jason had left the bed and had returned with a damp washcloth, the moist heat moving over her face and limbs and between her thighs. The need for sleep was overwhelming. He pulled the covers over them both and she felt herself sinking into layers of inviting darkness.

"I'm coming back to you, Justine," she heard him say. "You know that, don't you?"

"You promised you wouldn't."

"You'll want me to." When she didn't answer, he held her more closely. "Don't be afraid," he whispered.

Justine had every reason to fear for both of them. The safety she felt in his arms was only an illusion. But she would take it for now.

The shriek of the alarm clock woke Justine into a state of heart-pounding alertness. With a muffled exclamation, she crawled across the mattress and hit the snooze button. Collapsing onto her back, she groaned at the prospect of starting the day.

After a long, shivering stretch, she yawned and glanced around the room. Thin morning light had seeped through the shutters, casting the room in muted colors like a vintage postcard. Her gaze was attracted by an incongruous splash of red . . . three bundles of hemp rope on the nightstand.

Mortified color spread over her as images flashed through her mind. She wished she could have claimed that the previous night had happened as a result of one glass of wine too many. Because no one had that kind of sex while sober. Crazy sex. Off-the-chain sex. I-can-never-see-you-again sex.

Justine inched lower on the bed and tugged the sheet up to her nose. Had those bundles of hemp not been left out, she might have convinced herself it had been a dream. Unfortunately she could recall every detail. The way Jason had gripped the ropes to pull her body onto his, the way he had traced and kissed the marks on her skin afterward. The sight of him so deliberate and intent, a flush of passion on his face. His smoke-and-brimstone whisper . . . *"You owned me."*

She had felt it. She'd had him going hard, all wrapped up in her, taking her mouth with hard sweet kisses and breathing her name in between, every muscle in his body straining to get closer, deeper. At the end, a sound had caught in his throat as if something had hurt him. Unable to hold him in her arms, she'd gripped him down below, a tight caressing clasp while he spilled inside her.

Remembering, Justine let out an unsteady sigh. Her chest was heated with a leftover erotic glow.

The warmth faded, however, as she reminded herself that Jason was gone. Spirits willing, he would be safe now that he was away from her. *Don't think about him.* Don't miss him or his blinding smile or those long kisses or how his skin always seemed hotter than normal, like a perpetual low-grade fever.

How did you stop yourself from loving someone? You could end a relationship, but you couldn't end the feelings that had fueled it. Only time could do that . . . maybe.

Sitting up, Justine pushed back the tangled sheaf of her hair and reached over to the nightstand for her necklace, the long chain with the copper key.

It wasn't there.

Had it fallen? Frowning, she slipped out of bed and hunted for the chain on the floor. She looked behind the nightstand. Still nothing.

She felt sick, covered in adrenaline stings, the way it felt when she was about to fall but had caught herself, nerves zinging with the anticipation of pain. Her mouth and throat went dry. She was too numb even to feel her heartbeat. Before she brought herself to look under the bed, she knew what she would find.

The Triodecad was gone.

Nineteen

....

The only fortunate aspect of the situation was that with the guests gone, no one was there to hear the howl of outrage coming from the back cottage. Nor did anyone witness the explosion of an alarm clock, two lightbulbs, and a toaster.

By the time Justine had regained control, the cottage was filled with a light acrid haze of smoke and she was huddled on the floor. Her eyes were hot and bone-dry with fury. She was going to kill Jason Black. Creatively. *Slowly.*

Clasping her head in her hands, she tried to think through the red cloud of rage.

How could Jason have stolen her spellbook? No one could take it from her . . . it wasn't possible. And yet somehow he had.

"I swear I won't come back unless you ask me to."

The bastard had known that she would want him to come back, if only to return her spellbook. She let out a guttural cry of rage.

What the hell did he think he was going to do with the Triodecad? Did he think he could just open it and recite a spell like he was reading a Betty Crocker recipe?

No. Whatever else Jason was, he wasn't stupid. He knew he would need a crafter to help him. The concept of paying someone to cast a spell—magic for hire—was as old as time. From Jason's point of view, stealing the Triodecad was a Hail Mary play, a gamble with no downside. As he had told her the previous night, he was already living on borrowed time. He intended to do exactly as he pleased, and then talk Justine into forgiving him. *Fat chance,* she thought darkly.

Struggling to her feet, Justine went to her bedroom. She pulled on some leggings and an oversized tee. Her gaze went to the dark space beneath the bed, and her chin trembled. She hadn't been separated from the Triodecad since Marigold had given it to her.

Justine left her cottage and went to the empty inn. The Inari group was gone, and Zoë wasn't coming until the afternoon. Four of the rooms had been booked for the weekend, but that was a couple of days away.

Bounding up the stairs, Justine went to the Klimt room. Jason had left nothing behind. No note. No message on her phone. The covers had been drawn up neatly over the bed. Justine sat on the mattress and dialed Priscilla. It was especially galling that Justine didn't even have Jason's cell number and had to reach him through his assistant.

"Stupid, stupid, stupid," she said to herself through gritted teeth. "Justine Hoffman, do not *ever* sleep with a man without getting his phone number first."

At the moment, Priscilla and Jason and the others were on

the company plane, flying back to San Francisco. Or maybe the Inari group was going to San Francisco and Jason was heading somewhere else. With the Triodecad. Damn him, what was he going to do with it?

The call clicked through to Priscilla's voice mail, directing her to leave a message. "Priscilla," she said tersely, "have Jason call me as soon as possible. He has something that belongs to me. I want it back."

Ending the call, Justine flopped back on the bed. She tried to think of what to do next. Undoubtedly she should call Rosemary and Sage for guidance, but the idea of having to confess how *monumentally* she had screwed up . . . that she had lost possession of one of the most revered grimoires in the Tradition . . . *no*. No way. She would handle this on her own. It was her mess, her fault, and she would deal with the fallout.

Continuing to lie on the bed, she redialed Priscilla and left another message. "It's me again. This is important, Priscilla: Tell Jason he doesn't know what he's doing. He's going to put himself and possibly other people in danger. Make him call me *right away*."

Fuming, Justine ended the call and stared at the ceiling. Priscilla had to know something about what Jason was planning. He had probably put her in charge of finding someone who could work a spell. And Justine was pretty certain that Priscilla wouldn't let the questionable morality of Jason's plans bother her. She was too ambitious to let anything get in the way of her career. Whatever Jason wanted, Priscilla would do without hesitation.

I have to reach him before he tries anything.

Arrogant, lying lowlife . . . the question of what Jason might do with the Triodecad in his possession, given half a chance . . . the possibilities were appalling.

As she tried to keep from thinking the unthinkable, Justine was infuriated to discover that she was unconsciously rubbing her cheek against Jason's pillow, subconsciously trying to derive comfort from the scent of him. *Hades' bones.* Grabbing the pillow, she hurled it against the wall.

To expend some of her rampaging energy, Justine spent three hours replacing a couple of old damaged floor planks in the dining room. It was a project she'd kept on the back burner, until she found the right time to take care of it. Now was as good a time as any. She took particular enjoyment in pounding the new planks into place with a rubber mallet, imagining she was hammering parts of Jason Black's anatomy.

When her phone rang, Justine's heart began to slam hard against her ribs. An unfamiliar number appeared on the tiny screen. She fumbled to press the "accept call" button, and held it up to her ear.

"Hello?"

Conflicting emotions coursed through her as she heard Jason's infuriatingly calm voice. "You know why I did it."

"Yes, I know why. And it doesn't make you any less of a sneaky, self-serving shithead. Where are you?"

"Traveling."

"Traveling to where?"

"East Coast."

"*Where* on the East Coast?"

"We'll talk about that later."

Justine burned with indignation. "I want my book back *now*. The Triodecad isn't going to do you any good. You don't understand the first thing about magic—this is a disaster waiting to happen."

"You'll have the book back soon."

"The next time I see you, I will Taser you with my bare hands!"

His tone turned gently cajoling. "I understand why you're upset."

"Yeah, funny how I tend to overreact when I'm *robbed*."

"I didn't steal it. I borrowed it."

"Oh, *please*," she said wrathfully, and hung up.

In fewer than thirty seconds, her phone rang again. Justine answered it without preamble. "Tell me who's going to do the spell-casting, or I'll hang up again."

He hesitated for a long moment. "Priscilla."

Priscilla? Justine's fingers went to her mouth, mashing her lips against her teeth. When she could manage to speak, she said unsteadily, "Fiveash. I knew her last name meant something. She's a crafter. She's . . . *My God.* Is she natural-born?"

"Yes. Inexperienced . . . but she has the creds."

This wasn't heartache. This was a body-and-soul ache. A toxic mixture of shame, anger, hurt, mainlining into her veins. "You used Priscilla to come here and *prey* on me. You were planning to take the Triodecad from the beginning. Before you even knew me!"

At least Jason didn't insult her by trying to deny it. "After I met you, the reasons changed. Before, I was going to do it out of self-interest. Now it's because I want to be with you. Because I—"

"I don't give a damn if your reasons changed, or what your

228

motivation is," she said hotly. "Your actions are the same. And whatever you try with my grimoire is going to backfire."

"I'll take my chances."

"I'm not just talking about you, you self-absorbed ass! It could backfire on Priscilla, or me, or someone else down the line who had nothing to do with this. Listen to me: The burden of proof falls on the crafter to make certain the spell won't harm anyone. You don't know who will be affected."

"I know there are risks if I go ahead with this. But if I don't, Justine . . . I have no chance. No sand left in the hourglass. And to be with you—for as long as possible—is all that means anything to me now."

"You can't use magic to screw around with matters of life or death. The spirits will find a way to turn it against you."

"Then you make the choice," Jason said coolly. "You love me. We know the consequences of that. You want me to sit back and wait for the anvil to drop?"

"I don't love you," Justine tried to say, except that she was forced to stop between words and take a painful extra breath, and to her disgust, she was fighting not to cry.

Love, she reflected bitterly, wasn't something you bargained with or negotiated terms with . . . it lived by its own rules. Love appeared when you didn't want it and refused to go. It was like an invasive species that entered your garden without warning, and proceeded to grow wildly out of control, resistant to every method employed to kill it.

Basically, love was pigweed.

"All I want," Jason said, "is to take care of this and come back to you. I'll do whatever you ask from then on. I'll give you anything you've ever wanted."

"Don't you dare try to buy me!"

"I'll rub your feet when you're tired. I'll hold you when you're lonely. I'll love you like no woman has ever been loved on this earth." He paused. "You just have to give me a pass on this one little thing."

Her brows rushed down. "You don't get a pass for stealing my grimoire."

"Borrowing."

"You'll do the same thing again when you decide you need some handy spell to fix something."

"I won't."

"And I'm supposed to believe that? How stupid do you think I am?"

A long pause. "You're not stupid," he said quietly. "You care about me, and I took advantage of that. And I'm sorry."

"You're not sorry for anything you've done. You're only sorry that I'm angry."

"I'm not sure what kind of sorry it is. I only know I feel a lot of it."

"If that's true, then don't let Priscilla try to cast a spell from the Triodecad. Send it back to me."

"And then what?"

"I'll find a way to keep you safe. I'll stop . . . caring about you. I'll cut my heart out if necessary."

Silence, and then a slow exhale. "You can't do that," he said. "You've already given your heart to me."

The call ended.

"Jason? Jason—" Frantically Justine went to the recent calls list and autodialed the number. She was sent directly to voice mail. "Oh, you *bastard*." As she glared at the supplies and equipment piled around her, she trembled with the urge to do something drastic, destroy something.

A woman in this mood, she thought vehemently, should not be left alone with power tools.

Twenty

· ·

"Another message from Justine," Priscilla said grimly, sliding her phone back into her bag. "She's madder than an Amish electrician."

"She'll get over it."

"I wouldn't, if I was her." Priscilla looked down at the bulk of the Triodecad, smoothing her hand over the linen that covered it. The book and the cloth were saturated with the pleasantly dry, sweet scent of white sage. Although Jason had suggested that she put the heavy volume in one of the backseats, she had insisted on holding it on her lap.

"You seem nervous," Jason said, driving the rented Nissan away from Little Rock National Airport. The afternoon light was strong and yolk colored, causing him to squint through the lenses of his polarized sunglasses. "Is it because you don't want me to meet your family, or because you're not sure the spell-casting will work?"

"Both, I guess. My kinfolk take some getting used to. Most of 'em have always lived within ten miles of Toad Suck Park."

"I won't have any problem getting along with them, and . . . Did you say 'Toad Suck'?"

"That's where we're headed. Toad Suck, Arkansas. People call it a town but it's really an unincorporated community."

"Where did the name come from?"

"The story is that back in the old days, the steamboat crews would hole up at the tavern and wait for the Arkansas River to rise. Local folk said those rivermen would suck on a bottle till they swelled up like toads."

Jason grinned, turning onto I–40 to head north.

"There's another story," Priscilla continued, "that the original French settlers called the area Tout Sucre, which means 'all sugar.' Over the years people kept pronouncing it different ways until it turned into Toad Suck."

It was easy to understand why the settlers had first called it Tout Sucre—the land was abundant and fertile, hills covered with hardwood trees, valleys rich with alluvial soil. Forests of sugar maples were starting to turn, their branches clouded with fire-colored leaves. Scores of creeks cut from the Ozark plateau through the river valley and down to the Ouachita Mountains.

"The Fiveashes have lived in Toad Suck for as long as anyone can remember," Priscilla said. "They work hard, go to church, and send their kids to school. They shop at Dollar Tree because they don't want to get dressed up for Walmart. They think eating local means shoot your own squirrels. And when my kin start talking, you'll wish they came with subtitles."

"There won't be any problem," Jason said, mildly surprised by the defensive note in her voice. "You know I'm not a snob."

"Yes, sir. All's I'm saying is, you thought I had rough edges when I started working at Inari. Well, compared to the rest of the family, I'm Princess Di."

"Understood," Jason said, inwardly amused. "There won't be any problem, Priscilla."

She nodded, still looking troubled. "You're not going to meet my mama, by the way. Ever since Daddy died, she wanted nothing to do with the craft. We're going to Granny Fiveash's double-wide. You're going to meet her and my great-aunt Bean and my uncle Cletus. Cletus won't help with the spell-casting, of course, since he's a man."

"Is there such a thing as a male witch? A warlock?"

"No, that's just a myth. It says in the *Malleus Maleficarum* that—"

"What's that?"

"A witch-hunting book written by a Catholic priest in the fourteen hundreds. It says the devil tempted women by sending handsome fallen angels to seduce them . . . and the women became his handmaidens. That's how witches were started. Hypothetically. But there's nothing satanic about the craft now."

"Does it bother you to think about the witch's bane?" Jason found himself asking. "It must. You must worry about falling in love with someone."

Priscilla looked disconcerted, her color rising. It was rare for them to have such a personal conversation. "Actually, I don't. My whole life, I've been single-minded about getting away from Toad Suck. Getting educated, working my tail off . . . no time for romance." She looked thoughtful as she added, "Even though I don't live here anymore, it still feels like I'm trying to get away. I've always wanted something different. Not sure what. Money,

I guess. Mama says I'll never be happy till I have enough money to burn a wet mule."

"No," Jason said quietly. "When people are driven to make a lot of money, it's never about the money."

Priscilla fell silent as she pondered that.

After a couple of minutes, Jason said, "Don't get worked up over this spell-casting. Just do your best."

"Easy for you to say. I'm the one who has to get it right. Magic isn't like mathematics where there's a right answer. Sometimes it's a choice between a lot of bad answers. Or worse, a lot of right-sounding answers."

Jason tried to think of something that might lessen the pressure for her. "Priscilla, do you know what the most difficult shot in golf is?"

"The windmill," she said decisively.

"The what? . . . No, I'm not talking about Putt-Putt. I mean real golf. The most difficult shot is the long bunker shot." Glancing at her blank expression, Jason said, "When the ball gets stuck in a sand pit. You have two ways to handle it. You can either pitch it or blast it. Pitching is a short, low-risk shot, just to get it out of the pit. Blasting it with a long power swing ends in either glory or total defeat."

"So you're saying when we try this magic spell tonight, you want to take the big risk."

"No. Play it safe. It's too important to risk everything. Just go for the short pitch, get me out of the damn pit. If you can buy me a few years with Justine, I'll make them count for a lifetime."

Priscilla stared at him in wonder. "You're in love with her."

"Of course I am. What did you think?"

"I thought you were just shining her on to get the spellbook."

He shot her an affronted glance. "Why is it so hard to believe I might fall in love with someone?"

"Because every time you break up with a woman, you tell me to buy some expensive jewelry and have it wrapped up for her. Your Tiffany's bill caused the economic bubble in the precious metals market."

Jason scowled, keeping his gaze on the road. "Justine's different from the others."

"Why? Because she's a witch?"

"Because she's Justine."

Priscilla stared down at the Triodecad, smoothing circles over it. "Is she in love with you?" she asked carefully.

"I think so." Jason swerved slightly to avoid a vulture feeding on roadkill. "And I'd like to live long enough to try and deserve it."

"Then I'd better find an extra-strength spell" came her tart reply.

After a thirty-minute drive, they took the exit for Toad Suck Park. Priscilla directed him along a series of turns, the roads getting narrower and rougher, until they reached a private drive lined with eroded gravel, the car wheels dipping into deep potholes. They pulled up to a double-wide tucked into a grove of dogwood trees. The trailer home was fronted with a patio improvised from a sheet of buckled plywood and a set of plastic lawn chairs. A dog of indeterminate breed lazed on the corner of the plywood, his scraggly tail thumping as he saw the car approach.

"They'll probably seem a little crazy at first," Priscilla said as Jason stopped the car. "But after you get to know 'em . . . they'll seem even crazier."

"No judgment," Jason assured her. It was one of the things he'd learned from living in San Francisco for nearly ten years. A person with rainbow hair and multiple piercings could be a millionaire, or someone who'd dressed as if he'd harvested his clothes from a Dumpster, a respected community leader. Preconceptions were useless, not to mention foolish.

Getting out of the car, Jason was struck by the serenity of the area. All he could hear was the tapping of a woodpecker in a nearby thicket of pine and cedar, and the trickle of a creek. The air steamed as if it had been freshly ironed. A flat, languid breeze was stitched with the smells of cooked grass and stewed pine pitch.

The silence was shattered by the cacophony of a pair of elderly women emerging from the trailer, both of them clattering with jewelry. Neither of them was a day under eighty. They were dressed similarly in flip-flops, brightly colored tunics, and cropped pants. One of them had hair swirled like a vanilla cone from Dairy Queen, and the other, a shock of flamboyant red. Whooping and chattering, they both hurried to Priscilla and hugged her between them.

"Prissy, honey, you're all skin and bones," the red-haired one exclaimed. "Don't they feed you out there in California?"

"'Course they don't," the other woman said before Priscilla could reply. "All them West Coast hippies eat is kale chips." She beamed at Priscilla. "We cooked you up some *real* food, girl. Hot dog casserole and fried apple biscuits."

Priscilla laughed and kissed her leathery cheek. "Granny, Aunt Bean . . . I'd like you to meet my boss, Mr. Black."

"He own that computer company you work at?"

"Video games," Jason said, walking around the car to reach

237

them. He extended a hand to the red-haired woman. "Please call me Jason."

"Computers will be the ruination of this world," she said, ignoring his outstretched hand. "We don't bother with handshakes, honey, we just do hugs." She threw her arms around him, enveloping him in a bewildering mixture of scents: hairstyling product, perfume, deodorant, body cream, and a distinct tang of bug spray. "I'm Priscilla's granny," she told Jason. "You call me that, too."

The vanilla-haired woman came to hug Jason, as well, her torso strong, short, and barrel-round. "I used to be Wilhelmina, but folks took to calling me Bean when I was a kid and it stuck."

Since neither of the women seemed inclined to release his arms, Jason went to the trailer with Granny and Bean on either side of him. Priscilla followed with the spellbook. A blast of icy air hit them as soon as the front door was opened. An airconditioning unit hummed in a window space, chilling the interior of the trailer to an arctic level. They entered a living room, the main wall covered with tin license plates.

The home was clean but packed with tables and shelves of collectibles; figurines, vintage hook and flies, bottle caps, cookie jars. It made Jason, who preferred spare and uncluttered space, feel vaguely claustrophobic. As he saw that both kitchen windows were fully blocked with rows of beer glasses and metal thermoses, he was forced to take a calming breath.

"Now," Granny said to Priscilla, "let's have a look at the spellbook."

"It's very old," Jason said, uneasy at the sight of Justine's treasured grimoire being set on the same dining table as a foil-covered casserole reeking of hot dogs and ketchup. "I can't let anything happen to it."

"We'll be careful." Granny gave Jason an astute glance. "Never thought I'd see one of these, specially not one with a name."

"We never learnt our magic from a grimoire," Bean said, following Jason's gaze to the casserole. She took the dish from the table, turned to set it on a kitchen counter, and wiped her hands on her tunic. "Only the elite-type crafters have those. We've always kept our spells and formulas on recipe cards."

"A book like this," Granny said, "has more power than what's written on the pages."

The older women let out little breaths of appreciation as Priscilla unwrapped the Triodecad. The leather cover gleamed with a black-plum finish. A copper keyhole was centered in an unusual clock face design. Even if Jason hadn't known the supernatural value of the book, he would have instantly recognized it as something ancient and priceless.

"Why a clock face?" he asked.

"It's not a time clock," Granny replied. "It's the phases of the moon. The earth is here at the center." She traced invisible lines from the keyhole to each of the points of the outer circle. "First quarter moon at the top . . . waxing gibbous next . . . full moon right there . . ." Her finger moved to the edge of the cover. "The sun would shine from this direction."

A perturbed frown crossed Priscilla's forehead. "It's a full moon tonight, Granny. Is that the right time to cast a spell?"

"Depends on the spell. We'll need to read some, you and me and Bean, to figger what's best." Granny turned to Jason and said, not without sympathy, "Prissy told me what we're dealing with. Between the lack of a soul and the witch's bane, you got more problems than a math book. And we can only cast one spell at a time, or they start canceling each other out." She paused. "Who's got the key?"

"I do," Jason said, fishing out the chain from beneath his polo shirt.

Granny received it from him with a businesslike nod. "Bean, before we open the book, I think we'd best sweep the kitchen with the besom broom."

"I'll find it," Bean said, and hustled down the narrow hallway.

"Jason," Granny continued, "we'll be reading for a while. Put your feet up, if you like. You could watch TV. The Razorbacks are playing the Aggies."

"Would you mind if I took a walk?"

"Go right on."

As Jason picked up his sunglasses from the table and turned to the door, Bean hurried up to him with an aerosol can and started spraying. He backed away reflexively while Bean directed the spray over his pants legs and even reached for the hems to mist his ankles. The smell of insect repellent filled the air in a noxious cloud. "No. Really. I don't—"

"You need it," Bean said with authority, going behind him, spraying busily without stopping.

"You don't know about Arkansas skeeters," Granny told him. "In ten minutes they'll bleed you dry as a hog on butchering day."

"My, my" came Bean's voice from behind him. "This is what I call a superior posterior."

240

Jason slid a narrow-eyed glance at Priscilla, who appeared to be repressing a grin. "Thanks," he muttered, and fled as soon as Bean was finished.

"One more thing," Granny called after him. "If you see Cletus upstairs, don't pay him no mind." The door closed.

Jason stopped in his tracks. "There's no upstairs on a trailer home," he said aloud.

Slowly he wandered around the rickety structure. He discovered that the dogwood trees at the front of the trailer had concealed a camping chair, a plastic cooler, and a tiki umbrella, all arranged on a corner of the flat roof. The chair was occupied by an elderly man wearing a fishing hat, shorts, and a tee that proclaimed NOT ONLY AM I PERFECT, I'M A SOUTHERNER, TOO. The man stared intently at a cell phone in one hand and held a beer in the other.

"Cletus?" Jason asked cautiously.

The man replied without taking his gaze from the phone. "That's me. You the fella Priscilla brung for a visit?"

"Yes. Jason."

"Come on up and have a cold one." He pointed to a ladder braced against the trailer.

Jason climbed up to the roof, which was covered in a thick blanket of rubber that reeked of new tire smell.

He approached the old man, and they shook hands briefly. Cletus's eyes were hard blue chips beneath two silvery caterpillar brows. His skin was as brown and textured as a dried tobacco leaf. Most people of Cletus's advanced years wouldn't have been able to make the climb. But he was tough, weathered, with ropy arms and a wiry build.

Reaching into the cooler, Cletus pulled out a dripping can of beer and handed it to him.

"Thanks." Jason sat on a patch of roof beneath the tiki umbrella.

"Guess you're here to get Granny and Bean to work a spell for you," Cletus said.

"That's the plan." Jason opened the can of beer and drank deeply. "You're Priscilla's great-uncle?"

"By marriage. My twin brother, Clive, was married to Bean, a long time back. He died from a bee attack six weeks after their wedding."

"He was allergic to bees?"

"Allergic to curses, more like. Clive knew the risk, marrying Bean. Everyone knows about the Fiveash women. Black widows, all of 'em. They can't help it. You mate one and then you die."

"Why did Clive marry Bean, if he knew about it?"

"Bean was a looker in those days, and Clive went crazy over her. Said he had to have her, curse or no curse. No one could talk sense into him, not even Bean. He was a goner the first time he laid eyes on her."

"I know the feeling," Jason said without humor.

Finishing the beer, Cletus crumpled the can and tossed it off the roof. "The curse follows all the Fiveash females. I hope you're not sweet on Priscilla."

"No, sir."

"That's good. Keep it that way. You don't want to end up like Clive. Or Granny's husband, Bo, neither."

"How did he die?"

"Struck by lightning on the Toad Suck ferry landing, back

242

when there was still ferries." Cletus paused reflectively. "A week before it happened, Bo told me that wherever he went, clocks stopped ticking. His watch froze. Hell, even the kitchen egg-timer hourglass shattered when Bo got near it." He pulled up the stay-tab on a new can of beer. "Strange thing was, Clive told me he had the same problem, right before his accident. Showed up on time to work every day of his life, but started punching in late, 'cause every clock in the house had stopped. A week later, Clive was gone."

Jason stared at him alertly. "They each died a week after the clocks stopped?" His gaze lowered to his stainless-steel watch. Relieved to find that it was still functioning, he let out a controlled sigh.

Before he looked up, he heard Cletus say gently, "Boy, you're in a mess o' trouble, ain't you?"

After keeping company with Clive for about an hour, Jason climbed down and went back into the trailer. The three women concentrated intently on the Triodecad.

"How's it going?" Jason asked.

"This book is unbelievable," Priscilla said. "There are spells for nearly everything you could imagine."

"Did you find anything to counteract the witch's bane?"

Priscilla shook her head. "Nothing specific. Which makes no sense, because through all the generations of natural-born witches, *someone* must have tried to fix this problem. Why didn't any of them write something down?"

"Bean and me tried to save our husbands," Granny said.

"When it didn't work, I figured our magic was too weak, since we never got educated in spell-casting. But I thought a book like this would have the answer."

Jason focused on Priscilla. "What about pitching the bunker shot?"

"We found a longevity spell," she said. "A powerful one, from the looks of it."

He kept his expression neutral. "Any drawbacks to a longevity spell?"

"None that we could think of. Everyone wants to live longer, don't they?" She frowned. "But you're asking the wrong person. None of us have been trained at this level of magic. Basically you're asking someone who only makes Hamburger Helper to whip up an entrée from *Mastering the Art of French Cooking.*"

Jason hadn't forgotten Justine's warning about the longevity spell . . . that someday he could end up begging for death. At this moment, however, longevity was the answer to everything. It would allow him to be with Justine, and it was his best chance at being spared from the witch's bane.

"There's another spell we want to add to it," Priscilla said.

His brows lifted. "I thought the rule was only one spell per person."

"The second one isn't for you. It's for Justine."

Jason was silent, listening closely.

"We want to bind a geas to her," Priscilla said quietly. "As close to the original as possible. It wouldn't be quite as good, but we think with the three of us—"

"No."

"She'd be better off. And so would you."

244

"Not open for discussion."

"You'd have what you wanted at the beginning," Priscilla persisted, turning red. "You'd have more time to live *and* you'd be safe from Justine."

"If the fate of the whole earth hung in the balance, I wouldn't have a geas bound to Justine again."

"You're still young," Bean said. "You could find someone else."

He shook his head. "It's Justine or nothing."

Priscilla glared at him. "You're acting as crazy as a sprayed roach. You haven't known her long enough to make that choice."

Jason met her gaze without blinking. "Of course I have. Someday your life will change in one second flat. Something you never could have expected will hit you like a two-by-four. And there won't be enough time to figure out how or why it happened. You'll just have to go with it."

"No, I'll remind myself that some things are over before they start," Priscilla said.

Jason glanced at Granny's and Bean's sober faces. "Give me your best shot at the longevity spell, and I'll double the price we agreed on. But leave Justine out of it."

"I don't think—" Granny said.

"Triple," Jason told her.

Granny and Bean looked at each other.

"Let's git'r done," Granny said briskly. "Priscilla, you're in charge of casting the circle. Bean, we'll need the chalice and altar cloth."

Bean went to the windowsill to retrieve a thick-walled mug printed with the Budweiser logo.

"That's a chalice?" Jason asked blankly.

"Sure is. We've done some of our best magic with it." Reaching into a drawer, Bean pulled out a dish towel and spread it on the counter.

After glancing at the cloth, which was printed with a silhouette of Elvis playing a guitar, Jason gave Priscilla a look askance.

"It doesn't matter what the altar cloth looks like," she told him in an undertone, while the two elderly women busied themselves with preparations. "Let them do it their way. They know what works best for them." After a brief pause, she added, "And don't throw a fit if they mention Dionne Warwick a couple of times during the spell-casting. It makes Bean happy, and the spirits won't mind it a bit."

Twenty-one

By the third morning after Jason had left the inn, Justine was struggling to stay angry. Anger had given her the energy to get ready for the new influx of guests: maintenance such as fixing a broken toilet, resetting a television remote control, resupplying each room with soaps and toiletries. Anger had also propelled her through the tedium of bookkeeping and bill paying, ordering new supplies, and sending e-mail confirmations to guests who had reserved rooms.

The problem was that Justine wasn't certain what would happen if she let go of the anger. She didn't want to soften toward Jason. And she didn't want to view his actions in context: Love was not a mitigating circumstance. She had to focus exclusively on what he had done, and ignore his reasons for doing it. Which was why she had confided as little as possible about the situation to Zoë, who was a big believer in context. And love.

In the middle of laundering linens and toweling, Justine

received a call from Priscilla, who until then hadn't returned any of her wrathful messages.

Justine had waited for that call, had kept herself awake at night rehearsing long eviscerating rants that would leave Priscilla in an apologetic heap. But as she answered, Justine was furious to discover that all she could manage was a choked hello. All the vehement words had tangled up with each other like fine chains.

"Jason has no idea I'm talking to you," Priscilla said. "He'd kill me if he knew."

"Where is my spellbook?" Justine asked tightly.

"Jason's got it. He's taking real good care of it. He'll bring it to you by the end of the week."

"Where is he now?"

"There's a conference in San Diego. One of those big gaming shindigs. He has to do a charity fund-raiser and—"

"Are you with him?"

"No. He stayed in Little Rock the night before last and left yesterday for California."

"Little Rock?" Justine repeated, bewildered. "Arkansas?"

Priscilla's voice was subdued. "My granny and great-aunt are crafters. They helped figure out the spell to use for Jason."

"Using my Triodecad," Justine said tautly. "That's just great. What spell did you use?"

"Longevity."

Justine's anger dropped like a climber abseiling a rock face. Down into a thick fog of gloom. She closed her eyes and leaned against the clothes dryer, needing its heat. She had to take a few deep breaths before she could speak. "You used high magick?"

Priscilla's tone was cautious. "Granny said she thought it

248

took. So there's nothing to worry about. You'll have your book back and then—"

"There are two things to worry about," Justine said sharply. "One is if you cast the spell wrong. The other is if you cast it right."

"I don't understand."

"Let me put it this way: Just because you can do something doesn't mean you should. There's no way of knowing exactly what you've set in motion. We'll only find out when it's too late. And if you've done it right . . . Jason's going to suffer for it later. Supernatural longevity is a *curse*, Priscilla. You wouldn't wish it on your worst enemy. There's no guarantee against illness or dementia or any of the terrible things that can happen to a human body. The only guarantee is that you'll live, and live, and live, until you would do anything to end your misery." Her throat clenched. "I've already told this to Jason, the stubborn idiot!"

"He did this because he loves you," Priscilla burst out.

"Give me a break. He was going to do it anyway, for his own selfish reasons."

"He loves you," Priscilla repeated.

"Why do you think that?" Justine asked sarcastically. "Because he said so?"

"Because it's the truth. Everyone knows you'll be the death of him. The longevity spell won't hold out against the witch's bane. But Jason doesn't give a damn—all he wants is to buy more time with you." Priscilla let out a frustrated breath. "My daddy died young, same as yours. People warned him never to marry my mama. They told him to run like hell so that curse could never touch him. I always wondered why he didn't listen.

I couldn't figure out how a man could be so in love that he'd rather die than live without it. Well, now I'm seeing it firsthand. There's no way to save Jason. He's found something he wants even more than a soul, and that's you. If you won't have him, he'll wait."

"He'll spend the rest of his life waiting," Justine snapped.

"I told him that."

"And what did he say?"

"'Then waiting is how I'll love her.'"

Justine was silent, her hand curling into a fist against the warm metal surface of the dryer.

"I hope to Goddess no man ever wants me that way," Priscilla continued. "And I'm sorry for my part in all this. But I'm calling to tell you where Jason is, in case you don't want to waste time. Because even if that spell worked . . . you don't have forever."

"Don't worry about a thing," Zoë said cheerfully, placing folded clothes into the open suitcase on Justine's bed. Not only had Zoë agreed when Justine had asked if she could cover for her, she'd been positively enthusiastic. In fact, Zoë had insisted on helping her pack for San Diego.

"Nita's sister is coming in to help with the cleaning," Zoë continued, "and Annette will be here early to help with breakfast in the morning, and we only have a few rooms booked. So stay the whole weekend."

"You're all trying to get rid of me," Justine grumbled.

Zoë smiled. "You deserve this. None of us can remember the last time you went away for a romantic weekend."

"It's not going to be a romantic weekend. I'm going there to get my spellbook from Jason, and then I'm going to yell at him and stay in my own room. The only reason I'm not leaving the same day I arrive is because all the return flights were full."

"Take an extra outfit just in case. And something cute to wear for dinner." Zoë pulled a little black dress from the closet. "This will be perfect."

"I'm not going to dress for dinner. I'll have a hamburger in my room."

"Where are your strappy sandals?"

Justine scowled in the face of Zoë's determination. "At the back of the closet."

"What about a necklace?"

"I don't have one that goes with that dress."

"Here. This will be perfect." Zoë took the antique crystal brooch pinned to her retro-styled sweater, and fastened it to the lowest point of the dress's neckline.

"Zoë, thanks, but that's totally unnecessary. I'm not going out to dinner with Jason or anyone."

Zoë folded the dress carefully. "You never can tell."

"Jason doesn't even know I'm doing this. I'm only going there to tell him good-bye forever, and then I'm coming back here to resume my life of quiet desperation. I didn't know how good I had it."

"Why do you have to tell him good-bye in San Diego?" Zoë asked gently. "You could leave a message on his voice mail. Or text him."

"You can't text 'good-bye forever' to someone," Justine said indignantly. "It has to be done in person."

"In strappy sandals," Zoë added with satisfaction, dropping the shoes into the suitcase.

The Hotel del Coronado had earned an instant iconic status upon its completion in the eighteen hundreds. Despite the massive size of the Victorian beachside resort, the broad swaths of white-painted verandas, pavilions, and terraced colonnades gave it a light and airy quality. Justine had never visited the Del, as it was called by San Diego residents, but she had read about it while studying hotel management.

Countless celebrities had stayed at the Del in its history, including Hollywood royalty such as Rudolph Valentino, Charlie Chaplin, and Greta Garbo. The hotel had also hosted U.S. presidents, foreign royalty, and legends such as Thomas Edison and Babe Ruth. There was even a resident ghost, with sightings reported ever since an unaccompanied young woman had died there in 1892.

Walking into the plush lobby with its towering vaulted ceiling, red and gold carpeting, and gleaming dark wood finishes, Justine briefly regretted her casual attire. Although nearly everyone else in the lobby wore jeans as well, it seemed like the kind of place where people should be dressed to the nines.

Standing in a line that had formed in front of the reservations desk, Justine set her overnight bag by her feet. Priscilla had given her Jason's room number and a copy of his schedule. The gaming conference was located at another hotel, which meant Jason was probably out at the moment. But when he returned, she was going to tell him exactly what she thought of him. How low he was for stealing the Triodecad, and what a fool she'd been for sleeping with him, trusting him—

Her thoughts were interrupted as a feeling of warmth bristled along the back of her neck, all down her spine. She slid a guarded look around. The others standing in line looked unconcerned. People in seating areas continued to laugh and chatter idly.

A small group of men had left the old-fashioned cage elevator to walk through the lobby at a relaxed pace. Engrossed in conversation, they paused at the huge round table weighted with the largest flower arrangement Justine had ever seen. One of the men was sexy and sophisticated in a slim dark suit, radiating a charisma that almost—but not quite—crossed the line from confidence into swagger. His black hair had been neatly brushed but was beginning to fall into casual disorder over his forehead. She remembered the feel of that hair beneath her hands, the sweet, firm pressure of his mouth against hers.

Justine turned away and ducked her head. She was appalled by the strength of her pleasure just to be in the same room with Jason. Her heart had begun the clickety-clack rhythm of a runaway locomotive. She focused on staying still, when all her muscles had tensed with the urge to bolt . . . toward or away from him, she wasn't entirely certain.

She thought he might be looking at her . . . she could almost feel his gaze. But the lobby was full of people, and Jason wasn't expecting her to be there. It wasn't likely he would spot her. After a moment, she risked a quick glance at the group. They were gone.

The line moved forward, and she bent to pick up her bag.

A pair of gleaming black lace-up shoes came into view. Straightening slowly, Justine felt her heart rise in her throat. She looked up at him, her thoughts tumbling in a confusion of eagerness and need.

Jason spoke in a casual tone, but his gaze was caressing. "You can't get a room here. They're all booked up."

The inside of her throat felt as if it had been coated with honey. Justine swallowed hard before replying. "I have a reservation."

He took the overnight bag from her nerveless fingers. "It's been canceled. You can share my room."

Their electric mutual awareness had communicated itself to the others around them. A few gazes followed them, some curious, some envious.

Guiding Justine to the partial concealment of a tall potted ficus, Jason set her bag and his briefcase aside. He surveyed her intently. "Why are you in San Diego?" Before she could reply, he added, "Let me make it clear that I'm not complaining. I'm happy as hell to have you here."

"You're not 'having' me here. I've come to get the Triodecad."

"I was going to bring it to you the day after tomorrow."

"I couldn't wait that long."

"For the spellbook," he asked, "or me?"

She had already decided in advance that she would not flirt with him, would not smile or relent or succumb to his charm. "I want my book."

Wordlessly Jason picked up his black leather briefcase and gave it to her.

Bemused, she asked, "You've been carrying it around with you?"

Jason smiled faintly. "Like it's the nuclear codes."

Turning away from him, Justine opened the briefcase and peeked inside. She reached in to pull up a corner of the linen cloth. A sigh of relief escaped her as she saw the grimoire's familiar cover.

Jason drew close behind her. His head bent, his mouth lightly caressing the side of her neck.

A sensual shiver ran through her. "I'm still going to fry your ass."

"Yes, do it," he said, right before she felt his teeth in a gentle bite. "With both hands."

Fuming, Justine turned to face him. "You lied to me."

"Not technically."

"Bullshit. If nothing else it was a lie of omission."

"It was the only way I could be with you."

"And the end justifies the means?" she asked caustically. "You haven't even justified the end."

Jason studied her with outward calm, but she sensed the force of strong emotion locked beneath the surface. "This is why you got rid of the geas," he said. "You wanted love. Now you've got it. I love you enough for a dozen people. Maybe there's something I wouldn't do to have you—some rule or law I wouldn't be willing to break—but I'm damned if I can think of one. I know I'm not perfect. But if you—"

"You are the *opposite* of perfect." Justine clutched the briefcase and stared at him unhappily. "And I didn't want the kind of love where people get hurt and things go wrong and you're not even sure who you are anymore."

Jason had no right to look so sympathetic, when he was the cause of her misery. He reached for her hand, his grip warm and firm. "Let's go somewhere, honey. I'm not comfortable discussing my innermost feelings behind a potted plant in a hotel lobby." Picking up the overnight bag with his free hand, he pulled Justine toward the concierge desk.

Seeing their approach, a man emerged from behind the desk, radiating an air of confident knowledge befitting a concierge of a world-class hotel. It was said that a great concierge was part Merlin, part Houdini, able to solve a wide spectrum of problems with lightning speed. The issue could be anything from replacing a lost toothbrush to chartering a private jet. There was only one word that a well-trained concierge would seldom, if ever, say to a hotel guest . . . the word "no."

"Good afternoon, Mr. Black. Is there something I can help you with?"

"Yes, thank you. As it turns out, I need a different room."

"Of course. May I ask if there is a problem with your current room?"

"No, it's fine. But I need something a little more spacious. I'd like to change to one of the beach cottages."

"We don't need a beach cottage," Justine said hastily.

Jason ignored her. "One with as much privacy as possible," he said.

"If I'm not mistaken, there is an available suite at the end next to the Sapphire pool. Quite private. It's a one-bedroom king with its own patio, fire pit, hot tub, and gated access to the beach."

"That sounds expensive—" Justine began.

"We'll take it," Jason said, giving him Justine's overnight bag. "Would you have this brought to the cottage and move my stuff there, as well?"

"Give us half an hour to forty-five minutes," the concierge

said, "and we'll make up some new room keys and have you all settled in. Would you care to sit at an outside terrace while you wait? Perhaps I could send out some wine and refreshments?"

Jason looked down at Justine. "How does that sound?"

"Oh . . . are you asking me something?" Her tone was pure saccharine. "You want my opinion? My *preference*?"

The concierge's expression was politely blank as Jason turned to him. "I think we'll go for a stroll on the boardwalk," Jason said. "Just give me a ring when the cottage is ready. Oh, and please cancel my friend's room reservation. She'll be staying with me."

"Yes, sir." The concierge smiled and looked at Justine expectantly. "May I ask for the name on the reservation?"

"Justine Hoffman," she muttered.

"Miss Hoffman. Welcome to the Del. We'll do everything possible to make certain you have an enjoyable stay."

Justine accompanied Jason through the lobby of the main Victorian building. As they neared the entrance of the garden patio courtyard, a bellman dressed in a uniform complete with a red vest and a black bowler hat recognized Jason. "Mr. Black. Need the car brought around?"

"Not at the moment, thanks."

"Have a good one, sir."

As they continued through the lobby, Justine frowned at Jason. "I am *not* impressed by the way people suck up to you."

"Yes you are. Even I'm impressed by it. Here, let me carry the briefcase."

"I'm just staying for one night," she said, handing it over. "I'm leaving tomorrow morning."

"Stay the whole weekend," he coaxed.

"Sorry, I can't."

257

"You still haven't forgiven me for borrowing the spellbook," he said rather than asked.

"You took the most treasured possession I own without asking. I had a heart attack when I saw it was missing. You took ten years off my life."

"Tell me how I can make it up to you."

"There's nothing you can do."

"I'll hire a skywriter to write an apology over all of San Diego. I'll take you to the Taj Mahal. I'll start a charity for wounded kittens."

She gave him a disdainful glance.

"You like books," Jason continued, undeterred. "Did you know that L. Frank Baum wrote *The Wizard of Oz* while living at the Del?"

"Yes, I knew that. What about it?"

"Right now there's a display of *Wizard of Oz* memorabilia in the lobby. Including a first-edition copy autographed by the author and the entire cast of the 1939 movie."

"That's cool," Justine said. "I'd like to see that. But why are you—"

"I'll buy it for you as a souvenir."

She stopped in her tracks, obliging him to stop, as well. Had he really made such an outrageous offer? "That's not a souvenir. A souvenir is a T-shirt or a snow globe."

"You'll need something to read on the way home."

"A book like that would cost a *fortune*," she said, adding in a highly insulted tone, "How many times do I have to tell you that I can't be bought?" She paused. "The entire cast?"

"Including Toto." Seeing her expression, Jason pressed his

258

advantage. "His cute little paw print is right on the inside of the front cover."

Had a woman ever faced such temptation? "I don't want the book," Justine forced herself to say. "Not even if the ruby slippers came with it."

"What if I take you to dinner tonight? A table by the ocean, the two of us watching the sunset."

Justine wanted to prolong her coolness toward him. However, she was hungry and tired, and the prospect of a fine meal with an ocean view was too tempting to resist.

"That might be nice," she said grudgingly. "But even if I have dinner with you, it doesn't mean you're forgiven."

"Am I at least a little bit forgiven?"

"Maybe a barely-measurable-by-science bit forgiven."

"That's a start." Jason fished his cell phone from the inside of his suit jacket. "I'll make the reservation."

"All by yourself?" Justine asked in mocking awe. "You're not going to have one of your minions do it?"

He gave her a sardonic glance and began to dial.

"Wait," she said, recalling his schedule. "You have plans for the evening."

"I'm completely free."

"You're supposed to have dinner with some computer-simulation guys tonight."

Jason looked up from his phone. "How do you know that?"

"Priscilla gave me your schedule."

He glowered down at the phone. "Bad minion," he muttered.

"It's no problem. I'll just relax in the private hot tub while you go out for your business dinner." Justine paused before adding,

"I hope there are no rules about nudity. I didn't bring a swim-suit."

She heard his breath catch. "I'm canceling dinner."

"At the last minute?"

"I cancel dinners all the time," he informed her. "It's part of my elusive charm."

Justine couldn't help smiling. "'Elusive' is one word for it." As they reached the boardwalk, she paused to take in the view, the flat sand beach silvered with a heavy infusion of mica, the water, startling Pacific blue. "No wonder L. Frank Baum wrote such a great book while he stayed here," she said. "It's a magical view, isn't it?"

"Yes." But Jason was looking at her. "Did you ever read *The Wizard of Oz*?"

"When I was little. Did you?"

"No, but I saw the movie at least a half-dozen times." Gently he smoothed back her hair as a breeze toyed with the loose locks. "Incidentally . . . I always rooted for the witch."

The beach cottage was sophisticated and luxuriously appointed with hardwood floors, an abundance of glass windows, and deep comfortable furniture. A color palette of creams and neutrals gave it a fresh open feeling, with the blues of the sky and ocean visible from every room. There was a gourmet kitchen, a dining room, and a main living area with a fireplace surmounted by a flat-panel TV. The king-size bed in the bedroom was covered with heavy slick linens. A huge marble tub dominated the adjoining bathroom, which also featured a separate glass shower.

After investigating every room of the elegant villa, Justine went back to the main area.

Jason had removed his suit jacket and was draping it over the back of the chair. She had caught him in an unguarded moment. He was tired, she saw, his handsomeness a bit lived-in, worn around the edges. Somehow that made him even sexier, more human, a man with flaws and needs.

"*You wanted love,*" he had told her in the lobby. "*Now you've got it.*"

No matter how angry or hurt she was, Justine knew it was the truth.

And the echo of Priscilla's words were still with her: "*Even if that spell worked . . . you don't have forever.*"

Could she afford to waste a moment of love? Could anyone?

Jason looked up as she approached him. The self-possessed mask was instantly resumed. "Do you like the cottage?" he asked. "Because if you don't—" He broke off, his only reaction a quick double blink as Justine deliberately stripped off her T-shirt and tossed it to the sofa. His gaze locked on to her slim form, dressed in a white cotton bra and jeans. "Justine," he said raggedly, "I want to make it clear that there's no obligation . . . that is, you don't have to . . ."

"You're trying to say I'm not required to sleep with you in exchange for room and board?"

"Exactly." He didn't move as she reached for his tie, her slender fingers unknotting the length of silk.

Justine tossed the tie aside. "So when you canceled my reservation and insisted that I stay in this cottage with you, there was no thought of sex lurking in your mind?"

261

"Not lurking," Jason said, breathing unevenly as she began to unfasten his shirt. "Stampeding. But you still don't have to sleep with me."

Justine let the front of his shirt hang open and slipped her bra straps down. Reaching for the back fastening of her bra, she arched her breasts toward him. "So if I asked you to take the sofa tonight, you'd be fine with that?"

"Yes."

She let the bra drop to the floor. Standing on her toes, she slipped her hand behind his taut neck. "Doubtful," she whispered, and pressed her parted lips to the underside of his jaw. "But you get points for trying to be a gentleman." The familiar warmth and scent of his skin was her undoing. All trace of melancholy was driven out by a relief so sweeping and giddy that it felt like being drunk.

Jason brought his mouth to hers in a slow, hot kiss. His long fingers spread over the contours of jaw, cheeks, nose, forehead, as if he were blind and could perceive her only by touch. The kiss turned deep and ravenous, until they were both panting, fumbling to undress each other.

Soon a trail of clothes marked the path to the bedroom. Standing by the bed, Jason held her close and cupped her breast. He shaped the plush contour, his thumb and forefinger gently pinching the tip until it was hard and deep pink. He bent to soothe it with his tongue. At the moment her balance faltered, his arm was there to support her, lowering her to the wide bed covered with cool white sheets.

There was nothing in the world beyond this quiet room with the shutters drawn closed. No time, no spinning earth, no deep blue ocean, no broken magic or fate bestowed by unfriendly stars. There was only this man. Her lover, her charmer, binding her heart with invisible cords.

He pressed her back and bent over her breasts, kissing the swollen tips. Sensation darted from her breasts to her groin in vibrant flashes. His hand went to the soft place between her thighs, one of his fingers wriggling into the tightness, his thumb resting lightly on the aching peak. He began to massage her in slow, teasing circles, inside and out. Pleasure began rolling up to her, gathering momentum. *Not yet.* She wrenched free and bent over his lap to take him into her mouth, letting her tongue circle the stiff silky tip. The taste of him was intensely arousing, a hint of saline freshness like the ocean.

Jason went still. His eyes closed, and his hands clenched into fists as if he were being tortured. Soon he moved to stop her, pulling her head away with unsteady hands.

He pushed Justine to her forearms and knees, his palms sliding along the taut lines of her body. As he moved behind her, the hard, hair-roughened texture of his legs intruded between hers, spreading them wide. She jerked at the touch of intimate hardness, a blunt stroke all along the open cleft. Moaning, she gripped handfuls of the sheets, waiting blindly. He lifted her hips into a high upward tilt as if she were a stretching cat.

They breathed in unison, hearts and lungs laboring. Without warning, he entered her in a demanding thrust. She writhed and backed up against him, her flesh throbbing reflexively around the insistent pressure. He set a relentless rhythm, every movement roughened with pure carnal feeling. Her inner muscles clenched and unclenched in the opposing tensions of pleasure and need. Another slippery-hard plunge, another, deepening until there was no part of her he hadn't reached.

Too much pleasure, her face burning with it, her flesh aching. She was so close, just a few heartbeats away.

"Jason. Please—" She broke off with a whimper as his hands came to her bottom, rotating to make her feel the taut circling pressure of him inside.

"Tell me," came his dark whisper. "Tell me what you need."

She found herself gasping out words that had spilled from a heart cracked wide open. "Love me. I need you to love me."

She felt his response, a deep shiver, a hot jolt inside her. He answered with a rasping word. Leaning over her, he murmured endearments, gathering her hips more tightly up against his. His hand slipped between her thighs, kneading in counterpoint to the deep centering thrusts. A climax broke over her, immolating and blinding.

Pressing her face against the mattress, she made raw pleasured noises, her flesh squeezing and pulling at him. He drove deep and held, not moving, not even breathing for a moment as the release pumped through him. A shudder, a growl, as he luxuriated in the hot clasp of her body.

As they lay together afterward, groggy and spent, Justine realized what he had said to her in that ultimate moment.

Always.

Twenty-two

. . . .

Since neither of them was inclined to leave the bed, Jason canceled their dinner reservations. He paused to stare at the long lines of Justine's body. She was stretched out on her stomach, the sheet gathered up to her slender hips. "Your skin is so beautiful. Like white violets." He ran his fingertips along her spine, marveling at the perfect paleness of her back. She blushed easily, the fever-color lingering. He found a delicate rosy shadow on her shoulder, and another on the side of her breast. "After I've made love to you," he said, "these sweet little pink patches appear everywhere, especially on your—"

"Don't embarrass me," she protested, burying her face in the pillow.

Jason bent to kiss every patch he could find, and continued to stroke her with proprietary hands. "Making love . . ." he mused aloud. "I've never called it that before. Too old-fashioned. But with you, the other words for it don't sound right."

Her voice was muffled in the depths of the down pillow. "Trust me, there's nothing old-fashioned about the way you do it."

Jason smiled, pressing kisses at intervals along her spine. "Are you hungry?"

Her head lifted. "Starving."

"We could call for one of the hotel's master chefs to cook something here in the cottage."

"Really?" Justine considered it. "But I'd have to put on clothes."

"No, never mind. Let's get room service." He left the bed, hunted for a leather-bound menu in the dining room, and brought it back to Justine. "Order something from every column," he said. "I missed lunch."

"So did I." She looked over the menu with evident pleasure. "You want me to order for you?"

"If you don't mind."

He stretched out beside her, content to watch her expressive face as she read. He loved the way she wore her feelings on the outside like a price tag she'd forgotten to remove. But even so, her motivations weren't always clear to him.

His hand caressed her upper arm. "Justine."

"Mmmn-hmmn?"

"Why did we just have sex?"

"You would rather have done something else?"

"No," he said fervently, "but it was sooner than I expected. I was going to give you all the time and space you needed. I wouldn't have said one word of complaint if you asked me to sleep on the sofa."

"I realized that time is too important to waste." Gently her finger traced the lines of his nose and mouth. "Even though a relationship between you and me is crazy and inconvenient and basically doomed . . . none of that matters. Because I love you anyway."

Jason took her hand and pressed her fingers to his lips, and held them there.

"I've always believed love couldn't be real if it happened too fast," she told him ruefully. "That's what makes this whole thing so confusing. You can't just meet a person and *know* he's the one . . . you have to spend time together, ask a lot of questions, observe him in different situations."

Jason spoke through the screen of her fingers. "We did that."

"For two days."

"That's not long enough?"

"No, falling in love should be a process. Not like a thunderbolt . . . there's a French phrase for it . . . coup de something . . . coup de gras?"

"Coup de foudre," Jason said. "A bolt of lightning. Love at first sight. A coup de grâce is when you deliver a death blow to someone. Which, for us—"

"Don't joke about it," she warned, covering his mouth firmly. When Jason fell obligingly silent, she removed her hand. "Aren't you supposed to pronounce it 'coup de gras'?" she asked. "In French, you leave the last letter off."

"Yes, but the word is 'grâce.' A 'coup de gras' means a 'blow of fat.' As in death by bacon."

Her stomach growled, and she grinned sheepishly. "I'm going to order a coup de bacon," she said, and turned her attention back to the menu.

In a couple of minutes, she dialed the concierge and ordered several items off the menu, including a bottle of wine. As she considered ordering dessert, the concierge offered to send the ingredients for s'mores, to roast over the private fire pit.

She put her hand over the mouthpiece and asked Jason, "Do you like s'mores?"

He looked at her gravely. "It hurts my feelings that you would even have to ask."

Grinning, Justine said to the concierge, "Yes to the s'mores."

After Justine had set the phone back into the cradle, she told Jason, "I hope you're good at roasting marshmallows . . ."

"I am."

". . . because I always burn them."

"I know."

Justine wrinkled her nose at him. "How?"

"Because roasting marshmallows takes patience."

"Are you implying that I'm impatient?"

He walked his fingers along her sheet-covered thigh. "I'm stating it as a categorical fact," he said, and she grinned.

Dinner had arrived by the time they had left the bed and showered. Justine put on a hotel robe and stayed in the bedroom while Jason, who had dressed in casual clothes, let the room service attendants into the cottage. They set out a feast of exquisitely prepared dishes, decanted the wine, and left discreetly.

"How does it look?" Justine asked, venturing out of the bedroom.

"Fantastic," Jason said, his gaze taking in the sight of her in the hotel robe.

She smiled at him. "I meant the dinner."

"The dinner, too." He poured the wine and seated Justine at the table. They started with sun-ripened tomato slices drizzled with delicate green olive oil and flaked sea salt, followed by salads of crisp fennel leaves dressed with jammy slices of mission figs. Justine's entrée was osso buco, rich braised meat melting off the shank. For Jason she had ordered a vegetable ricotta tart topped with pine nuts and slices of smoked Meyer lemon. It was seriously good food, the flavors so sublime that you would remember them later and be sorry if you hadn't eaten every bite. They did justice to the meal, hunger tamping down all but the most necessary conversation until they were finally satisfied.

They went outside to sit by the fire pit, orange flames dancing against the darkness and warming the air pleasantly. Jason roasted a steady supply of marshmallows, each one perfectly golden, the toasted sugar-skins breaking to reveal melting white interiors. When Justine was too full to eat another bite, she went to Jason, took the skewer from him, and set it aside. "No more," she said, sitting on his lap. "I've eaten so many marshmallows, I feel like a giant s'more."

"Let me taste." Having noticed a bit of fluff on her thumb, Jason took it into his mouth and licked off the sticky sweetness. "Perfect. I just need to layer you with chocolate."

Settling back against him, Justine shivered pleasurably at the contrast of the fire and the cold night, and the sound of chilled Pacific waves against the shore. The hard masculine arms around her, the heartbeat at her back.

They were both quiet, relaxing deeply as warmth accumulated between them. An unfamiliar feeling stole through her. She realized it was joy, burnished with the bittersweet awareness of its transience. "I didn't know happiness came in these flavors," she said absently, her head on his shoulder.

"Marshmallow and chocolate?"

"And you. My favorite flavor." She turned her face until her lips brushed his ear. "Do some people really get to have this for a lifetime?" she whispered.

Jason was quiet for a moment. "Not many," he said eventually, and she didn't complain even though his arms were a little too tight.

"Don't you want to go sightseeing?" Justine asked late the next morning, in the aftermath of a leisurely lovemaking session that had begun with Jason kissing every inch of her body.

He stretched out at the foot of the bed to play with her toes. "I've been sightseeing you."

"I guess your mother never told you to look with your eyes instead of your hands." One of her sensitive feet jerked as he pressed a kiss to the arch. "No tickling! I'm declaring my feet off-limits."

Jason caught her ankle in his hand, keeping her still. "You can't. I've just discovered a latent fetish."

"You have enough fetishes. You don't need a new one."

"But look at these feet." He stroked the glossy surface of her big toenail, which was painted violet-purple-cream and adorned with a tiny pink bow decal. He bent his head, and Justine squeaked as she felt his tongue flicker into the space between her toes.

"Stop it," she protested, yanking uselessly at her captured foot. "I'm not putting up with you and your . . . your foot-related perversions . . ."

"Podophilia." Another wet little flick made her squirm and giggle.

"Wh-what?"

"The word for the love of feet."

"You," she said severely, "play too much Scrabble."

"Insomniac," he reminded her.

They went for a long walk on the beach, their feet sinking into sand as soft as talcum powder. Closer to the edge of the water, the flat terrain turned moist and biting cold. The tide had gone out fast, stranding a small constellation of spiny sand starfish. Spying the bleached white circle of a sand dollar, Justine picked it up and brushed away the sediment to examine the star shape of pinholes.

Jason had stopped a few yards away to look out at Glorietta Bay. Navy ships, tourist boats, and merchant vessels passed slowly beneath the arc of the two-mile-long steel girder bridge that linked San Diego and Coronado. Approaching him from behind, Justine slipped her arms around his lean waist and opened her hand to show him her find.

"What's the plan for the rest of the day?" she asked against the back of his shirt.

Taking the sand dollar, Jason turned to face her. His eyes were concealed behind sunglasses, but his mouth held a relaxed curve. "The plan is to do whatever you want."

"Let's get sandwiches at one of those boardwalk shops, and go back to the cottage to take a nap. And then I'll need some time to get ready for the cocktail party tonight."

His mouth flattened into a hyphen. "I need to cancel that."

"According to the schedule Priscilla gave me, you're listed on the invitation as one of the hosts. And it's for a cancer charity. So there's no way you can cancel."

"I'm considering faking an illness."

"Tell them you have severe localized swelling," Justine suggested

271

innocently. "Tell them the only cure is to go straight to bed. I'll vouch for you." Giggling at his expression, she scampered colt-ishly along the beach, obliging him to follow.

After they had returned to the cottage and showered the powdered grit from their legs, Justine promptly dove into bed. Jason spent a few minutes sending texts and e-mails to business associates, and went to set the alarm to wake them in an hour.

He went still as he saw that the digital numbers on the clock were flashing.

12:00

12:00

12:00

For a moment he couldn't breathe.

It happened all the time, Jason told himself. An interruption in power, or someone pressing the wrong button, a hotel maid forgetting to reset the clock. Nothing to worry about.

But he'd gone cold all over, his heart starting to slam. He went to the dresser, where he'd put his Swiss Army watch. The second hand had frozen. The watch had stopped at 2:15.

"Come to bed" came Justine's dozy voice from among the heap of pillows. Jason was vaguely surprised he could hear her over the chaos of his thoughts. He forced himself to act normal, stay calm.

Shedding his robe, Jason slid in beside her and took her into his arms. She fitted against him bonelessly. "Did you set the alarm?" she asked.

"No." His hand passed gently over the satiny river of her hair. "The clock stopped. Don't worry—I won't sleep for long."

He wouldn't sleep a wink.

"That's weird," Justine mumbled. "Did I tell you about the clocks at the inn?" She yawned again and settled more deeply against him.

Jason's hand stopped in the middle of a caress. "What?" he asked softly.

She was quiet, drifting off.

"Baby, don't go to sleep yet. What about the clocks?"

She stirred and made a protesting sound.

Jason fought to keep his voice gentle. "Just tell me about the clocks at the inn."

"It's no big deal." Rubbing her eyes, Justine said, "A couple of days before I left, all the guest room clocks stopped working. It was strange because the wall clock in my cottage stopped working, too, and that one's not plugged in. It runs on batteries."

"Why do you think that happened?" Jason asked carefully.

"I have no idea. I'm going to sleep now." She yawned hugely. In a couple of minutes her body had gone heavy and relaxed, and she was breathing deeply.

She'd said it had been happening for two days. Jason hadn't noticed anything of the kind, until now.

His watch had frozen at a quarter past two . . . which was about the time he had met Justine in the lobby the previous afternoon, when she'd been about to check in.

What if the clocks had stopped not because of his presence, but because of Justine's? A hideous thought came to him: Was it possible that when the longevity spell had been cast, the effect of the witch's bane had somehow transferred to Justine?

A nightmare feeling unrolled over him in a chilling blanket.

A man's most primal instinct—an instinct no less compelling

273

than the need for food or sex—was to keep his woman *safe*. From anyone and anything. Horror consumed him as he realized that he not only might have failed to protect Justine . . . he might have set her death in motion.

Twenty-three

· ·

Jason was suffused with fury, directed exclusively at himself, for putting what he wanted—namely, Justine herself—above what had been in her best interests. He had tried to engineer the outcome he'd wanted, as if life were some damn game he was directing.

It was a mistake he would never make again. But it might be too late to correct.

Sweet Jesus.

This was what Justine had feared doing to him. This was what her mother and Sage and Priscilla's grandmother and Bean had all suffered. Killing what you loved most. The devil knew how any of them had survived it.

He realized he had never truly been terrified of anything until now.

Over the past ten years he'd become accustomed to the idea of his own mortality. Although he had resolved to do as much as possible to prolong his life, he'd never allowed himself the luxury of imagining himself in the future, at an advanced age. But it was crucial, *imperative*, for Justine to have the life she was meant for. He would not be responsible for taking a single minute of it away from her.

Slowly he eased away from Justine's slender body and left the bed. He dressed in the semidarkness, grabbed his phone, and went out to the patio. After closing the glass doors, he made a call.

He heard Sage answer. "Hello?"

"Sage," he said quietly. "It's Jason. Justine's friend."

"What a delightful surprise."

"I'm afraid you're not going to find it delightful after I tell you what I've done. Do you have a few minutes? It's important."

"Yes, of course."

"Can you put Rosemary on the line, as well?"

Sage put him on hold and went to find her partner.

As Jason waited, he knew he was going to have to confess everything to the elderly women, including the fact that he'd borrowed . . . stolen . . . the Triodecad from Justine.

He rubbed his forehead with the pads of his fingers as if to erase the self-loathing thoughts. It was one thing to rationalize your actions in the privacy of your own mind. But when you had to explain your actions to someone else, they became a lot harder to justify.

He heard Rosemary's voice. "Is there a problem with Justine?" she asked without preliminaries.

"Yes. I think she's in danger because of me. I'm sure of it. I need you both to help me put things right."

The private cocktail party was held at a penthouse suite of the convention hotel, while tournaments and demonstrations took place in the massive banquet rooms below the lobby. A floor-to-ceiling wall of glass revealed a view of the port's Embarcadero redevelopment project, with pavilions, parks, and a waterfront promenade.

Justine felt comfortable in the unpretentious atmosphere of the party. The crowd consisted of San Diego locals and people in the video-game industry, all of whom seemed friendly and down-to-earth. Some were dressed in designer fashions, some in T-shirts and khakis. Justine was grateful to Zoë for having insisted on packing the little black dress—it was perfect for an evening like this.

"I didn't think I was going to be able to talk with anyone," she told Jason. "I expected the conversation was going to be way too technical, or that people would be standoffish. But so far they've all been incredibly nice."

"It's usually that way at conventions," Jason replied, smiling into her upturned face. "We all spend so much solitary time in front of the computer that hanging out with real people feels like we've been let out of the basement."

A laughing young woman's voice added, "It's why I refer to my computer as my square-headed boyfriend." The woman and two men, all of whom appeared to be in their twenties, had approached them.

"She refers to her actual boyfriend that way, too," one of them said. His face was narrow and foxlike, his eyes bright with good humor. "I'm Ross McCray"—he reached out to shake Jason's hand—"and these are my coworkers, Marlie Trevino and Troy Noggs."

As they each shook Jason's hand in turn, Marlie, a sturdy, rosy-cheeked blonde, said in a stage whisper, "We all work for Valiant Interactive."

Jason regarded them speculatively. "You guys have a game scheduled for release next month. Shadow Justice, if I'm not mistaken. The buzz is good."

The trio looked thrilled. "I'm a character artist," Ross said, "and these two are programmers."

"This is Justine Hoffman," Jason said, sliding an arm around her shoulders. "A very close friend. She owns a bed-and-breakfast in the San Juans."

"Cool," Marlie exclaimed, shaking Justine's hand. "Is this your first gaming convention? Take my advice—never go down to the meeting rooms completely sober. And do not, under any circumstances, sit in any of the beanbag chairs in the tournament room."

For a few minutes Jason listened as the trio described some of the graphical problems that had delayed the game's original launch date, and their worries over fans' reactions about having to download a patch the first time the game was played.

"I wouldn't worry," Jason said. "If a day-one patch makes the gaming experience better, they'll bitch for five minutes and then they'll forget about it." He looked down at Justine. "Can I get you something to drink?"

"White wine, please."

Glancing at the other woman, Jason asked, "Would you like a drink, Marlie?"

She seemed pleased and surprised by the offer. "Thanks, yes.

I'd love to try one of those blue drinks I've seen people carrying around."

"I'll be right back."

Marlie was nearly preening as Jason went to the bar. Turning back to Justine, she said, "Oh, my God. I just met Jason Black and he's getting me a drink. I'm having a total fan-girl moment."

"I'd always heard he was a genius in the body of a male model," Ross said, perfectly deadpan, "but I just don't see it."

"That's because you're blinded by his charisma," Troy said.

"It's not like he's a rock star," Justine said, laughing.

"He's more than that," Troy said. "He's a legend." Seeing her reaction, he said, "No, seriously. Cult-figure level."

Justine gave him a skeptical glance. "I thought there were a lot of people who did what Jason does."

The remark was received as near-blasphemy, with all three of them hastening to enlighten her. Yes, there were thousands of great game directors and developers, but Jason did epic RPGs—role-playing games—better than anyone else in the business. He had taken them to a level so far beyond what others were doing that, at the moment, he didn't really have a peer. His work was often cited as an example of video games as an art form, offering up worlds so compelling that anyone who played an Inari game was helplessly pulled into its sad, sinister beauty.

Although Inari games had earned a reputation for technical wizardry, like the stunning realism of water effects or the details of character's faces, the true magic was in the way the games created emotional connections.

"Inari always puts you through the wringer," Marlie said. "Skyrebels made everyone cry like a baby at the end."

"I didn't," Ross said.

279

"Oh, come on," Marlie said. "When the guy fatally wounds the dragon and he realizes it's his wife?"

"And she takes off to go die somewhere alone," Troy added. "You felt *nothing*, Ross? Really?"

"I may have misted up for a second," Ross admitted.

"He sobbed until he was dehydrated," Marlie told Justine.

As Jason returned with a glass of wine for Justine and a cocktail for Marlie, Justine told him, "I may have to try one of your games. They were just telling me how amazing your work is."

"The credit goes to my group at Inari—they're the best at what they do."

A new voice entered the conversation as a pair of young men approached them. "How come you only say that stuff behind our backs?"

"Too much praise is demotivating," Jason replied, reaching out to shake hands. He introduced them as Inari game designers who had been part of a panel discussion earlier in the day. Grinning, they proceeded to inform him that so far, a demotivating level of praise was not something they or anyone else at Inari had experienced.

Noticing that one of the other hosts was gesturing for him to come to the other side of the room, Jason slid his hand beneath Justine's elbow. "The mayor and the port commissioner just arrived," he said in an undertone. "Would you go with me to meet them?"

She smiled at him. "Of course."

Jason spoke to the group around them. "If you'll excuse us, Justine and I have to go mingle."

"You're not going to spend the entire evening with us?" Troy asked, looking mildly perplexed.

280

Jason grinned. "It was nice meeting you. Good luck on the launch next month."

But just as he began to turn away with Justine, Marlie asked bashfully, "One quick thing . . . Jason . . . is there any way I could get a picture with you? I've got my camera phone right here, and it would only take a second."

Jason looked apologetic. "Sorry, but I avoid having my picture taken like the plague."

Marlie covered up her disappointment with a smile. "I figured as much. Thought I'd give it a shot anyway."

One of the Inari designers said slyly, "We have a theory about Jason's camera phobia. He secretly fears it's going to steal his soul."

Jason glanced at Justine, a flicker of private amusement in his eyes.

"One more thing," Marlie said. "After the cocktail party, a bunch of us are going to one of the events downstairs. Feel free to come with us if you'd like."

"Which event?" Justine asked.

"The Miss Klingon Beauty Pageant."

"I used to watch *Star Trek*!" Justine exclaimed, pleased to encounter a subject she actually knew something about.

"It's a great pageant," Ross said. "During the talent portion, last year's winner did baton-twirling with a Klingon pain stick. But what really put her over the top was the evening gown competition, when she threatened the entire audience with blunt-force trauma."

"That sounds fun," Justine said, laughing. She glanced at Jason. "Should we go see it?"

"I would rather be beaten with the pain stick."

"We could stand at the back of the room," she wheedled. "No one will see you."

"I'm more worried about what I'll see," Jason said. But as he looked at Justine, he smiled ruefully and murmured, "How can I say no to you?"

After the cocktail party, they took an elevator to the banquet and conference rooms. The doors slid open to reveal a festival-like chaos in which it seemed that anything and everything was allowed. Nearly everyone was dressed in costume: Romulans, robots, Storm Troopers, warriors from Mortal Kombat and Assassin's Creed, even a pack of dogs dressed as the canine corps of Starfleet.

Keeping Justine's hand firmly in his, Jason pulled her through the packed crowd. The noise approximated the decibel level of an airplane runway. One of the common areas was especially tumultuous: It appeared that someone in a Jabba the Hutt costume had gotten stuck in the men's-room doorway, and by-standers were trying to pull him out.

Someone solved the dilemma by poking holes in the Jabba costume with a curved saber. The crowd was highly entertained by the flatulent deflation. When the costume had shrunk sufficiently, volunteers worked together to pull the man out of acres of latex and fabric. They all cheered as he was finally freed. "Let's all hug," one of the rescuers exclaimed to the others. "Can we hug?"

Giggling at the shenanigans, Justine glanced up at Jason. "This is fun."

"It's insane."

"Yes. I feel almost normal by contrast."

Jason put his arms around her, holding her protectively in the jostling crowd. It felt as if they were a still, small island in a turbulent sea. "You know," he told her, "there are better things to aspire to than being normal."

"Like what?"

Bending his head, he murmured near her ear. "Being exactly who you are."

"That's too easy."

He laughed quietly and amended, "Being exactly who you are and loving it."

"That's too hard." She reached up and curved her hand against the lean side of his face, the hard edge of his jaw. A wave of tenderness came over her, and in that moment all she wanted was to be alone with him. "Hey," she said softly, "what do you say we skip the beauty pageant and go back to the Del?"

"Are you sure? The ballroom is right over there."

"I'm sure. My feet are starting to hurt. And it's too noisy down here. Besides . . . if you've seen one Klingon interpretive dance, you've seen them all."

Justine awakened the next morning suffused with the kind of contentment that could only have come from two days of great food, sex, and sleep.

Unfortunately Jason didn't share her mood. He was preoccupied, brooding over something he apparently had no intention of discussing.

Last night in bed, she had been aware of him lying awake beside her, even though he'd been completely still.

"Would a nightcap help?" she had asked in the darkness. "I'm sure there's some vodka in the minibar."

"No, I'm okay."

"If you want to read or watch TV—whatever you usually do on sleepless nights—that's fine with me."

Jason had refused.

After a couple of minutes of taut silence, Justine had said, "I can *feel* you worrying. Can you just give me a hint? If there's anything I've said or done—"

"No, it's nothing like that." He had turned to his side to face her, his hand settling on the curve of her hip. "A work-related issue. Too technical to explain. I can handle it."

She moved closer to him, rising to her knees. "Do you need a distraction?"

"Maybe." His breath quickened as he felt the cool streamers of her hair trail over his skin. "Got any ideas?"

"Just one." She pressed him to his back and moved over him, prowling along his body. He lay beneath her, going taut in every muscle. Her mouth touched him here and there, as if she were adorning him with kisses. His hands went to her hair, playing gently.

She mounted him and lowered herself carefully, moaning at the delicious full invasion, riding slowly. He matched her rhythm until they were moving in fluid undulations like some protean creature, a tide of sensation buoying them upward in fresh swells. It was all that mattered, this pouring of heat into heat, love into love.

"Despite my best efforts," Justine said the next morning as they drank coffee in the kitchen, "you're still preoccupied."

Jason was scowling down at his cell phone, his fingers tapping swiftly at the touchscreen. "My phone keeps automatically switching time zones and dates. I've tried to reset it manually, but the fix only lasts a few seconds. I'm about to put it in the microwave and kill it."

Justine reached for her handbag on the counter and pulled out her phone. Glancing at the touchscreen, she said in bemusement, "According to my phone, we're in Beijing and it's eight o'clock at night. What's going on? The bedroom clock and now this. I wonder if—"

"Coincidence," Jason said brusquely. "The bedroom clock went out because of a power outage."

"What about the cell phones?"

"They probably received rolling software updates that screwed with data connectivity." Jason slid his phone back into his pocket. "Is your bag packed? We have to leave in a couple of minutes."

"You want to get rid of me?" Justine asked lightly, dropping her phone into her handbag.

"No, I want you to arrive at the airport with plenty of time to make it through security."

A bellman arrived to take their bags to the rental car in front of the hotel. While he and Jason went through the obligatory how-was-your-stay conversation, Justine looked through the cottage to make certain she hadn't left anything behind. She picked up the briefcase that contained the Triodecad and followed Jason outside.

"Do you think we'll ever come back?" she asked wistfully, taking a last look at Coronado Beach.

"If you want to." Jason took the briefcase from her and held her hand as they walked back to the hotel. "But I thought you didn't like to travel."

"I can be flexible. If you're willing to visit the island, I'll reciprocate by going to San Francisco or any other place you want. Both people need to make some effort in a long-distance relationship." She paused. "That's what this is, right? . . . A real relationship?"

"What else would it be?"

"Well, it could be one of those fuzzy relationships that looks and feels like a real one, except you're never sure if you can keep a toothbrush at his place. And you never say the word 'relationship,' you only refer to it as 'this thing that we're doing.' And you can't talk about being exclusive, even if you secretly want to."

"There's nothing fuzzy about this relationship," he said. "'Yes' to the toothbrush, 'no' to seeing other people."

Her hand tightened on his. He could be so straightforward at times. But there was still so much about him that was mysterious, guarded, complex.

"I woke up this morning thinking about something the Valiant Interactive guys were saying last night," she said. "They told me about the ending of one of your games, when a man wounds a dragon and then he finds out it was his wife, and the dragon flies away to die alone."

"Yes."

"That's so dark. Why does she have to die at the end?"

"She doesn't have to die. There's a secret level to the game. Some players stumble upon it, and others have heard rumors but don't know how to access it. But if you can manage to get to that level, the man has another chance to find his wife and save her."

"What's the secret to accessing the level?"

286

"During the time it takes to play through the game, you have to make thousands of choices about how your character lives, fights, works, sacrifices for others. You're faced with opportunities to take the easy way out, or stick to your principles. At the end, if most of your choices have been moral, the last level unlocks itself."

"So your character has to be perfect throughout the whole game?"

"He doesn't have to be perfect. Just good enough. He has to learn from his mistakes and put other people's interests before his own."

"But why is there a secret level? Why not tell people about it up front, and give them an incentive to make the right choices?"

He smiled slightly. "Because I like the idea that sometimes in life—or in fantasy—you get rewarded for doing the right thing."

Twenty-four

. . . .

". . . we've replaced all the batteries in the clocks, and checked the electrical circuits," Justine was saying, "and everything is still screwed up."

"I'm sorry, honey," Jason said into the phone, pacing as they talked. "I know you must be frustrated as hell."

"I think there might be a supernatural cause for this."

Jason stopped walking. "Like what?" he asked, keeping his voice casual.

"I'm not sure. I'm wondering if the inn could be haunted. It's a historic building. Maybe we're harboring a clock-hating ghost or something."

"You should ask Rosemary and Sage about it."

"Yes. I'm going to visit them soon, and I'll mention it to them. How is your work going? Did you fix the problem you were worried about?"

"I think it'll be resolved by tonight."

"Oh, good. Maybe you can come to the San Juans this week-end."

"I hope so."

"Do you miss me?" Justine asked.

"No," he said, "I spend all day not allowing myself to miss you. I don't let myself think about marshmallow-flavored kisses, or how soft the spaces between your toes are, or how I want to talk to you until we've used up all the oxygen in the room. And I especially don't dwell on the fact that wherever I am, there's always an empty place beside me that's exactly your shape and size."

He talked with Justine a few minutes more, keeping his eyes closed so he could savor the sound of her voice. He wasn't entirely certain what they were talking about, and it didn't matter as long as he could hear her.

What could you say to the woman you loved, the last time you might ever talk to her? *You're everything to me. You've given me the best days of my life.* One of the more ignominious features of love was that you could only express it with clichés . . . it made you sound like a fraud at a time when you were blazing with sincerity. But at the end of the conversation, he found himself saying, "I love you," and she said it back.

And it was enough. Those three well-worn, everyday words got the job done.

Ending the call, he went to the next room, where Sage was dusting and cleaning, readying the lighthouse for guests. Ten, to be exact.

"I swore I'd never lie to her again," Jason said. "Or go behind her back. And less than a week later, I'm doing both."

"For the best of reasons," Sage said.

Jason lifted the Jules Verne diving helmet so she could clean the shelf under it. "That's been my MO lately," he said. "Doing the wrong thing for the right reason. So far it hasn't worked out too well."

"Don't you worry." Sage patted his arm as he set the helmet back down. "We'll fix everything. Once we let the coven know what had happened, they all dropped everything to come here right away."

"It's not often a man gets to spend an evening with a dozen pissed-off witches."

"We prefer to be called crafters. Or coveners. And while some in the coven are less forgiving than others, everyone agrees that you should be praised for taking responsibility. Most men would have run away."

"Most men wouldn't have caused all this trouble in the first place."

"We've all made mistakes," Sage said gently.

In light of the circumstances, she and Rosemary had been far kinder than Jason had expected or deserved. When he had called them from San Diego, he had explained the situation with ruthless honesty, not trying to spare himself, offering no excuses. They had both been quiet, taking in every word he'd said, occasionally asking questions.

They had agreed that the situation was dire. Sage had confirmed that the stopping of the clocks marked the arrival of the witch's bane; the same phenomenon had preceded her husband Neil's death. Something would have to be done right away, or the consequences would be deadly for Justine.

The two women were intrigued and even incredulous that

Priscilla's grandmother and great-aunt had managed to cast a powerful spell from the Triodecad.

"Had anyone consulted us," Rosemary had said pointedly, "we could have explained why a longevity spell was a bad idea. However, the fact that they were able to pull it off at all is impressive."

"I should have consulted you," Jason admitted, "but I was hell-bent on forcing things to turn out the way I wanted. Obviously I'm asking too late—but what went wrong?"

"Even if one is able to ward off the witch's bane," Rosemary had explained, "that won't make it disappear, it only attaches to someone else. Which is what seems to have happened in this case. The longevity spell redirected the bane from you to Justine."

"How do we put things back to the way they were before?"

A discomforting pause had ensued.

"I'm afraid we can't," Sage had said. "Things can't ever go back to the way they originally were. There will be differences. I think we may be able to lift the longevity spell, but that is no easy thing to accomplish. Longevity is a unique category of magic. High magick. There are risks."

"That doesn't matter to me."

"*Significant* risks."

"I want to go ahead with it."

"You could die," Rosemary had said. "And since you have no soul, that would be the end of your existence."

"But Justine would be okay? She would be safe?"

"She would be safe," Sage said. "I don't know about 'okay.'"

They had decided to consult the coven. It had been unanimously agreed that they would participate as a group in the lifting of the longevity spell, and that above all it had to be done fast. They would meet at Cauldron Island and perform the ritual at Crystal Cove, at the old abandoned schoolhouse where they had conducted many successful rites and ceremonies in the past.

No one in the coven had objected to Jason's request to keep Justine out of it. There was no way in hell that Jason was going to put Justine in the position of having to make an agonizing choice, or trying to sacrifice herself for him. Protecting her from that was the very least he could do.

His thoughts were dragged back to the present as someone knocked at the front door of the lighthouse. The first witch . . . coverner . . . had arrived.

Following Sage into the main room, Jason saw Rosemary welcoming in a middle-aged woman, slender and tall, with artfully styled red hair and a fine-boned face. Her Stevie Nicks rock-glam vibe was enhanced by a crushed-velvet skirt, a skin-tight top overlaid with a delicate macramé vest, and studded wedge-heeled boots.

Rosemary and Sage both went to embrace her, and she laughed in apparent pleasure at seeing them.

As soon as he heard that distinctive throaty laugh, Jason knew who she was.

Looking over Sage's shoulder, the woman caught sight of Jason. The amusement died from her expression. The atmosphere chilled. Her eyes were crystalline and smoked with heavy makeup, her gaze unblinking as she approached him.

"Jason Black," he said, reaching out to shake hands, then curtailing the gesture as he saw she wasn't going to respond. "I'd hoped to meet you under better circumstances than this. But it's a pleasure to—"

"You can hardly do anything worse to a crafter than steal her grimoire," Marigold said crisply.

"I gave it back," Jason pointed out, careful to strip all defensiveness from his tone.

"You want credit for that?" Marigold asked acidly.

Jason kept his mouth shut. There was no way he or anyone could blame her for disliking a man who had put her daughter's life in danger.

He studied her, seeing hints of Justine here and there: the slim and leggy build, the shape of the jaw, the skin as perfect as bone china. But Marigold's face, for all its beauty, had a mask-like quality, a façade that concealed the propulsive bitterness of someone whose worst fears about the world had been confirmed.

"As I understand it," Marigold said, "you hired a pair of hillbilly crafters to perform a complex spell, and surprise, surprise . . . something went wrong."

Rosemary answered before Jason could reply. "The spell was cast very competently. In fact, the strength of the spell is the problem."

"Yes. The witch's bane has been transferred to Justine. Does she know about what's happening tonight?"

"No," Jason said. "She'd only try to argue with me. It's my fault. My responsibility. I'll take care of it." Jason paused before adding sincerely, "I appreciate you coming here to help, Marigold."

"I didn't say I would help."

Rosemary and Sage wore identical expressions of bemusement.

"I have one condition," Marigold continued. "I'll only do it if you promise never to see or speak to Justine again. I want you to disappear from her life."

"Or what?" Jason asked. "You'd let your own daughter be taken out by the witch's bane?"

Marigold didn't reply. But for a split second the truth was on her face, and it made Jason's blood run cold. Yes. She was fully prepared to throw Justine into the volcano.

"Marigold," Rosemary asked sharply, "is this bargain really necessary?"

"It is. He's the one who endangered her in the first place. And Justine is equally responsible for breaking the geas. I want her to learn a lesson from this."

"Teach her lessons on your own time," Jason said irritably. "Right now the goal is to extend her life beyond the next three damn days."

"So she can continue to screw it up?" Marigold stunned him by asking.

Jason gave her an incredulous glance. "It's her right to do so, isn't it?"

"If you were a parent, you would understand that sometimes the worst thing we can do is protect a child from the consequences of her actions. Justine may learn something from this comeuppance."

There was a strange and disturbing note of satisfaction in Marigold's voice. If Jason had had any questions about the estrangement between Justine and her mother, they would have been resolved in that moment. This was not a mother who would welcome back a prodigal child, unless that child came back crawling and decimated.

"Maybe," Jason said. "But if my child were facing her comeuppance, I wouldn't buy center-court seats and bring popcorn, and call it a great parenting technique."

She shot him a hostile glance and spoke to Rosemary and Sage. "This entire problem could be solved easily if we tossed him off the cliff."

"I would take a running leap if that was the only way to help Justine," Jason said. "But in the hopes of preserving what little time I might have left, I'd like to give the spell-breaking thing a shot first."

"Then give me your promise," Marigold insisted. "Tell me you'll leave Justine no matter what happens."

"I can't give a promise when I know I would break it."

Without another word, Marigold turned on her heel and headed to the door.

Rosemary hurried after her. "Marigold! Think carefully about what you're doing. Your daughter's life is hanging in the balance. You must do this for her."

Marigold's mask broke long enough to reveal a glimpse of anguished rage. "What has she done for *me*?" she cried, and slammed the door as she left the house.

Jason and Sage stood alone in the silence. "I've got one of those, too," Jason said after a moment. "Only it's my father."

Sage was bewildered. "Marigold didn't used to be like this."

"She's probably always been exactly like this. She's just gotten worse at covering it up." Jason shoved his hands in his pockets and went to the window, staring at the blood-colored sunset. "Can we still lift the spell without her, or should I start practicing my long jump?"

"We can still lift the spell. But . . . I'm sure Marigold will return to help. She won't turn her back on her own daughter."

He gave her an incisive glance. "Her back's been turned for four years, Sage."

Rosemary entered the lighthouse, looking aggrieved. "The water taxi was still waiting at the dock. Marigold had no intention of staying. She just came here for a bit of grandstanding. I told her if she wouldn't help the coven in a time of need, particularly when her own daughter's well-being is involved—there isn't much point in her belonging."

Sage's eyes widened. "How did she answer?"

"She didn't."

"She would never voluntarily leave the coven," Sage said.

"No. Which is why we're not going to ask her to leave voluntarily. After I talk to the coveners, I'm going to make certain she's thrown out on her ass." Catching Sage's expression, Rosemary said, "I've defended Marigold for years. I've always tried to focus on the good in her and overlook the rest. But this can't be overlooked, Sage. This makes it impossible to pretend, to Justine or ourselves, that Marigold cares about anyone but herself."

Distressed, Sage went to straighten a stack of magazines on the table. "I think she might show up tonight and surprise us."

Rosemary glanced at her partner with a mixture of love and exasperation. She turned her attention to Jason. "She won't show up," she said flatly.

"Personally I'm glad," Jason said. "My sixth sense tells me she would have added an extra step to my ritual. Like evisceration."

As the last smear of daylight faded from the dark lacquered sky, the coven arrived in groups of two and three. They were all dressed comfortably in jeans or long skirts, accessorized with colorful scarves and copper jewelry. They were a pleasant, chatty group, clearly relishing the opportunity to see one another. As they grazed among the food that Sage had set out, roasted red pepper dip with pita chips, artichoke and mushroom crostini, pumpkin dumplings on skewers, they could have been attending a monthly book club meeting.

"Jason," Rosemary murmured to him at eleven P.M., "we'll need to begin preparing the schoolhouse for the ritual. It's about two thirds of a mile from here. If you wouldn't mind driving the coveners there in groups of three, they can begin setting up."

"Sure. What's the significance of groups of three?"

Her tone was dry. "It's the number of passenger seats in the golf cart."

"Golf cart?"

"No one has cars on the island. The residents use bicycles or light electric vehicles. We keep ours in the green shed outside. Would you mind backing it out and pulling it up to the front door? We'll have the first group of coveners and supplies waiting."

"No problem," Jason said.

Her gaze was speculative and kind. "This isn't the usual weeknight activity for a man in your position, is it?"

He smiled slightly. "Chauffeuring witches in a golf cart to an abandoned schoolhouse at midnight? Not really. But it's a nice change in the routine."

One of the crafters, an elderly woman with white hair and bright blue eyes, approached Rosemary and gently tapped her on the shoulder. "It's getting late," she said. "Shouldn't Marigold have arrived by now?"

"Marigold isn't coming," Rosemary said, her mouth tightening. "It seems she had other plans."

After a couple of maddening attempts at trying to fix the time and date settings on her phone, Justine gave up and downloaded a Scrabble app. Maybe playing a few rounds against the computer would give her some insight into why Jason was such a fan of the game. Curling up in the corner of her sofa, she adjusted the setting of the game to "easy" and started to play.

A half hour later, she had reached a few conclusions: She would be a much more successful player if the Scrabble dictionary would allow the use of certain four-letter words, that quat was the name of an African evergreen shrub, and that there was something seriously addictive about the sound of the electronic tiles being clicked.

She was mulling over her deficiency in words starting with *z* when she heard a knock at the cottage door. Wondering if there was a problem with a guest, or if Zoë had decided to drop by, Justine hopped off the sofa and went to answer the door in her sock feet.

Opening it, she felt her heart stop as she was confronted with the last person she expected to see.

"Mom?"

Twenty-five

. . . .

Whenever Justine had tried to envision a reunion with her mother, she had thought it would take place in cautious increments . . . an e-mail, a letter, a phone call, a brief visit. She should have known better. Marigold had always been a creature of impulse, following every whim and doing whatever was necessary to avoid the consequences. Showing up at the front door was to Marigold's advantage; the surprise of it would throw Justine off balance.

Justine had always hoped that someday she and her mother might come to a new understanding and acceptance of each other. Some resolution that didn't involve winning and losing, but instead . . . peace. But after four years of estrangement, her mother's eyes were hard with the same anger that had underpinned every moment of Justine's childhood. No visible signs of softening.

"Mom, what are you doing here?" Opening the door, she stepped back to allow Marigold inside.

Marigold ventured just past the threshold and looked around.

There was a time when Justine would have worried about her mother's reaction to the cottage, the inn, the life she had built. She would have desperately wanted Marigold's good opinion, so seldom given. It came as a revelation that she no longer needed her mother's approval. It was enough to know that she had made the right choices for herself.

"Is there a problem?" Justine asked. "Why are you here?"

Marigold's voice was threaded with contempt. "Is it hard to believe that I might want to see my own daughter?"

Justine had to think about that. "Yes," she said. "You've never liked my company, and I still haven't done what you wanted me to do. So there's no reason for you to visit unless there's a problem."

"The problem, as always, is you," Marigold said flatly.

As always. Those two words brought the past into the room with them as if it were a living presence. A giant standing over them both, casting an inescapable shadow of blame.

There had been no softening in Marigold's heart. She had ossified until, like a beautiful stone statue, any change in posture would cause her to break and crumble. She would never be able to turn her head to look in a new direction, or take a step forward, or hold her daughter in her arms. How terrible it must have been, Justine thought with a trace of compassion, to stay so rigid while life changed around you.

"Does this have to do with the geas?" Justine asked gently. "Rosemary and Sage must have told you by now. You must be angry."

"I made a sacrifice for you, and you threw it away. How should I feel, Justine?"

"Maybe a little like the way I felt, when I found out about it." She saw from Marigold's incredulous fury that it hadn't occurred to her to wonder about Justine's feelings.

"You've always been ungrateful," Marigold snapped, "but I never thought of you as stupid. I gave you what you needed. I did what was best for you."

"I wish you had waited until I was older," Justine said quietly. "I wish you'd explained it to me first. Maybe allowed me to have a say in it."

"I suppose I should have asked your permission before feeding you, clothing you, taking you to the dentist and the pediatrician—"

"That's different. Those things are all part of raising a child."

"*Ungrateful*," Marigold spat.

"No. I'm grateful that you took care of me and raised me. I have to believe you did the best you could. But the thing is, you made a decision for me that wasn't yours to make. Binding a lifelong curse to your daughter doesn't fall under the category of dental visits or polio vaccinations. And you know that, or you would have mentioned something about it to me."

"I kept it secret because I knew if you found out, you would ruin everything. I knew you would do something stupid. And you have." The bleached white of Marigold's face contrasted sharply with the red fury of her hair, the ruddy slashes of her brows over hard eyes. She burned like an angel of vengeance as she continued. "I've just come from Cauldron Island. They're performing a midnight rite because of you and your selfishness. And if they don't succeed, you're going to die. The witch's bane has turned on *you*."

Justine discovered that her heart wasn't entirely safe, after all. One human being could always find a way to hurt another.

"You fell in love with a man who betrayed you," Marigold ranted, "and the witch's bane is going to kill you unless they do something. It's your fault. You deserve this."

Justine tried to gather her wits. Her own voice seemed to come from far away. "What are they doing? What kind of rite?"

"They're trying to lift a spell from the man you're involved with. He's there at this moment. I met him. He might die for you. And if that happens . . . the blood is on your hands."

When the last group of coveners had been delivered to the old schoolhouse, Jason accompanied them inside.

The crafters had been busy. The place looked like a set for a horror movie, with black cloth draped everywhere and a wealth of flickering candles. Incense burned in a pedestal bowl, thickening the air with aromatic smoke. A huge pentagram had been chalked onto the floor, with handfuls of crystals placed at various places around the central star. Chalices and wands had been set all around the pentagram.

The hair rose on the back of Jason's neck.

Violet, a crafter in her mid-thirties, came forward to take his arm and give it a comforting squeeze. "Sorry. I know it looks creepy. But we want to do the very best we can for you, so we didn't hold back."

"Tim Burton would be impressed," he said, and she smiled.

As he glanced at the faces of the women around him, Jason was reassured. They were trying to help him, and in doing so, they would help Justine. "There's something I need to know," he said, and was surprised when they all fell silent and looked at him. A couple of coveners paused in their sweeping, while another who was arranging crystals looked up from her task. "I need to know that the results of what I did won't cause problems for Justine in the future. In other words, whatever you have to do to make sure that Justine will be safe . . . go for it. No matter what the consequences to me. Do you understand what I'm saying?"

"We understand." Violet regarded him with patent concern. "Rosemary explained the risks, yes? This spell is hard to remove. Like separating sand mixed with sugar. And once the witch's bane is focused on you again, you might have very little time left. No one knows what condition you'll be in when the spell is lifted, or what will happen."

"That's fine," he said gruffly. "Just tell me what I have to do."

Sage came to him and took his hand. "Just sit in the middle of the pentagram while we do our work. Try to relax and let your mind clear."

Jason went to the center of the chalked circle and sat, while the crafters gathered at the edges of the pentagram.

"Once we begin," Rosemary told him, "you have to be quiet. No interruptions. We'll all need to maintain our focus."

"Got it. No talking, no texting." He looked at the group around him. "Has everyone turned off their cell phones?"

Rosemary looked stern, but the corner of her mouth twitched. "That'll be enough from you. Unless you have any questions."

"Just one."

"Yes?"

"What is that knife with the curved handle for?"

"For cutting herbs."

He looked dubiously at the foot-long knife.

"It's midnight," someone said.

Rosemary looked at Jason. "Let's begin."

Sage had already explained to Jason that the ritual would involve a series of chants, blessings, and invocations before the actual spell-lifting would occur. "If you could possibly go into a meditative state during the rite," Sage had told him, "that would be very helpful to us. Focus on your breathing, let your thoughts go—"

"I can meditate," he had assured her.

He sat up straight and focused his attention on the flow of his breath. He tried to focus on a single image. His mind touched on one memory after another until he found the dark-sliding surf of Coronado Beach at night, the endless soothing rush of water, the way he had relaxed and listened with Justine's warm weight in his lap, her head on his shoulder. Waves turning over on themselves, salt-burled rhythm making its way from the blackest depths up to a moonstruck shore. A sense of calm pervaded him.

He heard women's voices calling to unseen spirits, summoning and beguiling. A cool, dark energy seeped into the air around him. He took it inside with every breath, feeling it cleanse the lingering thoughts and anger and fear until his mind was spread like the fingers of open hands and the place where a soul should have lived was left raw and exposed. The truth came to him between the space of one breath and another.

He had no time left.

He received the revelation with wonder and a brief, blind instinct to struggle. Not yet. Not now. But in the absence of a soul, his heart compensated with aching beats of acceptance . . . Let go, let go, let go.

Justine was not in a mood to take no for an answer. When no water taxis were available, she called a friend who owned a small trawler and desperately talked her into taking her to Cauldron Island. "I know it's late, I'll pay anything, do anything, if you'll just get me there, you know it's not far—" The friend had said yes, seeming to understand that Justine wasn't going to give her a choice anyway.

In ten minutes Justine had scrambled to the Friday Harbor docks and boarded the waiting trawler. Every minute that passed before launching was another agonizing tug at her nerves until the reverberations made her entire body sing in panic. Jason had gone behind her back again, and the coven, too. They had all locked her out of something that would affect her more than anyone else. The longevity spell was infinitely more dangerous to remove than to cast in the first place. A spell like that could work its way down inside you with backward barbs, until it would kill you to pull it out. Almost like love.

The boat parted from the dock at idling speed until it had left the no-wake zone. The motor growled with rising ferocity as the bow ate through serrated water while the wind huffed and struck Justine's face and tangled her loose hair. The weight of the Triodecad, contained in a canvas tote bag, thumped hard against her thigh.

Her mind was in high gear. She had talked with Jason earlier that day, and Jason had said nothing. He'd let her think he was in San Francisco. He must have been at the lighthouse right then. He'd been relaxed and casual, not revealing a hint about what he was planning.

She heard Marigold's voice: *"The witch's bane has turned on you."*

That was the unknown consequence. A blood sacrifice was required, that was the price of love for her kind. Someone had to pay, and Jason had decided it would be him.

The blood is on your hands.

How easy it would be to turn into Marigold. All she would have to do was let herself. And when all that bitterness had eaten up her insides, the only direction it would be able to go was outward.

The trawler docked at Cauldron Island just long enough for Justine to leap onto the slick weathered boards. She climbed the endless stairs with punishing upward lunges until her thighs knotted and burned, but she ignored the pain and kept going. The lighthouse was silent, unoccupied, the yard cemetery-dark and still. Clouds piled over the waning moon like discarded laundry, slowly obscuring the gibbous curve.

Still panting from the hard upward haul, Justine went to the outside shed and pulled out one of the pair of bicycles. She headed down the ragged trail to Crystal Cove, wheels jolting on stones that protruded like knuckles, then dipping into shallow scoops that sent the bike upward for stomach-lifting seconds.

The schoolhouse windows flickered red and black, blinking slowly at her as the bike wheels rolled and spat sand. Justine was off the bike before it had even stopped, the metal frame clattering to the ground.

She shoved hard against the door and barged in.

The rite had just ended, the circle of coveners broken up, two or three of them huddled in the middle of the pentagram.

"Justine," she heard Rosemary say in an odd tone.

306

"Someone turn on a light," Justine said impatiently.

The light from a portable lamp flared, a pool of unnatural white pushing the shadows on the floor right up against the seams of the walls.

Jason was sitting in the center of the pentagram, arms loosely curled around his bent legs, forehead resting on his knees. He didn't move or even look up as she approached. Sage, Rosemary, and Violet were crowded around him.

"Get back!" Justine cried. She rushed to Jason, dropped the Triodecad, and fell to her knees beside him. "Jason? Jason, what is it?" He made no sound that let her know he'd heard her. She cast a wild glance at the coveners. Whatever they saw in her face was enough to make them retreat. She saw that Jason was sweating heavily, the hair at the nape of his neck wet. "What did you do to him?" she demanded.

"The spell's been lifted," Rosemary said. "You're safe now, Justine."

"You shouldn't have done this without me," she said fiercely. "You knew I'd want to be told."

"It was his decision."

Turning her attention back to Jason, Justine touched the back of his head, his neck, trying to coax him to look at her. "Let me see you," she said. "Jason, please—"

She broke off as his head bobbed up on the uncertain support of his neck. His complexion was gray, gleaming with sweat, his eyes not quite focused. Pain had tightened the skin over his bone structure, turning the cheekbones into blades. Every breath was a short, dry gasp.

"What is it?" she asked urgently. "Where does it hurt, what's the matter?"

307

She saw that he wanted to say something, but his teeth were clenched too hard to allow for words. His right hand gripped the upper part of his left arm, fingers digging into the muscle. Instantly she understood.

Heart attack.

"His time is up, Justine," she heard Sage say in a choked voice. "He was warned—"

"*No.*" Justine grabbed wildly for the Triodecad, yanking it from the tote bag. "I'll fix this. I'll find the right spell. Just hang on, I'll take care of it, I promise. I promise—" At least that was what she was trying to say, except the words were shuddery and cracked. She wasn't aware that she was crying until she saw the heavy splats of water on the ancient pages, the ink blurring, her eyes swimming. Frantically she fumbled with the book, paper crumpling and ripping beneath her frenzied hands.

"Justine," she heard Sage cry out in dismay. Some of the crafters began to move toward her.

"*Stay away from me.*" She stared at them with wild eyes, her hand extended in midair like a weapon.

She felt Jason touch her arm. Letting go of the Triodecad, she turned to him. His deep brown eyes stared into hers. Through the glaze of pain there was a quiet glow of understanding. He leaned closer to say something, and she steadied him with her arms.

His whisper was hot and gentle against her ear. "Never would've been enough time anyway."

His head dropped to her shoulder, and his weight eased against her as he collapsed slowly into her arms. She breathed in the familiar and tantalizing scents of his skin and hair. His body was heavy and racked with shivers.

308

"You're going to be fine," she said desperately, screwing her eyes shut, racking her brain for any kind of spell, *anything*.

Jason's fingers tangled in her hair, pulling her head down to his. "Worth it," he whispered.

She could feel the life pouring out of him as if from a sieve, even as she tried to contain it with her hands, her palms pressing on his chest, back, arms, head. "Don't, don't, don't—"

"Kiss me."

"No." But she did, finding his mouth with hers, soft and warm, while her tears slipped onto his face, his closed eyes. His lips pulled in a grimace of pain, and her arms locked around him. She would hold him so tight that death couldn't take him. She would keep him with her, harbor him inside herself.

One last breath, a quiet exhalation. The fingers in her hair unclenched, and his hand slid away, dropping to her lap. Time stopped, seconds caught and collided like raindrops in the cup of a leaf.

Easing him to the floor, Justine stared down at his expressionless face, the way his lashes lay against his cheeks, the gray tinge of his mouth. The force of a terrible energy built inside her, racing through bones, cartilage, nerves, blood. A wild pulse threatened to burst her veins. He would not disappear. She would hold him in the space between life and nothingness, she would keep him *somewhere*.

Her face streamed with sweat and tears. She put her hands to his chest. His body jolted as a shock of energy blazed through him. She heard the horrified exclamations of the coveners around them.

"Justine, no—"

Again and again, while she kept her hands on him and let the fatal voltage sear through them both. She heard Rosemary begging her to stop, it was no use, she would hurt herself. But no one dared come near . . . she and Jason were surrounded with blue-white energy, hot as the heart of a dying star. They had formed a circuit, fused and burning out bright and fast. Let him take her with him. Let her soul carry them both, so he could never leave her and she would never have to mourn.

She crawled over him, gripping his head in her hands, her mouth coming to his. The brilliance flared, followed by startling black.

No pulse, no sensation, no vibration of energy. Only the cry of her soul in the silent oblivion.

Where are you?

A force more powerful than gravity pulled her out of the darkness, drew her into a steep ascent, a billowing forward roll, love tumbling into love.

Here.

He was with her, impossibly, irrevocably.

And time began again.

Slowly she returned to herself, her eyes opening. She was aware of the coveners nearby, of the walls of the Crystal Cove schoolhouse, the flickering light of candles and glass lamps. But her attention was riveted on Jason, his still features, her hands pale brackets at the sides of his face. She said his name carefully.

His lashes lifted in the amber veil of lamplight, the dark irises soft and drowsing.

"I couldn't let you go," she said, stroking his cheek, the edge of his jaw.

He held her gaze, his eyes filled with wonder as he perceived what she already knew. "Something's different," he said hoarsely.

She nodded and lowered her forehead to his. "Somehow," she whispered, "we're sharing a soul. But I think half of it was yours all along."

Something soft brushed her forehead. Justine ignored the feathery touch, trying to remain comfortably asleep. Another tender stroke, this one on her cheek. With an irritable sound, she turned to snuggle deeper into the fat, downy depths of her pillow.

"Justine." A velvety murmur . . . Jason's voice . . . his lips playing near her ear. "It's almost noon. Wake up so I can talk to you."

"Don' want to talk," she mumbled. Her exhausted brain sorted through memories of the previous night. What bizarre dreams she'd had . . . seeing Marigold, fearing for Jason's life, racing to Crystal Cove . . .

Her eyes flew open, and she looked at the masculine face right above hers. Jason was propped up on one elbow, a faint smile on his lips. He was freshly showered and dressed, his face smooth-shaven. "I've been waiting for you to wake up," he said, his fingertips slowly following the shape of her collarbone to the curve of her shoulder. "I couldn't stand it any longer."

A cursory glance at their surroundings revealed that they were in the Cauldron Island lighthouse tower bedroom. She was naked beneath the sheets, her body relaxed and more than a little fatigued. "I feel like I've run a marathon," she said dazedly.

"Not surprising, after last night."

She sat up, keeping the sheets pulled up over her breasts.

311

Efficiently Jason propped up pillows behind her. Just as she realized that her mouth was incredibly dry, he gave her a glass of water.

"Thanks," she said, drinking thirstily. "What exactly happened last night?"

He looked at her closely. "You don't remember?"

"I do, but I'm not sure what was real and what I might have imagined."

"Do you want the long version or the short?"

"Short." She gave him back the glass, and he set it on the bedside table.

"For me the evening kicked off with a midnight spell-lifting ritual, followed by a near-death experience and a bare-handed cardiac resuscitation performed by you, after which you apparently lit up the schoolhouse like a Las Vegas casino. The coveners said they'd never seen anything like it—I'm sorry I missed the show."

"I think you were the show," Justine said. "Where is everyone now?"

"Rosemary and Sage are taking a nap. Some of the coveners left late last night. A few of the others stayed and talked until breakfast, and left a little while ago. I never knew witches kept such insanely late hours."

"Something they have in common with insomniacs."

Jason smiled, reaching out to smooth the wild mass of her hair. He was so handsome that it almost hurt to look at him. Everything that had been appealing and dynamic about him before seemed to have amplified, if that were even possible.

"What did the coven say?" she asked.

"About which part?"

"About any of it."

"The one thing they all agreed on was that somehow I've been given an impossible gift. By you." He looked into her eyes, making no effort to conceal a mixture of adoration and awe. "Sage thinks that somehow you infused part of your soul into me, in the same way that one flame can start a new one. But no one's ever heard of it being done before. And no one can figure out how you did it."

"I don't know," she said, abashed. "I just . . . wanted you. I had to keep you with me."

"You've got me," he said. "In fact, you'll have me even when you want to get rid of me."

She smiled and shook her head. "Never." The word was crushed between their lips as he leaned over to give her a hard kiss.

Drawing back, he stared at her tenderly, his expression more difficult to interpret. "The coven also discussed something else," he said. "They think that the witch's bane may no longer apply in our situation . . . because a sacrifice was made." At her questioning glance, he said, "Can you try to do your snapping thing? Set something on fire?"

Bemused, she focused her energy and snapped her fingers. The expected spark wasn't there. She blinked in surprise and tried again.

Nothing.

Twin notches of concern appeared between Jason's brows. "I can't remember the supernatural words they used," he said. "But basically you may have exceeded your capacity. Blown a circuit." He paused, his gaze searching hers. "Would you be unhappy if you had no more power?"

"No, I . . . I just never imagined . . . *no*. Especially not if it saved you." She tried to make herself comprehend it fully. If she no longer had the powers of a hereditary witch, she could probably still work a few simple spells, mix a potion now and then. *For all the good it's done me in the past,* she thought wryly. A giddy feeling swept through her as she said aloud, "I don't need magic to be happy." It was the truth.

Jason cupped her flushed cheek in his hand, his gaze caressing. "What do you need to be happy?" he asked. "Give me the longest list you can come up with. I won't rest until you have everything on it."

"It's a short list," she said.

"God, I hope I'm on it."

She shook her head as if the comment were absurd. "You're all of it."

Jason pulled her close for a long moment, kissing her lips, cheeks, throat, pressing endearments against her skin. "Justine," he asked eventually, pulling back just enough to look at her. "How did you find out what was going on last night? I'm glad you did, but . . . I didn't want to put you through any of that. I was trying to protect you."

She made herself frown, which wasn't easy when happiness was dancing in every nerve. "We're going to talk about that later," she said. "You promised not to do anything behind my back again—"

"I'm sorry. There were extenuating circumstances."

"You're still in trouble."

"I know. Tell me how you found out."

Justine described Marigold's abrupt and confrontational visit as pragmatically as she could, while Jason listened with quiet sympathy. "She doesn't love me," Justine finished, trying to sound matter-of-fact.

Jason gathered her into the warm strength of his body, giving her all the comfort she could have wished for. His hand swept gently along her naked back. "If she can't," he said, "it has nothing to do with you. The first time we met, I loved you without even trying."

"I love you, too."

He continued to soothe and caress her, until the embrace began to seem somewhat more lecherous than comforting. "You know," he said thoughtfully, his hand slipping beneath the sheet, "this whole relationship has moved so damned fast, I don't see any point in slowing down now. I'll ask you the right way later, but Justine, sweet love . . . you're going to have to marry me." He paused. "That wasn't an order, incidentally. It was . . . imperative begging."

"Marriage," she repeated, stunned. "Oh, let's not even go there. It's too soon."

"We're already sharing a soul," he pointed out. "We may as well start filing joint tax returns."

Justine let out a rueful laugh, knowing that once Jason set his mind on something, he was nothing short of relentless. "I can't begin to imagine how the logistics would work."

"Logistics are easy. Full-on marriage, twenty-four-seven, living in the same house and spending every night in the same bed. We'll spend most of our time on the island, but occasionally you'll spend a week in San Francisco with me. We'll hire a manager to help take care of Artist's Point whenever you're gone."

"But not just anyone can do what I do," she protested. "Usually guests at a bed-and-breakfast expect a warm and personal experience, like they're visiting someone's home."

"We'll hire a warm and personal manager. I'll have Priscilla find someone."

"I do not want any help from Priscilla."

He asked gingerly, "You're still annoyed with her for helping me borrow the Triodecad?"

"Steal. And yes, at the moment she has all the appeal of finding a hair in a biscuit."

"None of it was her fault. I was the devil who made her do it."

"Yes." She let out a breathless laugh as he tugged the sheet away from her. "But you're *my* devil."

"And you're my gorgeous little witch."

"A witch with no magic," she said, but she was smiling as he pulled her onto his lap.

"There's magic in every part of you," he told her.

"Prove it," Justine said throatily, linking her arms around his neck.

They both knew that Jason Black was not a man to back down from a challenge.

CHRISTMAS EVE AT FRIDAY HARBOUR

When Mark Nolan is given custody of Holly, his young orphaned niece, he moves back to Rainshadow vineyard, the Nolan family business, to provide a secure life for her. Although he does his best to take care of her, the trauma of losing her parents has made her increasingly withdrawn. And when Mark stumbles upon a letter Holly has written to Santa asking for a new mum, he is determined to kiss goodbye to his bachelor lifestyle and marry a woman who will be the 'right kind' of mother for her.

Then one afternoon Mark and Holly wander into an intriguing shop called the Magic Mirror and meet the free-spirited and unconventional owner, Maggie Flynn. There is an instant attraction between Mark and Maggie, but having suffered a tragic heartbreak of her own, Maggie has vowed never to risk loving again. She offers to help Mark fulfil Holly's Christmas wish and introduces him to a warm, attractive, traditional woman – just what Mark had been looking for, until he fell under Maggie's spell . . .

RAINSHADOW ROAD

Lucy Marinn is a glass artist living in beautiful, inspiring Friday Harbour, Washington. Creatively fulfilled and in love, she is content with her life, until she is stunned by the worst kind of betrayal: her boyfriend Kevin announces he's leaving Lucy to be with her younger sister.

Facing the disapproval of Lucy's parents, Kevin asks his friend Sam Nolan, one of the owners of the Rainshadow vineyard, to 'romance' Lucy and help her get over her anger. But when Sam and Lucy begin to fall in love, things become complicated, especially when Kevin starts to have second thoughts. And when Lucy discovers that the new relationship in her life began under false pretences, her world is shattered, and she is forced to question everything.

DREAM LAKE

Zoë Hoffman is as gentle and romantic as they come, and when she meets the startlingly handsome Alex Nolan, all her instincts tell her to run. But something about him intrigues Zoë, so she attempts to make Alex open his mind to the possibility that love isn't for the foolish.

Alex Nolan is about as bitter and cynical as they come, battling his demons with the help of a whiskey bottle, until he is visited by a mysterious ghost. Has Alex finally crossed over the threshold to insanity?

The ghost doesn't know who he is, or why he is stuck in the Nolans' Victorian house. All he knows is that he loved a girl once. And Alex and Zoë hold the key to unlocking the mystery that keeps him trapped there.

Do you love historical fiction?

Want the chance to hear news about your favourite
authors (and the chance to win free books)?

Mary Balogh

Charlotte Betts

Jessica Blair

Frances Brody

Gaelen Foley

Elizabeth Hoyt

Eloisa James

Lisa Kleypas

Stephanie Laurens

Claire Lorrimer

Sarah MacLean

Amanda Quick

Julia Quinn

Then visit the Piatkus website and blog
www.piatkus.co.uk | www.piatkusbooks.net

And follow us on Facebook and Twitter
www.facebook.com/piatkusfiction | www.twitter.com/piatkusbooks

piatkus